BLAZE

www.chellebliss.com
CHELLE BLISS
USA TODAY BESTSELLING AUTHOR

Publisher © Chelle Bliss June 2nd 2020
Edited by Lisa A. Hollett
Proofread by Read By Rose & Deaton Author Services
Cover Design © Chelle Bliss
Cover Photo © FuriosFotog
Cover Model - Jacob Wilson

PRAISE FOR THE HEATWAVE SERIES

"I loved this book!!"
-Corinne Michaels, NYT bestselling author

"This book will blow your mind."
-Chelsea Camaron, USA Today bestselling author

"Fast-paced, twist, turns, and a whole lot of FLAME" -Kaylee Ryan, NYT bestselling author

"Blown away!" -Fiction Beer & Cupcakes

"I inhaled this engaging tale!" -Books & Bindings

"Absolutely had me wanting more!" -Angel Payne

"Oh my. Just wow!" -My Timeout

"Holy cow!! What an absolutely awesome book"
-Cat's Guilty Pleasure

"What a freaking amazing read."
-Bookhaven Book Blog

"HOT. HOT. HOT."
-Ruth Cardello, NYT bestselling author

1

LILY

THERE'S ALWAYS a moment in my day when I want to smack someone in the face I'm just about there, but I'm doing my best to hold it together, because today, that someone is my father.

He's taken me under his wing since I dropped out of college, teaching me everything there is to know about Inked and the piercing of every type of body part imaginable—and even some I never thought possible.

The man is the quintessential helicopter parent, hovering around me every second of the workday and even at home. I thought it was cute when I was a little girl. It didn't even bother me when I was in high school because the big lug loved me and he showed it.

But now, at twenty-one, it's old. Really old.

Then there's the fact that I'm Lily.

The sweet one.

The good girl.

The only person in the family who doesn't say how I feel,

always wanting to keep the peace—or at least, not draw extra attention to myself.

"Dad, I know. You've watched me do it hundreds of times already," I huff, resting my chin in my palm, staring out the front windows of the shop. "I seriously can do this on my own now."

His eyes widen as he jerks his head back like I've slapped him with my words. "I know, sweetheart." He nods. "I know."

I know there's a but in there because there always is. My father doesn't know how to agree with anyone without adding the big old but, throwing in his opinion whether he's right or wrong.

"But..." And there it is. Predictable.

I roll my eyes.

"Fine," he says quickly after he glances down, catching me. "You can do the next client through the door all by yourself."

I sit up straight, mouth hanging open, because my dad's never this easy. "Really?"

He taps his finger against the large calendar sitting on the front desk. "It's a simple nipple piercing in an hour. You could do those in your sleep."

"At this point, I can do them all in my sleep," I tell him, pushing his finger out of the way so I can see the other appointments for today. The shop has only been open an hour, but so far, it's been extremely quiet. The rest of the day is booked, but not overbooked...nothing I can't handle on my own. "Why don't you take the day off, take Mom somewhere nice, and let me handle this today?" I bat my eyelashes, begging for him to say yes, because if there's one thing I know about my dad, he's a sucker when it comes to me.

He reaches back, rubbing the back of his neck as he

glances around the empty waiting room. "I don't know, Lily. It's a big step."

"Everyone's here." I motion toward the back area where everyone's busy setting up or working on their first client of the day. "If I have a problem, I'll ask Uncle Joe or Anthony. And—" I smile, placing my hand on his chest "—Mom's off today and the house is empty."

Barf. I can't believe I'd stoop so low as to entice my father with an empty house and my mother to get a little space. But times like this call for drastic measures, even if that includes your parents doing the nasty.

Dad's face brightens. "She'd probably like to grab some lunch."

"Yeah," I mutter as he kisses the top of my head, no longer concerned with leaving me alone for the first time ever. "You'll make her day."

"Mine too," he whispers in my hair.

Still gross, but it's working.

"It's just easy piercings today. A few nipples, a couple ears, and two belly buttons."

"Sounds like a blast." I don't even try to hide the lack of enthusiasm from my voice. Who knew so many women had their nipples pierced? Not me, but the number is staggering and growing each day.

The front door opens, and I gasp. The man walking inside is like a ghost. Someone I haven't seen in over five years because he's been away, serving in the military. Or at least, that's what I heard from Aunt Suzy.

"Oh my God, Jett!" I screech, pushing out of my father's arms and running toward the boy I had the biggest crush on as a kid. "You're alive."

"Sweetheart," he says, holding out his arms to me,

catching me as I smash into him, almost climbing his body. "Why wouldn't I be alive?" His laugh is deep, rich, and damn…it's sexy too.

When he left, he was a boy. One I had a very serious crush on, but I never said a word to anyone. He was the older, cool kid, and I was…not. If it weren't for Tamara and Gigi, I would've eaten lunch in the library, opting for solitude and fiction over the sad reality of my real life.

But Jett was popular. The girls wanted him, and the boys wanted to be him. He always had a cool factor. Something I never, even to this day, could figure out how to get a piece of for myself.

"No." I laugh, slapping him on the chest when my feet finally touch the floor. "You left, and we never saw you again." I shrug and snort all at the same time. I grimace and take a step back because, fuck me, why in the name of God did I have to sound like a little pig when I laughed?

As soon as I peer down at the floor, trying to avoid his haunting gaze, he moves his fingers under my chin, forcing my face upward. "I never had an extended enough leave to stick around town for very long. When I was home, you guys were away at school, getting smarter and prettier, while I was getting my ass kicked."

Oh my God. Oh my God. Did he just say I was prettier?

No. He can't be talking about me.

He's just being smooth, Lily.

This is Jett after all, and he's a world-class flirt.

Of course he's not talking about me.

Maybe Tamara or Gigi, but not me, because I'm Lily, the nerd and the least cool chick in high school or, hell, the entire city.

"I dropped out," I blurt, having no filter around him just like back in high school.

Some things never change. That's why I avoided him back in the day. Any time he was around, I literally had verbal diarrhea, saying the most embarrassing shit I'd ever heard come out of any girl's mouth when a hot guy was around.

His fingers tighten near my neck as his eyebrows rise. "You what?"

"I dropped out of college," I whisper like it's a dirty secret I can't bear to say any louder, "and moved back home."

"Jett, Jesus. Look at you, kid," my dad says, stalking across the room until he's at our side.

My father's shadow, along with his outstretched hand, causes Jett to drop his hand away from my face. "Mr. Gallo. You never change. It's great to see you, sir." Jett smiles, and I swear to God, the whiteness of his teeth and the sparkle of the sunshine off those babies could light up a room.

My dad shakes hands with Jett, and with his other hand, he totally feels up Jett's bicep. "The military made a man out of you, son. A real man."

Jett's mouth twitches as my father gropes him because the man is obsessed with muscles. Back in the day, Dad was a total meathead and a hotshot fighter. But now, he's all about his family and Inked.

"Thanks, sir," Jett tells him.

Dad cranes his neck toward the back as he finally releases his hold on Jett's ample arms. "Joe, Jett's here."

"Jett?" Uncle Joe yells out from the back like he heard his brother wrong, but he didn't.

He's here, all right. Live and in the flesh and looking more delicious than ever. There isn't an ounce of the man that isn't drop-dead gorgeous. Even his feet are cute, and I *hate* feet. His face is tanned and covered in the most perfect five-o'clock shadow even though it's early afternoon.

I stand there, staring at Jett like he's a celebrity and I'm an awkward fan too starstruck to form words. Jett peers over at me, winking, and I nearly faint.

"Holy fuck," Uncle Joe says as soon as he walks into the waiting area at the front of the shop, catching sight of Jett. "It's been two years since I've seen your ugly ass."

"Uncle, you're no prettier either, but sure as fuck are a lot older," Jett teases him, giving my uncle a quick bro hug.

Uncle Joe holds on to Jett's shoulder, soaking him in like he's one of his own kids he hasn't seen in forever. "Sophia didn't say you were coming home."

"I surprised her and Dad this morning."

"Lily, want to go over the books one more time?" my dad asks, but I shake my head and wave him off, not answering with words. "Or would you rather me stay here all day?"

That's all he has to say to get me moving. Pretty boy or not, I don't want my father sticking around here, hovering over me like a rain cloud.

I turn my back, leaving Uncle Joe and Jett to talk as my father goes over the schedule one more time. I sneak a peek at the hottie, pretending to be staring at the books, but I am really watching his hands move and the muscles on his arms as they flex.

"What are you doing here? I don't have any openings today, but I could probably fit you in."

"No, Uncle. I didn't come for some ink, but if I did, I'd only want you to do it."

"We're good, Dad. I got it. Now go home and spend time

with Mom," I say, finally turning my attention to my father, trying to push him toward the door.

"If you run into trouble, baby, just call me." He kisses my cheek and is one step closer to being gone.

"Then what's up?" Uncle Joe asks Jett.

"I wanted to get pierced."

My father's foot stops in midair like someone grabbed the damn meat stick and held him there. He turns, eyeing Jett, with one hand on the door handle.

"Well, Lily's here." Uncle Joe ticks his head my way. "Do you know what you want to get?"

Holy shit. Holy freaking shit. Jett wants to get pierced. That means me. I'm going to pierce the hottest boy in school. The one I daydreamed about on the regular.

Jett smirks, glancing in my direction. "A Prince Albert."

My eyes widen.

My father's eyes do not just widen, they almost bug out of his eye sockets. "I'm staying," he announces, dropping his foot back to the floor and letting go of the door handle.

"Like hell you are," Uncle Joe says, coming to my rescue. "You were leaving, so leave. Lily can do this. She's trained and has done them before."

I blush, thinking about the times I've done it with my dad watching over my back while I held a cock in my hand. Talk about awkward. Besides being walked in on while having sex with someone or taking a poop, I can't imagine anything more embarrassing.

Uncle Joe pitches his thumb over his shoulder. "If she needs help, Anthony's here or Pike can assist."

My dad shakes his head. "Jett's junk is too important to let someone like Lily do it alone."

I giggle—hearing my dad talk about Jett's penis just sets me off, and me doing *it* alone.

"Listen to yourself, man." Uncle Joe swats my father's shoulder before pushing him backward. "Don't worry about Jett's junk. I know Lily can handle just about anything, including a penis."

"Lemme die," I whisper, covering my face with my hands to hide my red cheeks.

"It's Jett's penis," my dad argues, shaking his head.

Uncle Joe crosses his arms, glaring at my father. "And his penis is special because...?"

I peek through my fingers, still too mortified to look anyone in the face, especially Jett, who's staring right at me.

"Because it's Jett." My dad shrugs.

"Get out of here, or else I'm calling Mia and telling her you could've spent the day with her but decided to babysit your twenty-one-year-old daughter instead because she had to touch a penis."

Oh my God. I wish everyone would stop saying penis. Especially when they're talking about Jett's penis.

My dad throws his hands up. "I'm going, but I want a full report and expect some text messages too."

"What details do you want?" Uncle Joe sighs, rolling his eyes. "You want to know his length or some shit?"

"I'm out," Dad says, pushing through the front door, arms flailing around as his mouth moves.

I drop my hands from my face, gawking at the front door as it swishes and my father storms out. I can't hear him once the door closes, but the string of curse words spilling from his lips before was fierce, creative, and nothing short of profane.

"You got this?" Uncle Joe asks me, ticking his chin toward Jett.

I nod, still mute and embarrassed.

"Good." He smiles and grabs Jett's shoulder. "Are you okay with her doing the piercing?"

Jett moves his gaze to me again. "As long as she knows what she's doing and won't lead to me getting an amputation, I'm game. How about you, Lily? You up for it?"

"I know how to handle a penis." I smile, not realizing what the hell I just said and how freaking dirty it sounded.

That's until Jett's smile widens, and he winks at me again. What the hell did I say?

I know how to handle a penis? Fuck my life.

When Jett's around, it's like my brain disconnects from the rest of my body. This is going to be a long, long day, and it's barely started.

"Well, she's your girl." Uncle Joe ignores my idiotic statement as he moves toward me with a straight face. "Just holler if you kids need help."

I stand there, gaping at Jett. My mouth is opening and closing like I'm a goldfish out of water, gasping for air.

"Jett?" Gigi's voice is filled with shock as she stands next to me, gawking at Jett too. "Am I seeing things? Are you really here?"

All I can do is blink. It doesn't matter that Gigi seemed to come out of nowhere. I never saw or heard her walk into the waiting room. All I can think about is Jett. Jett's penis. My hands. The needle. Oh my God. I am finally going to see the one body part I've dreamed about on this guy but never seen.

"Hey, sweetheart." He runs his fingers through his beautiful hair, doing the smooth, cool thing he always has.

She's in his arms a second later, kissing his cheeks frantically. "I didn't think you'd come back alive."

Jett moves his head to avoid her kisses. "Stop, Gigi." He laughs, gripping her arms, trying to put some space between them. "You're killing me, smalls."

She swats his chest. "You disappear for years—no letters, no phone calls, nothing. You just vanish into thin air, and now I'm not supposed to kiss you." She wipes her cheeks like she's crying and being overdramatic. "You're like seeing my long-lost brother. I'm getting my kisses before you disappear again."

Jett's parents, Sophia and Kayden, have been best friends with Aunt Suzy and Uncle Joe since way before any of us were born. From what I understand, Sophia and Suzy were roommates before she met Uncle Joe. I find it hard to believe because Sophia's kind of kick-ass and Aunt Suzy…well, she's more like me.

Jett smiles. "I'm not going anywhere. I'm back for good."

My heart almost leaps out of my chest with the news. Not that it should matter because it's not like we've ever run in the same circles. And then there's the fact that he's Jett and I'm boring Lily.

Gigi slaps Jett's shoulder and nearly vibrates with excitement. "We have to celebrate, then. Tamara will be home this weekend from school. You game for a little party like old times?"

Like old times. I never had any old times. The parties they went to in high school, I didn't attend. I stayed home, knowing my dad wasn't going to let me go anyway, and read books. I studied on weekends or helped my mom at the clinic. I could've been the poster child for boring.

Jett looks over Gigi's shoulder. "Only if Lily's coming," he says, staring straight at me.

I blink like I'm in a trance or daydreaming, trying to wrap my head around what he's saying. Maybe I'm imagining things. Why in the world would the town hottie want me there? I'm about as fun as watching paint dry on the walls. I know it too, and I've accepted my blandness.

"She's totally coming," Gigi answers for me.

"Maybe she has a date or something," he says.

Gigi snorts. "Lily doesn't date."

"I date." I give Gigi the death glare.

"Oh. Okay," she laughs, rolling her eyes in my direction. "Are you free this weekend?"

I don't answer right away as I stare at Jett, our eyes locked and my body beginning to overheat. "I think so." I shrug, trying not to commit to anything in case I chicken out.

Gigi hugs Jett one more time. "We're doing this, and it's going to be epic."

"Yeah," Jett says as Gigi wraps her arms around him, but his eyes are on me.

"I better start prepping," I say, stepping backward toward the piercing room. "So much to do." I smile nervously, feeling the heat of his gaze.

"What are you doing at Inked?" she asks him when I turn my back, almost running away from them.

"I'm getting a Prince Albert."

Gigi gasps. "No. Fucking. Shit. Are you shittin' me?"

"I never joke about my dick, sweetheart."

Once inside the small room, I close the door, plastering myself against the cool metal for support. I can do this. It's just a penis. I've seen so many at this point, I've lost count. What's another one, right?

2

JETT

LILY HASN'T LOOKED me in the eye since the moment I stepped foot in this room. She's busied herself with getting supplies, prepping a small table nearby, and hyperventilating.

"What made you drop out?" I ask. I'm trying to get her mind off whatever's making her have a mini panic attack and the fact she's about to put a hole in my cock.

I don't know why I thought today was the day to get the piercing, but as I drove by Inked, I figured it was as good a day as any. I'd wanted the piercing for years but never could bring myself to do it.

She stops moving, turns her head, and finally looks at me. "It just wasn't right for me."

I jerk back my head like her words slap me. "You were always a good student, though. The smartest girl in the whole school."

There wasn't anyone who could beat Lily in a debate. The girl was on fire when she put her brains on full display. Senior year, I snuck into the debate team matches more than once to watch her in action, but I made sure I left just as quietly so she'd never know.

She blushes as she moves her gaze back to the supplies in her hands. "I know I'm a nerd, but that doesn't mean I was happy in college. I realized I was going to medical school to make my parents happy and not because medicine was my passion."

"You've got to do what brings you joy."

"I know."

"And you're not a nerd, sweetheart."

"I am." She sighs, running her fingers over a package with the biggest needle I've ever seen. "But it's sweet of you to say I'm not."

I reach out and grab her wrist, stopping her from moving. "I've never seen a nerd as beautiful as you."

The blush on her cheeks moves down, coating her neck. "You're such a flirt, Jett, and a shit liar."

I love a girl who doesn't know how pretty she is. So many women I've been with were vain, spending more time on their looks than anything else. Lily barely wore makeup in high school and still doesn't, besides a little lip gloss and mascara.

"One thing I don't do is lie, Lily."

"You don't have to flirt with me. I'm a sure thing," she says, her eyes widening as she stops breathing.

The smile on my face is immediate.

God, she's so freaking beautiful. I know she wasn't talking about sex, but the look on her face says she knows exactly how it sounded. "Relax," I tell her, leaning back in the chair, trying to be cool when I'm nothing but a ball of nerves.

I've been in some crazy situations in my life. The military

isn't for the faint of heart. But never, and I mean never, have I been this nervous.

My penis is like my best friend who's never failed me, and now, I'm about to put another hole in him at the hands of a newbie? I've got to be fucking mental.

But it's Lily, right? If there was ever a newbie in the world to trust your most valuable treasure to, it would be her.

While most boys were daydreaming about slutty porn stars, I was getting busy thinking about my favorite bookworm and her flowing brown hair and those haunting blue eyes. I had it bad for Lily, but she was always too young, too aloof, and way too good for me to ever really have a shot.

"Are you sure you want to do this?" she asks, sitting on the small stool between my legs. "I mean, this is drastic and painful as hell."

I suck in air between my teeth as she talks about the pain, something I've been telling myself is a myth. But, this is my cock, and jamming a needle through it is going to suck. "I'm sure."

"We're ready, then," she whispers, glancing away from me. "You can either pull your pants down or remove them completely. Whatever you're more comfortable with."

In all the fantasies I've had about Lily, this was not one of them. I never thought the first time she saw my dick, we'd be in a cold, sterile room, and never would she be fully clothed.

"I can take them off," I say, never having been shy about my body. There is no point in keeping my pants on. She is going to see my dick anyway. She is going to touch it too. *Shit.* I didn't think this through. What if… I shake my head. "Lily."

"Yeah?"

"What happens if I..." I swallow, not able to say the words.

There's no way I can have her so close, with her hands on me, and not get hard.

No fucking way.

She blinks, looking sweet, innocent, and completely delicious. "If you what?"

I peer down, staring at my crotch. "What if I get... hard?"

Her smile is immediate, and so is the redness in her cheeks. "It won't be a problem," she tells me.

I groan. "No, I'm being serious. What if you touch me, and I get hard?"

She giggles like I'm crazy. "I'm sure that's not going to happen."

She doesn't know it yet, but I'm already fighting an unwinnable battle. "Trust me, it will."

"If it does, I can work with it. It wouldn't be the first time. I know penises often have a mind of their own." She pats my leg. The gesture is innocent enough but has the opposite effect than she's going for. It doesn't comfort me but sends the wrong signals straight to my dick. "Just take off your pants so I can see what I'm working with and can start making out on it."

I jerk my head back, and my penis gets even more excited. "What?" I choke.

"Jesus. Marking on it," she says quickly, squeezing my knee so tight, her knuckles turn white. "I'm so sorry. When you're around, I swear I turn into the biggest idiot and my words get all jumbled. You make me so nervous."

I slide my hand over hers, covering her fingers as I study her. "I make you nervous?"

She nods and glances down, avoiding my eyes. "You always have."

"Lil, there's nothing to be nervous about around me. You've known me your entire life. We're friends. Always have been, always will be. If you can't be yourself around me, who can you be yourself around?"

"Maybe," she whispers. "But you'll always be one thing I'm not."

"Which is?" I squeeze her fingers, trying to get that beautiful pout off her face.

She peers up, her eyes twinkling as they lock with mine. "Cool."

I chuckle, wishing I could wrap her in my arms and kiss away the pout. "When you're as pretty as you, Lil, cool doesn't matter."

She rolls her eyes and pulls her hand out from under mine, ending whatever moment I was trying to have with her. "Would you like me to leave the room while you undress?"

"You're going to have to look at my cock sometime, babe. Might as well stay for the grand unveiling."

She sucks in a breath, her beautiful breasts jutting out, making the entire situation in my pants worse. I have to think about something shitty to keep my cock under control. Something so horrible, my boner will have no choice but to fuck right off. "Just talk to me while I do it. Keep my mind off what you're about to do."

She nods like she understands, but she really has no idea. She's always been clueless with me. No matter how many times I flirted with her, she never caught on. Not because she's stupid, Lily's smart, but because she never thought I was serious. "So, are you living back home with your parents?" she asks.

I stand, moving my hands to the waistband of my sweatpants. "For now. I'm trying to find a place, but everything is either full or too expensive for me to afford on my own until I find a job."

"Me too," she says as she watches my hands like she's waiting with bated breath for whatever she's about to see. "Gigi and Tamara have a two-bedroom, and I crash there when Tam's at school. But I want to find something more permanent."

"We should move in together. We can share the rent and be roommates," I blurt out as I push my pants down my thighs, giving her nothing but a face full of dick.

She stares right at my junk, blinking slowly and breathing shallowly again. "Are you freaking kidding me?" she says softly.

"About living together?" I shake my head. "I need to get out of my parents' place. It's been a day, and I'm already climbing the walls. You need a place. I need a place. What could be more perfect?" I say all this with my cock out, waving at Lily like the slut he is.

She peers up, biting the corner of her lip, making my boner worse, before she glances back at my dick. "This is a lot to take in."

She's freaking killing me. I don't know if she's talking about my dick or my idea. "Which part?"

"All of it." She waves her hand toward my crotch. "Your cock is big, no shocker there. But damn, the bend." She swallows, blinking a few times while I hold in my laughter. She suddenly pales, covering her face with her hands. "Did I just say that out loud?" she mutters into her palm. "Oh God, I did. Let me die. Someone kill me now."

I want to comfort her, but if I take one step closer, my cock won't just be waving, he'll be tapping her on the cheek. "I like that you don't have a filter, Lily. It's refreshing."

So many of the women I've dated expect me to be a mind reader. But Lily's inability to hold in her thoughts is intriguing and could be a ton of fun. This is the first time she's expressed any real interest in me, even if it's only when she's face-to-face with my other head.

Her face is still hidden behind her palms as her shoulders roll forward until her elbows are on her knees. "I can't live with you. I would be a constant mess, blurting out crazy things. I'd annoy you within a day."

"You could never annoy me." I toe off my tennis shoes, followed by yanking down my sweatpants to my ankles. From the waist down, I'm buck naked, standing in front of the hottest chick I've ever known and have never had. Funny how life works out like that. "Just think about it."

"Oh, I am," she murmurs, still hiding her face. "Thinking long and hard."

"You're fucking killing me, babe," I laugh, shaking my head as she stays hidden behind the safety of her hands.

What the fuck am I doing, asking her to move in with me? Talk about a hot mess.

Not her, but me.

I could never bring a woman home with Lily in the house, feeling like I'd be cheating even though we weren't a couple. And with Lily, if she ever brought a guy home, I'd want to punch him in the face at the very least.

"Maybe I should come back when your dad's here."

Lily's back straightens, and her hands fall away from her

face as her eyes snap to mine. "I can do this. Trust me, it'll be worse if he's around. Imagine me holding your cock with my dad breathing down my neck, watching my technique, critiquing me on the job I'm doing."

But then I wouldn't have to worry about the boner I can't seem to get to go down, not even at the mention of her father watching the entire thing. "It would be awkward," I tell her.

She motions toward the table before turning to grab a pair of gloves from the tray. "Just lie down. We'll go slow, make sure you're comfortable with everything before I do anything irreversible."

I climb up, happy to have a moment where she's not eye level with my dick, and chastise myself for being a complete idiot. *We should move in together.* What a freaking moron. In what world would that work out? Not mine. That much is for sure.

When she comes to stand next to me, she looks like an angel bathed in light. "Tell me where you've been for the last five years while I figure out exactly where we're placing this and make marks to see if you're satisfied. After that, we'll begin, but not until you're completely comfortable."

I nod and close my eyes because, dear God, I can't watch her touch my dick. I can't. There's no way I'd make it through the next however many minutes seeing her fingers on me. "After boot camp and A School," I start to say and nearly rocket off the table as her latex-covered fingers touch my cock.

"Relax. You're in good hands," she says in a soothing tone, holding the head of my penis between her fingers. "I promise to give you my best."

I exhale, thinking back on my time in the service, pulling

from my bank of awful memories to get my mind off my cock, and Lily too. "I was stationed in San Diego. I did two deployments..."

"Where did you go?" Her warm breath skids across my skin when she speaks, making my boner rock hard.

I sneak a peek, seeing her tongue poking out from between her lips and her luscious mouth so close to my dick, it takes everything in me to keep my hands to myself. "Middle East and Asia. Never spent any real length of time in any one place, though."

"Sounds exciting."

Not as exciting as this. "It was okay. It's not everything they promise. Join the Navy, see the world. Biggest bunch of horseshit I've ever heard." I clench my fist, bearing down like I'm in physical pain because Lily's touching my junk, which is something I've always daydreamed about, but never like this.

The sensation of the marker against my cock is a cruel form of torture. I concentrate on my breathing, not because I'm scared, but because I'm turned on. "I think this is the best placement based on the slight curve of your penis. Open your eyes and tell me what you think."

"Lily?" I crack open an eye and stare at her.

"Yeah, Jett?" She smiles, giving me her eyes.

"Can you let go before I look?" I hold my breath, knowing if I look and see her hands around my dick, I'm liable to do something stupid.

Her hand is gone immediately. "Sorry. Sometimes I get a little lost in what I'm doing. I just want this to be everything you want it to be."

"You can't fuck it up," I tell her, finally opening both my

eyes. I lift myself up on my elbows, staring down at my dick instead of gawking at her. "What am I looking for?"

She moves forward, reaching for my shaft before pulling her hands back. "May I please touch it?"

Jesus. Do you know how many times I'd wanted to hear those words from her lips? I'd done some bad shit in my life, but I don't know if any of it rose to the level to deserve this special kind of torture. Maybe it's payback for the shitty way I treated most of the women I've slept.

She blushes and peers down at the floor, rocking back on her heels. "I mean, show it to you so I can explain the placement and the logistics."

"Go ahead. Touch away," I tell her because, at this point, what's the difference? My dick can't get any harder.

Feeling her hands on me with my eyes closed is very different from watching as her slender fingers touch my cock, wrapping around the tip. I suck in a breath as my body tightens, needing a release.

She tips my cock back, almost flattening it against my belly. "The Prince Albert will come out here." She swipes her fingertip over the underside of my cock, right where the small purple circle she drew is. "Is that good for you?"

"It's all good for me." I collapse backward, the visual and soft caress of her fingers too much for me to handle.

"Great. Just give me a minute to get new gloves and everything I'll need, and we'll be done in a jiffy."

I lie there for what feels like forever, waiting for Lily to come back. There's the sound of metal moving and then the snap of the latex against her skin. I turn my head, staring at her backside, soaking in her long, tanned legs, wishing I could crawl between them and live there forever.

"Ready?" she asks, turning with the biggest fucking tube of some sort and needle I've ever seen in her hands.

"Uh." I laugh nervously as my boner, which had been out of control, suddenly seems to fade. "As ready as I'll ever be."

"Just take a deep breath when I tell you to, and you won't feel a thing. I'm going to be quick and make this as painless as possible."

She doesn't know it, but the pain, the deep ache I feel isn't about the hole she's about to put in my cock, but because of her.

"Now," she says, gripping my dick. "Close your eyes. Think of something relaxing like the beach on a warm summer day. Now inhale—" she pauses for a moment, her sharp intake of breath matching mine "—and exhale."

I'm damn near hyperventilating when I finally close my eyes, picturing Lily in a tiny bikini, lying on the sand next to me as the waves crash nearby.

"Inhale slow and deep, Jett, and you won't feel a thing."

But she's wrong...I feel it all.

3

LILY

"SHUT THE FUCK UP." Tamara covers her mouth as her hazel eyes widen. "You saw his penis?"

I nod. "Touched it too." The grin on my face has been there since the moment he staggered out of Inked yesterday, promising he wasn't in too much pain and thanking me profusely for doing an amazing job.

He didn't cry like some men do when you jam a giant hollowed needle right through their shaft. The sound he made was somewhere between a moan and a growl, both sexy and scary at the same time.

"You touched Jett Michaels's cock?" Tamara asks again like she just can't process what I've said.

"Yep." I stare at my beer bottle, scratching at the half-torn label down the front. I leave out the fact that it's a work of art, thick and long and quite possibly the most beautiful one I've ever seen.

My experience with dicks has been limited, outside of work. I'd always been too busy with school or too scared I'd get knocked up. While my college friends were at frat parties, drinking, and having fun, I kept my butt in my dorm, studying and staying out of trouble.

"She's going to touch a lot of dicks with her job," Gigi says as she sits down at the table with us.

I groan. "Don't remind me."

To an outsider, seeing dicks every day sounds exciting, but when you're putting holes in them, it kind of kills the fun. Most of the time, the man attached to said cock isn't worth the time of day.

"Lucky asshole." Tamara shakes her head. "Jett Michaels," she whispers like he's a celebrity.

"You want to know the weirdest thing of all?" I blurt out, wanting to stop talking about his beautiful cock.

Tamara sobers for a moment, blinking at me like I'm insane, or at least lying. "There's something weirder than you touching your high school crush's junk?"

"He wasn't my crush," I lie, earning me a glare from Tamara. "Fine. Fine. Maybe I liked him a little."

"A little." Gigi laughs, elbowing Tamara. "Liar."

I don't know why I'm lying. No one knows me better than Tamara and Gigi. While they always agreed he was hot, they didn't have the same feelings about him I did. They said he was too much like a little brother and the very thought of kissing him made their skin crawl.

"We're not talking about how I felt about him, jerks," I grumble, unable to look at them anymore.

If I did, they'd see that I still have a crush on the man. Maybe even more so now than I did five years ago when he disappeared.

"What's the weirdest thing?" Gigi asks, knowing I've always been touchy about my feelings for him.

I look at Tamara and then back to Gigi, fully aware

they're going to flip their shit when I tell them. I brace myself, placing my hands on the table, because it's about to get loud. "He asked me to move in with him."

Gigi blinks, her head jerking back like she heard me wrong. "He what?"

Tamara tilts her head, gawking at me like she's trying to translate my words because I'd just spoken in a different language. "Say that again."

"He asked me to move in with him." The words still seem foreign coming off my lips. I've repeated the moment when he said those words over and over again since he walked out the door.

Why me? That was my biggest question. Why would *the* Jett Michaels want to live with me? I'm boring. I embrace that fact about myself. I've never tried to be something I'm not.

Tamara turns her head and stares at Gigi. "Did I hear her right?"

Gigi shrugs. "If you heard he wants her to move in with him, then yeah."

"Did she hear him right?" Tamara asks, rubbing her forehead and crinkling her nose. "I mean, there's a high probability she didn't because this is party-animal, manwhore Jett Michaels and good-girl, bookworm Lily Gallo we're talking about."

They're talking about me like I'm not even here. Or maybe they think I'm delusional and made up the entire conversation.

But I know.

I know what he asked me. I was just as shocked as they are now, but I was good at hiding my disbelief.

I glare at them, flipping them each a middle finger. "I

heard him right."

Tamara gives me her full attention, and she's no longer laughing. "What were his exact words?"

"'We should move in together. We can share the rent and be roommates,'" I repeat his words verbatim. They're burned in my brain, playing on repeat because even I can't believe he said them to me...still.

They both blink at me like they have something in their eyes they're trying to work out.

"He..." Tamara's mouth opens and closes as she stares at me in disbelief. "He..."

"Holy shit," Gigi whispers. "He really said that?"

"Yeah." I glance down to my bottle to avoid their gazes. "But of course, I won't. I mean, can you imagine what it would be like to live with someone like him?"

There's nothing but silence. Something there never is when Gigi and Tamara are in the same room. These two can talk nonstop about everything, and they never seem to run out of things to say either. But now, they're suddenly speechless.

I peer up, still picking at the label on my beer, as they stare at me like I have two heads. "What?"

Tamara crosses her arms, shaking her head like she can't believe I'm going to say no to him. "If you don't say yes and get on that man, I'm going to beat you."

"Do it," is all I get from Gigi.

"It would be awful." I'm trying to convince myself more than them. "It wouldn't be good."

Gigi moves her hand to my forearm, giving me a light squeeze. "What wouldn't be good?"

"Where do you want me to start?" I roll my eyes and sigh. "Living with a man. Living with Jett, specifically. I mean, imagine if he brings home a date and I have to listen to them…" My voice trails off, and I grimace, thinking about him having sex with some woman in the bedroom next to mine.

Tamara taps her long fingernails against the tabletop, and I can almost hear the wheels spinning in her head. She's coming up with a plan. A plan for something I'm not going to follow through on. "Hmmm. Maybe you need to make rules. Set boundaries. Like, no women at your place if you're home."

I laugh. "Yeah, like that'll work."

"You're right, babe. You can just keep going back and forth between crashing on our couch and staying with your parents," Gigi says, knowing exactly what to say to remind me I hate living at home. "I know your parents love having you around."

I loathe living with my parents again. They're great people and even better parents, but they treat me like I'm still in high school. I have a curfew, and they feel the need to know where I am at every moment, day or night. It's suffocating, especially after being on my own for over three years.

Tamara checks her phone, smiling when she sees a waiting text. "Mammoth's almost here. When are we headed out?"

"Can't we just stay in?" I groan, hating parties because there're always too many cool kids and I never fit in.

Gigi stands from the table, taking the beer from my hands that I've been nursing for an hour. "I already told everyone to meet at nine. Jett's supposed to be here any minute too, and then we can head out. We're not canceling tonight. So, put on some makeup, change your clothes, and be ready to go as soon as your roommate arrives."

"He's not my roommate," I grumble, rubbing the meaty part of my palms into my eyes.

Gigi barely even looks at me as she cleans the kitchen, tossing our almost empty containers of Chinese takeout. "Either way, get your sweet ass moving, babe. We have to celebrate Jett's return, and that includes you."

"Why?"

Gigi glances up, narrowing her eyes at me. "Because you're one of us. And anyway, since when do you ever pass up a chance to stare at Jett Michaels?"

"When I was sixteen."

Tamara pulls on my arm, trying to get me to stand. "I'll do your makeup. We'll make Jett want to be more than roommates."

I yank my arm out of her grip and sit back down. "We'll never be more than roommates. Hell, we're not even friends, Tam."

"We're going to change that tonight. You got a rockin' bod underneath those frumpy clothes you're always wearing. If we put a tight little dress on you, do up your makeup and hair, he'll have to see you as something more..."

"Fuckable?" Gigi adds, giggling.

"I don't want to fuck him." It's a lie. I've dreamed of the moment when Jett would undress me, peppering my body with kisses.

"Uh-huh. Sure." Tamara pulls on my arm again, not taking no for an answer. "Either way, we're sexing you up a little."

"I look nice," I argue, tipping my head down to stare at my outfit.

I'm never one to be overly "done up." My khakis and frilly

tank top, which doesn't show my breasts, are about as dressy as I get, preferring my comfy leggings and oversized T-shirt.

She steps back and releases my hand, eyes moving over my outfit. "You cannot wear that to a bonfire."

"What's wrong with it?"

"Khakis." Tamara scrunches her nose like the word alone offends her. "You're not an insurance salesman or a librarian. You need something a little more...daring."

There's a knock on the door, and we all turn our heads, staring at the slab of wood.

"I bet that's Jett. You better get moving before he sees you like that," Gigi says, walking toward the door.

"Looking like what?" I ask defensively.

Gigi doesn't stop moving and doesn't even turn around before she gets in her last dig. "Like you're about to do his taxes and not his dick."

"I hate you both," I grumble under my breath as Gigi places her eye against the peephole.

"It's Jett," she whispers. "Last chance before he sees you like that."

"I fucking hate you both so much," I mutter again before sliding out of the chair, almost running down the hallway as Gigi reaches for the doorknob.

I know it shouldn't matter. I have no shot with Jett. Never have and never will. We're friends at best, and even that's a stretch. Besides yesterday at the shop, if we've said one hundred words to each other in our lifetime, it would be generous. I watched from afar, while he barely knew I existed.

I stand in Tamara's room, watching her root through her closet, talking to herself. "Put these on." She throws a pair of jean shorts at me, hitting me square in the face. "They'll make your ass look great."

I peel the shorts away from my eyes and turn to look at my behind in the full-length mirror on her wall. "My ass looks great in these."

Tamara blinks at me, lips flat. "No one's ass looks good in khakis." She shakes her head and blows out a long, loud breath. "And I mean, no one."

I don't care what she says, my ass does look good in these pants. "Whatever." I roll my eyes.

"Take them off. We can use them as kindling tonight."

"You will not," I tell her, unfastening the button before sliding down the zipper. "These are my favorite pair."

She snorts. "Only you would have a favorite pair of khakis."

I stick out my tongue before yanking down my pants and stepping out of them. I fold them neatly and place them on her bed, giving her the side-eye the entire time because I don't trust her not to snatch them.

"Underwear too."

I gaze up, eyes wide because she can't be serious. "What?"

"You'll be picking your ass all night in those shorts if you wear underwear. Leave your cotton kid panties here with the pants. Trust me."

"But I've never..." I stand there, staring at her with one foot in the shorts, frozen and unsure what to do. "I always wear underwear."

"Fine, but I warned you."

That's all she says. Victory is mine. Although I'm not happy about the shorts, at least I don't have to worry about the world seeing my vagina every time I sit down or bend over.

Her jean shorts fit snugly, and I turn, getting a glimpse at the difference with my ass. I make a face as soon as I notice the very bottom of my ass cheeks peeking out from the hem.

"Better, right?" she asks, staring at my reflection in the mirror and totally checking out my ass.

"They're all right," I lie and bend over, cringing when I see my pink panties. There goes bending in any natural way because there's no way in hell I'm leaving this apartment without them on.

"Here." She throws me a black top, and this time, I catch the damn thing before she can hit me with another piece of clothing. "No bra, though."

Holding up the scrap of material, I gawk at it. "There's nothing here, Tamara."

She waggles her eyebrows. "That's why you can't wear a bra."

"What the hell?" I blink, still staring at the top. "I can't wear this in public." My nose scrunches all on its own because sheesh, there's barely anything to this top.

She places her hand on her hip, lifting her shoulder and giving me tons of attitude without even having to say a word. "You want Jett to notice you?"

"No."

"Liar."

"I don't. We're not even friends." Half my statement is the truth. We're not friends, but do I want him to notice me? Maybe. I don't know. I try to stay in my lane, and Jett Michaels is not even on my roadmap.

"For once in your life, act your age and have a little fun. If you don't catch his eye in that outfit, you never will."

"I could walk around naked, and he wouldn't notice me," I grumble, lifting my shirt over my head and glaring at

Tamara. "We both know it's true without me having to embarrass myself tonight."

"Why bother with clothes, then? It's just us. Walk out there with your tits out, and we'll find out."

"I never knew I could hate you more, but I do."

She giggles and slaps my ass as I turn my back to her to take off my bra. "You love me, and after you snag Jett, you can thank me."

I cover my breasts with my arm as I reach for the top. "I can't snag him. And anyway, he has a fresh piercing. He can't…you know."

"Fuck. I forgot." She slaps herself on the forehead. "Doesn't mean he can't please you, though."

"I don't do that. I'm not like…"

"Like me?" she says, finishing my statement.

"I didn't mean that in a bad way, babe. I've just never fooled around with someone unless we were committed."

She grimaces. "How many men have you actually slept with?"

"Actually sleep?" I ask quietly.

"No, Lily," she groans. "How many guys have you fucked?"

My head snaps back like she's slapped me with her vulgar language. "Well, I…" God, I don't want to tell her this. I've always skirted the issue with her and Gigi when they were talking about men. Going to a different college, I found it easy to hide my relationships—or should I say, the lack of any men in my life. But now she's putting me on the spot. "None," I whisper.

Her eyes widen, and her mouth drops open. "For real?"

"Yes." I give her a weak smile. "I just never found anyone worth giving my virginity to." I shrug and realize I'm half naked because my breasts make a surprise appearance from behind my arm.

"But you've touched so many dicks since you started at Inked." Now she's whispering. "How is that possible?"

"I was studying to be a doctor. And it's not like I've never seen a penis before, I've just never...you know." I waggle my eyebrows, the universal sign for getting freaky without having to say the words.

"Oh, girl. We've got to change this and fast."

"No, we don't." I lift my chin, hating when she tries to run my life. It's bad enough I'm letting her pick out my outfit; I won't let her decide when and who gets in my vagina too.

"Whatever you say, Lil. It's your pussy."

Yanking the tube top over my head, I let the bra fall to the floor and quickly cover my breasts. "It'll happen when it happens. You're you, and I love that you do whatever makes you happy. But I'm also me, and I don't sleep around. No offense."

She sits down on the edge of the bed and lifts her hands. "None taken."

"How do I look?" I ask her, pulling up the tube top to hide my cleavage but making my belly show.

"I'd fuck you," she giggles.

"I seriously hate you."

"Sit," she tells me, grabbing her makeup bag off the dresser. "This will only take a minute."

I sit in silence, glaring at her as she applies eyeshadow, telling me it's the perfect smoky eye, before applying lipstick and mascara.

She grabs my hand and starts to pull me toward the door. "Come on. Let's see what Jett thinks."

I try to yank my hand out of her grasp, but damn it, she's

so much stronger than me. I can't yell or make a big deal out of it because Jett would hear and I'd sound like a bigger weirdo than I already am.

"Here we are," Tamara says in the sweetest tone. "Did you miss us?"

I inch out behind her as her hand falls away. The smile on my face is forced and painful. All I want to do is run in the back, throw on my khakis, and rush out of here. But then I'd be a coward, and if Jett thought I was odd before, it would be nothing compared to what he'd think after I pulled a stunt like that.

"Hey, Tamara," Jett says, not even looking in my direction as he approaches.

"Hey, sugar." She grabs his forearms, giving them a good squeeze before kissing his cheek. "Sorry we're late. Lily and I had to finish getting ready."

That's when it happens. Jett glances over, his eyes flash, and I see the spark of something I've never seen before…possibility.

4

JETT

Lily Gallo.

Bookworm.

Straight A student.

Loner.

That's how I always thought of her. There wasn't a day in high school, and even before, when she wasn't off in a corner, head buried in a book. She pretended like I didn't exist, and when I tried to get her attention, she'd avert her eyes, tuck a lock of her pretty brown hair behind her ear, and go on ignoring me.

But now…this Lily, the one with short shorts and a tube top standing in front of me, is something else. She's not looking away but staring straight at me. A small but scared smile hanging on her lips.

"Wow, you look…" The words get lodged in my throat, and I'm suddenly aware of the new hole in my cock. I wince, unable to ignore the pain of the scab and dried blood pulling at my skin.

Her smile falls, and she takes a step back, paling. "I should change." She covers her body with her hands and bites her lip like she's ready to burst into tears.

"No. No." Tamara grabs her by the wrist, stopping her from going anywhere. "Stop it! Babe, you look great. Doesn't she, Jett?"

I force down the pain, focusing on Lily's outfit and trying not to focus on the fullness of her breasts or the smoothness of her thighs. Fuck my life. I finally get the nerve to get a piercing, and not only was Lily the one to do it, she's the first chick to give me wood since she jammed the needle into my cock.

"So fuckin' good," I say, but my voice cracks.

She backs up, glancing down at the tile floor. "Really. It's no big deal."

"Wait." I move to her and not gracefully because my fucking dick is killing me. "You really look amazing, Lily. I'm just not used to seeing you look like…" I'm completely and utterly speechless. Something I've never been around anyone, especially women.

"What the hell?" a man says behind me, causing me to turn and Lily to cover herself more. "Lily?" He squints, gawking at her from the doorway.

"Mammoth!" Tamara screeches, dropping Lily's arm and running toward the guy. He takes up the entire entrance. Tall, wide, and mean-as-hell looking. "I've missed you so much, baby." Her legs are around his waist, lips on him a second later, kissing him deeply.

"That's Tamara's boyfriend," Gigi tells me, throwing her hand in their direction as the guy gropes Tamara's ass. "Mine will be here any minute, and then we can jet." She starts to giggle as soon as she says the final word. "I mean leave." She laughs louder, covering her mouth. "Why in the world would your parents name you Jett?"

I shake my head, unable to stop my smile. "The real question is, why in the world do you still use the word jet, sweetheart?"

"Wait." Gigi looks around, and the room is empty except for us four. "Where the hell did she go?"

"Fuck," I hiss, knowing she ran off. Between my wince and the big brute's reaction when he walked through the door, we scared her away.

"I'll be right back." Gigi smiles and pitches her thumb toward the hallway. "I'll go check on her."

I'm in front of Gigi in two quick strides, moving her to the side. "No. Let me. It's my fault. Let me apologize."

The smile on Gigi's face is nothing short of salacious. "Would that include tongue or no tongue?"

"Shut up, weirdo," I tease, leaving her in the living room with Tamara and her boy toy as they suck each other's faces off.

"You know you want to play tongue hockey with her. Just admit it already," she whisper-yells down the hallway, loud enough for me to hear but not anyone else.

"Lily," I say softly, knocking on the only closed door in the apartment.

"What?" Her voice is strained.

I don't need to see her face to know she's crying.

Goddamn it. I'm an idiot. Add it to the long list of shit I can never seem to get right. Being around Lily, I always have the most awkward interactions, and it pisses me off. Any other chick in the world and I'm smooth as fuck, but her…no fucking way.

"Can I come in?"

"No!"

I lean against the door, resting my head on the wood. "Please, Lily. I need to show you something."

God, this is embarrassing. It was bad enough that I had wood before she pierced me, but this is worse. But I'm taking one for the team or, more specifically, Lily. Whatever I have to do to make her not so sad, I'll fucking do it. Even if it means embarrassing myself.

She doesn't open the door, but her voice sounds closer. "What do you want to show me?"

"I'm worried about my piercing." The words are barely out of my mouth before the door flies open.

"What's wrong?" Her gaze isn't on my face but firmly planted on my crotch. "Did you hurt yourself?" Her eyes flicker up, worry written all over her features.

"I don't know. It hurts like a bitch, though, and I don't know if there should be so much..." I wince again, catching sight of the swell of her breasts. "...swelling."

She pulls on my hand, slamming the door as soon as my ass clears the threshold. "Slow down," I say, walking quicker than I have since the big event yesterday. "I can't move that fast yet."

She nibbles on her bottom lip and slows down, her eyes moving back and forth between my face and crotch. "I'm so sorry. Let me see."

This is not how I ever wanted Lily to see my dick again. Not today and definitely not yesterday. I'd fantasized about her more than once, especially on deployment. Aunt Suzy had sent me some photos from Christmas, and front and center was Lily. I'd jacked off so many times to that photo, it eventually fell apart, leaving me with nothing but my memories.

"I just need to know how much is normal."

She falls to her knees, hands moving to my zipper.

"Fuck," I mutter, swallowing down the pain that's growing as fast as my cock as I touch her hands, stopping her. If she doesn't slow the fuck down, I'm going to end up in the damn emergency room. I'd always dreamed of her in this position, but never like this. "Wait."

She peers up, those big blue eyes piercing my soul. "I need to look so I can help. Come on, Jett. It's me. It's not like I haven't seen your penis before." She snorts.

I curse, dropping my hands to my sides because one way or another, she's going to get what she wants. The upside? She's not crying about what happened earlier.

"I'm in some crazy pain. It's why I made the face out there." I stare straight ahead, unable to look at her as she unzips my jeans in a flash. "Careful, babe," I warn because, goddamn, she's moving so quickly. Under any other circumstances, I'd think she was thirsty for my cock.

"Sorry." Her cheeks turn pink, and her tongue pokes out, sweeping across her bottom lip. She's concentrating and being careful, but fuck me if she doesn't make it all worse. "I'll go really slow." She even says the word at a snail's pace, moving her hands to my waistband even slower.

Torture. That's exactly what this is. "You can move a little faster."

"Bossy," she whispers into my crotch.

"You have no idea, sweetheart," I tell her, keeping my eyes trained on the wall behind her because, from this angle, all I see is tits. More specifically, Lily's amazing tits.

My jeans are down around my knees a few painful seconds later, and her hands move to the waistband of my boxers. "You okay?"

I glance down, gritting my teeth. "Just fine."

"You look pale."

"My cock, babe. It's killing me." I leave out the part that it's partially her fault. I mean, couldn't she stay in her khaki pants a few more days and give my dick a break?

Her eyes widen and flash with concern. "That's not good. Maybe you should lie down so I can get a better look."

I don't know why God hates me so much, but in this instant, no one could tell me any different. "I'm fine standing."

I don't look at her anymore. I can't. Her fingers dip into my boxers, and I close my eyes, thinking of bad shit. The worst kind of shit that gives people nightmares. The worst kind of shit that most certainly won't give me wood. Especially not Lily's breasts and ass hanging out of her clothes or in my hands. "Damn it."

She freezes. "Did I hurt you?"

"No." I'm a fucking liar, but there's no way I can tell Lily how I feel. She doesn't deserve someone like me. She deserves so much better. I promised myself a long time ago, I'd never sully her. I'd never put my dirty on her pureness. Up until yesterday, I'd planned on keeping that promise.

"So, can I keep going?"

"Take my cock out, Lily."

I always dreamed about saying those words. Never thought they'd be in a situation like this.

"Right. Your cock."

There's something so naughty about her voice when she swears. Something that licks up my spine, making the need to touch her even greater.

I squeeze my eyes shut, going back to all the bad shit. Anything to stop myself from touching her or from looking at her. She's quick. Her fingertips move gingerly against the bandages until the cool air hits my swollen, angry cock.

"Jesus," she murmurs. "It's huge."

I tip my head back, swearing under my breath at whoever is up there laughing their ass off at my torment. "Is it supposed to be like that?"

She's not touching my skin, but I can feel the heat of her breath. "I can call my dad and ask. He'd know."

I almost choke on my own spit as my eyes snap open. "No." Reaching down, I grab her hands, helping her off her knees. "That's not a good idea."

"Why?" She gives me those fucking doe eyes. The innocent look she always has. The one that's always driven me wild. "He's the most experienced and would know if this is normal."

"Lily," I say, trying to smile through my misery. "We can't call your dad and tell him you're looking at my dick again."

She giggles, leaving her hand in my grip. "He'll understand, Jett. My dad's super sweet, and he only wants the best for our clients."

I'm sure he does, but not this client. Not the one who was alone, cock hanging out, fantasizing about his little girl.

There's a knock on the door. "What's going on in there?" Gigi asks from the hallway.

My eyes are locked on Lily's, pleading with her for...I don't know what. "Don't open it," I whisper.

"Stop," she whispers back. "It's Gigi."

"So..."

"Jett's worried about his piercing!" Lily yells, holding my gaze. "Sorry."

"Oh shit!" Gigi gasps loud enough that not even an inch of wood can hide the noise. "How bad?"

"I don't know. Bad, I think." Lily shrugs as her eyes move to my dick again. "Really red and big."

I wish she'd stop talking about how big my dick is. I groan. "It's fine. My dick is fine."

"Wait!" Gigi yells back. "Mammoth has a Prince. Let me ask him what's normal."

"Fucking fantastic," I mutter, to which Lily giggles.

The sound is so sweet, whatever aggravation I have evaporates. I could never be mad at Lily. She doesn't have a mean, spiteful bone in her body.

"What's wrong?" the gruff voice asks, the handle starting to turn.

"Don't come in!" I yell, rolling my eyes and reaching for my pants with my free hand.

"How swollen were you after your piercing?" Gigi asks him, holding the conversation in the hallway so now everybody knows.

"It was pretty fucking angry for a few days. Totally normal as long as there's no pus or tons of bleeding," the guy who's been sucking Tamara's face says.

I blow out a breath, feeling relieved that my cock, while huge, is totally normal.

"Just don't get wood, or you'll be in a world of pain. Wrap it up tight too. Don't need that thing swinging around in your pants all day."

Lily breaks out in a louder fit of giggles. "He sure said it better than I did. I'm sorry."

Yesterday, when she was going over aftercare and what to expect, she turned a million shades of red, barely able to get the words out. I'd been too busy staring at her pretty face to really listen.

"My dick's fine. That's all a man can ask for."

"Want me to take a look?" the guy asks.

"No. We're good!" I holler, not wanting an audience.

"Thank fuck," he mutters before his heavy footfalls move down the hallway, growing quiet.

"No wood for you, mister," Lily says, trying to be cute and poking me in the chest.

I love her playfulness, but not at the expense of my cock. "Sweetheart," I whisper and pull in a deep breath, trying to steady my pulse. "Can we not talk about my wood anymore, yeah?"

Her laughter stops, but the smile's still on her face. "Sure. Not talking about your wood anymore. Got it."

When her gaze moves to the side, I realize I never let go of her, tethering her to me the entire time. "Sorry," I say, releasing my grip on her wrist and wishing everything were different.

"Do you want me to wrap it up?" she asks, tucking that lock of hair she always seems to have hanging loose behind her ear. "It would probably be easier if I helped you."

"I can do it." My answer is quick, drawing her wounded gaze. "It won't take me long. Go. I'll get this taken care of."

"Are you sure?"

"Yes, sweetheart. I'm sure."

She smiles for only a moment before it vanishes. She turns toward the door, her tits no longer an issue, but those legs and that ass a bigger one. She glances over her shoulder, catching me soaking her in. "Last chance for me to give you a hand."

"I'm sure." I nod, motioning toward the door with my chin. "I got this."

Her gaze drops, and I'm suddenly reminded that my cock's out and I'm doing nothing to hide it. "Holler if you change your mind and need help wrangling that back into your pants."

"Lily," I warn, on the edge of breaking.

Does she do this shit on purpose? Does she have any clue what she does to me, how she affects me? Maybe she gets a kick out of tormenting me, taunting me with her beauty, and in my current situation, her ability to give me a boner.

She shrugs, but there's no smile on her face. It's then I remember why I came in here in the first place, putting my embarrassment aside to make her smile.

"Lily," I call out before she can open the door.

"Yeah?" She casts her blue gaze over her shoulder.

"You look beautiful tonight. Always so beautiful."

Her cheeks turn the palest shade of pink as the corners of her mouth turn up. She walks out without saying another word, leaving me with my pants down, cock out, and no hope of satisfaction in sight.

5

JETT

"WHAT ARE your intentions with our Lily?" the guy with long hair, covered head to toe in tattoos, asks from my side as he nurses a beer and stares at the fire.

I lean back, resting my beer on my leg, glancing from side to side at the two guys I don't know. "*Your* Lily?"

"We're kind of protective of her. Someone has to watch out for her. If not us, then who?" the other guy says, brushing his fingertips across his beard. He's not glaring at the fire; he's staring straight at me.

"I've known Lily my entire life." I'm being defensive. I shouldn't be. She's not mine and never has been.

"Doesn't answer my question. What are your intentions with her?" the first guy, the scarier of the two, repeats and grunts like an animal.

"What's your name again?" I ask, because to have a conversation about Lily requires me to at least know the guy's name. It's not an easy talk to have, and for some reason, I feel like it's her father grilling me and not a perfect stranger.

"Mammoth."

I crack a smile. "You're shitting me."

"Don't listen to his bullshit. That's his MC nickname. His real name is Saint."

My eyes widen at that revelation. "Anthony didn't have an issue with his baby girl dating someone from an MC?"

"Joe didn't either," Mammoth, the biker, says, tipping his chin toward the guy on the other side of me. "Pike's from the same MC."

"Wait." I shake my head. Did I step into the twilight zone? What the hell happened in the last five years? I never thought they'd let their daughters date anyone, let alone guys from an MC. "Their fathers are okay with this?"

"I work at Inked," the guy who's here with Gigi says, lifting his beer in the air. "And for the record, I was never officially a member of the MC. I only lived at the compound for a few years. Now, Mammoth—" he tips his head toward the other guy "—is still a Disciple."

I scrub my hand down my face, at a loss for words. "Well, shit. Never thought I'd see the fucking day," I whisper to myself, and I clear my throat as soon as I realize I've said those words louder than I wanted.

"Not for long, Pike," Mammoth tells him. "A few more months and I'll be as free as I can be under the circumstances."

Pike nods slowly, lifting his beer to his lips and holding the bottle in front of his mouth. "It's not going to be an easy road."

"Never is, brother. Never is," Mammoth mutters.

Pike's eyes are back on me. "You show up out of thin air, and suddenly Lily's wearing skimpy clothes, obviously trying to get your attention. So, we want to know if you're honorable or just looking for a piece of ass."

I tip my head toward the three girls as they sit in the distance on Gigi's tailgate, talking and glancing our way every once in a while. "Look at her," I tell them, smiling when Lily's gaze finds me. "Does she look like a piece of ass?"

I've done my best not to look at her. Every time I do, I pay for the quick glance, catching sight of way too much skin. The one time she decides to show off her body is the only time I can't afford to be turned on.

Life can be unfair and ironic.

"In that outfit, yep," Mammoth says. "But she's delicate and sweet. I don't want to kick your ass for breaking her heart, but I'd do it if you did."

A lesser man would probably piss himself at this point, but not me. I've known men like Mammoth my entire life, and being in the military taught me how to handle guys with big egos and even bigger barks. "I'm not planning on breaking her heart."

"Gigi said you asked Lily to move in with you. Kind of a big step for a girl like her," Pike says, studying me.

Jesus Christ. This is like a Gallo family grilling but without the Gallo family sitting around me. Anthony and Joe had to like these guys—and probably because they were just like them. Protective, aggressive, and unafraid to speak their minds.

"I need a place to stay, and Lily said she was living at home and seemed miserable about it. Figured we could get a place together, split the rent for practical reasons, and..."

"And you'd have built-in pussy?" Mammoth adds.

I shake my head. "You said you know Lily. So, I'd assume

you also know she wouldn't just put out for anyone. She's not that kind of girl, and I'd never think she'd be there to be my sex slave."

Pike's fingers tighten around the bottle. "Maybe you just want a maid to clean up after the other pussy you plan to bring home."

"Listen." I rub the back of my neck, not liking where the conversation is going. "I don't want a maid either. I'm a grown man and can clean up my own shit. I also don't want to live with a messy guy who's just looking to party. I want to live with someone who's solid, who I know, who I trust."

Mammoth grunts. "She's that."

"I also know her dad well enough to know he wouldn't want his daughter living on her own. I figured it would be a win-win for us both."

"She likes you, you know," Pike says, ignoring everything I just told him. "More than I've ever seen her like someone."

"You think?"

"She's all dressed up for you." Mammoth smiles genuinely. "I'd say she more than likes you."

I gaze across the field, old friends dancing and drinking to the music under the ink-stained sky. Does she like me? She's never really shown much of an interest in me. The few times we've talked, she's never come on to me or even hinted that I had a shot at getting her.

"Just don't fuck this up, and we'll be fine," Pike mutters. "Even if she likes you, she's not that type of girl."

"I know," I groan and set my beer in the grass next to me. "Now, if you'll excuse me, gentlemen. I have to go see about a girl."

Mammoth laughs. "Watch the wood," he tells me.

I shoot him a thumbs-up, giving him a fake smile, because I can't forget about my dick, and I wish he'd stop reminding me about it every chance he gets.

"Hey," I say when I'm within a few feet of the three girls.

"Hey." Gigi gives me a chin lift, her eyes sparkling with trouble. "I better get to my guy and see how he's doing."

Tamara giggles, placing her empty beer on the end of the tailgate before hopping down. "Yeah, babe. Let's go check on our men. I'm sure Lily can keep you company."

Lily looks like a deer in headlights. Eyes wide, not moving, just blinking at me like I'm about to slam into her.

"You doin' okay over here?" I ask her, trying to find something to say that won't revolve around my dick.

She nods, biting down on her lip, chewing the soft skin. "Yeah. I'm good. You?"

God, she looks so damn beautiful right now with the moonlight falling across her skin. So damn good that under any other circumstances, I'd make a move and see if she really liked me. But I can't risk it. Not now. Not with my dick so angry.

"Yeah. I'm great," I lie, hiding my misery.

"You sure have a lot of friends," she tells me, doing her best not to look right at me.

"You know this place. Throw a party and everyone comes. It's not me they're here for, but the free beer."

She laughs, and it's the best goddamn sound in the world. "They're here for you. You were the most popular boy in school. All the girls wanted you, and the guys wanted to be you."

"Did you want me, Lily?"

Her laughter dies as she slides her gaze to me. Even under

the moonlight, I can see the pink stain her cheeks. "Jett," she whispers as her eyes shimmer. "I..."

"I always wanted you," I tell her honestly.

"I..." Her teeth are back at her lip, nibbling the skin I'd always dreamed of kissing. "You wanted me?" She crinkles her cute little nose, still not moving.

I nod, telling her the truth for the first time in my life. "I did."

"You wanted every girl." She waves me off, snorting. "You did your best to get them too."

She's blowing me off, throwing my shitty behavior in high school right back in my face. Sure, I slept around back then and maybe even more so while in the Navy, but they never satisfied me. Those women, the ones before now, meant nothing and didn't fill the void left inside me for one girl in particular.

I rub my neck, trying to hide my agitation. "You want to go for a walk? There's a cave nearby, and I bet with the full moon—" I tip my head back, glancing up at the cloudless sky "—the water looks beautiful."

"There're caves here?"

I nod, knowing some of them very well. They were always an escape when being around people became too much. They were the only place I could go where nobody would find me in a small town like this. "A few, but the best one isn't far."

She glances around, her finger moving to her lips. "You sure it's safe?"

I nod, hoping it's just as it was the last time I was there. "It's safe, and quiet too." I smile, knowing Lily prefers silence to a rowdy party. "We'll just go for a minute, and if you don't like it, we'll come back."

"I don't know, this is your party. We should really stay."

"No one cares. They're not even paying any attention. I've never shared this place with anyone before. It was always my little secret, but I want to show it to you. Come on. Sneak away with me."

She brings her head up, a smile spreading across her face. "I'd be the first?"

"The one and only, sweetheart," I promise, completely truthful.

She nods and pushes off the tailgate, standing straighter, looking more beautiful somehow. "Show me," she says.

I motion for her to follow me, and she does. "Stay close. It's a five-minute walk from here, but it's been a while since I've done this in the dark, and I don't have a gun or knife if something's in the woods." When there's no sound behind me, I glance back, seeing Lily frozen again.

"Something in the woods?" she whispers, staring off into the darkness in front of me.

"Sweetheart, it's Florida. There are more than a few things that want to eat you."

Namely me, but I don't say that. There are predators everywhere here. Alligators, bears, coyotes, but nothing more dangerous to Lily than me.

"That's why I'm not an outdoors type of person."

I turn and walk the few feet back until I'm right in front of her. "I'd never let anything happen to you. Trust me, if something comes after us, I'll let them get me before I'd let them get their paws on you." I hold out my hand to her. "Do you trust me, Lily?"

She peers down, staring at my open palm. "I trust you, Jett," she whispers, sliding her soft skin against mine.

Her words wash over me, bathing me in the sweetness

that is her. I close my fingers around hers, really touching her for the first time. I don't speak but tick my head toward the darkness. The moment doesn't call for words.

We walk in silence, our hands clasped together as we leave the loud music and people behind us. The farther we go, the quieter everything gets. Nothing but the sound of the animals rustling in the brush, Lily's breathing, and my heart pounding filling the air.

I realize then, I've never held a girl's hand. How odd is that? I've never been one to have a girlfriend, finding attachment just too much entanglement for a guy like me. But here, in this moment, nothing feels more natural.

"What was that?" Lily asks, slowing her pace as a branch cracks in the distance.

"Maybe a lion," I lie, squeezing her fingers. "Get closer to me so we look like one person, and maybe he'll think we're too big to attack."

She scrambles closer, plastering her body against mine.

Fuck, I really am a goddamn dumbass. *Get closer to me.* What the hell am I thinking? I'm not. That's the problem. I can't risk a hard-on, but here I am, telling the beautiful girl with half her body exposed to plaster herself to me. Smart. Real freaking smart. Obviously, I love torturing myself, or I wouldn't have opened my dumb-ass mouth.

"Are you sure this will work?" she whispers, her warm breath skidding across my shoulder.

"More than you'll ever know," I tell her and keep moving us forward to stop myself from grabbing her softness and tasting her.

When we make it to the opening of the cave, she pauses and yanks my hand back. "Are you sure it's safe in there?"

She peers into the opening like something is going to jump up and bite her.

"It's safe. I've been here a hundred times. Anyway, the water's too cold for gators."

"Oh, well," she mumbles, "that's comforting."

"I'll help you inside," I tell her before I climb down the small hill, testing out the ground in the darkness. Turning, I reach up, grabbing both her hands this time, and help her inside, careful she doesn't slip.

"This is really a place," she says, as if she didn't believe me but came anyway.

"Of course, it's a place. I wouldn't lie to you." I'm careful with her, holding on to her way too long, but I can't stop myself. "The water's over here."

The moonlight disappears for a moment, shrouding us in darkness as we move toward the light ahead. Any other time, I'd be on Lily, trying to taste her sweetness after a lifetime of starvation.

"Oh wow," she says, standing at my side as we find the water, blue and bright under the night sky and the opening above. "This is the most beautiful thing I've ever seen."

"It is," I say, but I'm not looking at the water. I'm only staring at her.

I turn and dip my head, wanting to kiss her, but she ducks and moves away. "How did I never know about this place?"

I run my fingers through my hair, tamping down my frustration. "Not many people do."

Lily crouches near the edge of the water, brushing the surface with her fingertips. "It's so peaceful here."

The music from the party is nothing but a soft vibration. No voices. No traffic. No other people. We're totally alone.

It's the reason I come here to think and get away when things in life become overwhelming or I need a break from others.

"It's my escape," I tell her, watching her as she stares into the water, studying the depths.

She turns her head, gazing at me, the moonlight reflecting off the water, illuminating her face. "An escape from what?"

I squat next to her, admiring her beauty as she turns back to gaze at the blue depths. "Anything and everything."

"That's why I read," she replies without taking her eyes off the water. "It's an escape for me. I can be anything, do anything, live through the characters instead of staying trapped in my life."

"Trapped? Do you feel trapped?" Her words surprise me. I never thought of Lily as trapped by anything. I always knew she liked to read, never seeing her without a book in her hand.

She shrugs, keeping her eyes straight ahead. "Sometimes, but not as much as I did before." Lily turns her head, peering at me for a moment but turning away as soon as she notices the way I'm staring at her. "When I dropped out of school, I felt like a giant weight was lifted off my shoulders. But sometimes—" she swallows, pausing for a moment "—I still feel the same way when I look around, realizing I'm back home, living with my parents like I was in high school."

"I was serious about you living with me," I tell her, holding myself back from touching her, but wanting to so badly.

"We barely know each other," she whispers. "Why would you want to live with me?"

"Why wouldn't I want to live with you?"

She shrugs again. "I'm boring, Jett, and we don't know each other that well."

"Yes, we do," I argue.

"Not really. This has been our longest conversation ever. I'm the least interesting person you know. I'd rather stay in, curled up with a book, than go out drinking and partying."

Clearly, Lily still sees me as the eighteen-year-old boy who walked away from this town five years ago, heading to boot camp. I'm no longer that person, just like she's no longer the sixteen-year-old girl too scared to even look at me.

"I don't want to drink and party. I had enough excitement in my life being in the military and hitchhiking around the country for the last year. I want quiet. I want boring. I want you, Lily."

Her head snaps up, and her eyes widen. "You want me?"

Shit. I do want her, but I don't want to scare her away. I didn't ask Lily to move in with me so I could get in her pants. If that happens, it's a bonus, but I couldn't think of anyone else who would be a quiet, considerate roommate except for her. Now, if she decided to walk around the house with very little clothing on, that would be another bonus.

"Of course, or I wouldn't have asked."

"Right, Jett," she whispers, my name sounding like heaven coming from her lips. "I do want to get out of my parents' house."

"Then say yes," I beg, reaching out and grabbing her hand. "Say you'll at least look at a few places with me and think about it. It would get you out of your parents' house, and you wouldn't have to live alone. It would be a win-win."

"Maybe," she mutters, her gaze dipping to where our hands are connected.

I squeeze her fingers. "Promise me you'll think about it."

God, if my dick weren't broken, I'd be all over Lily, kissing her smooth skin, tasting her sweet lips. But right now, just kneeling next to her holding her hand is painful. Any time she's around, my cock wants to remind me just how very lonely he is and how stupid the idea of a cock piercing was.

"I'll think about it, Jett," she says, making me so damn happy.

I give her fingers another light squeeze. "Would it be so awful, living with me?"

She shakes her head. "I've never—" she swallows as she averts her gaze away from me and back to the water "—lived with a man before."

"Well, I've never lived with a woman either, so we're even."

She giggles softly, the sound echoing in the small space like a sweet melody. "You're kind of crazy."

I smile, unable to stop myself because Lily is so damn adorable. "I've been called worse, and I've never claimed to be normal."

"Normal is overrated," she whispers, standing in front of me, staring up into my eyes. "I guess we would get along, and I'd feel safer with you than living alone."

"I would hope so. I'd never let anything bad happen. There's nothing better than having a man in the house."

"I do own a gun, Jett, and I'm not afraid to use it." She doesn't even blink when she says that, but I do. I never thought Lily would be the type to be packing, but knowing her family and her father, I'm not completely surprised.

"Well then, I guess maybe you'll be the one protecting me." I chuckle, unable to take my eyes off her big blue eyes.

"Don't worry," she tells me, leaning into me, and I hold my breath, thinking she's going to kiss me. She places her hand on my chest, smiling up at me. "I'd never let anyone hurt you."

But I wonder—who's going to protect me from Lily?

6

LILY

LAST NIGHT WAS WEIRD. There's no other way to describe it. Jett kept looking at me funny, and every time I thought he might kiss me, he didn't. Maybe I had made too much of his compliments. He had always been a nice guy. Was I confusing his kindness for something more? Possibly.

I've never been good at reading people. My social skills have always been awkward and clunky. I've never been outgoing like Gigi and Tamara, instead finding crowds exhausting and overwhelming. Around my cousins, I'm not shy, and I don't try to hide my weirdness completely. But around everyone else, including Jett, I'm a total dork.

Why I'm standing here, next to Jett, staring up a big yellow house, is beyond me. He called. I came. Simple as that. Last night, he asked me again if I wanted to move in with him, but I still thought he was joking. I mean, why would he want to live with me when almost anyone in town would jump at the chance to live with Jett Michaels.

"What do you think? I know the color's ugly as sin, but

the outside isn't too bad, and the inside is... You'll just have to see it to believe it," Jett says.

I keep my eyes straight ahead, not daring to look at him, but I can feel his body heat against my arm. "It's not so bad. It's the color of sunshine," I say, trying to be positive.

That's me. Always a positive person. Never a bad thing to say about anything or anyone. Sometimes it's exhausting, but why look at the glass as half empty when it's really half full?

"I saw the photos online and knew it was the perfect place for us."

I like when he says *us* like we're a couple, when in reality, we're not even friends. "We can look at it, but I still don't think this is a good idea."

His arm is around my shoulders as soon as I finish speaking, fingers stroking my skin. "Keep an open mind, okay?"

I nod, unable to find my words because he's touching me. The warmth of his body pressed against my side scorches me hotter than the sun overhead.

The front door opens, and a tall, slender woman steps outside, holding a folder. "Mr. Michaels," the woman says, face bright and eyes hungry.

I've seen the look a million times when women stare at Jett. He's not a person to them but a piece of meat. He's an experience, not a relationship. He's an orgasm waiting to happen if they could just catch his eye. This woman, even more than twenty years his senior, isn't any different.

"Ms. Monroe. Thanks for coming on such short notice."

I snort, earning me a look from Ms. Monroe and an arm squeeze from Jett.

"This is Lily, my friend."

Did he punctuate the word friend? Was he trying to tell

her something, or maybe he was reminding me that we are nothing more than that and never will be?

Ms. Monroe doesn't even glance my way; she's too busy soaking in everything that is Jett. Today, he's wearing a tank top, his tatted, muscular arms visible and glistening under the bright Florida sun.

"Wait until you see the top floor," Jett whispers in my ear, sending goose bumps across my skin like there's suddenly a freak cold front.

The smile I give him is tight and strained. I shouldn't be here. We shouldn't be here. There's no way I can live with Jett. First, my dad will blow a freaking gasket. Second, my dad will probably try to beat Jett's ass. Third, he's a player, and the line of women he'd bring home would be longer than my mind could handle.

Jett moves us toward the door, Ms. Monroe's thirsty eyes never leaving his body and face. I'm invisible to her. Even if Jett and I were an *us,* I'm pretty sure she'd still look at him like a fine piece of steak and not a taken man.

We step into the foyer, a staircase in front of us, along with open space and a direct sightline to the back of the house. There are floor-to-ceiling windows with the most stunning view of the Gulf of Mexico.

"How much is this place?" I peer up at Jett, still tucked under his arm, and swallow. It has to be a fortune. There's no doubt about it. No one rents a house on the water, even this far up north in the middle of nowhere, without a hefty price tag.

"Eighteen hundred a month. It's a total steal."

I gape at him. "What's the catch? It's too cheap."

Jett just winks at me. "Don't worry, babe. There's no catch."

There's always a catch when you're getting a deal, but this is Jett, and I'm not going to argue.

"Here's the kitchen." Ms. Monroe motions to the side, and I follow with my eyes, soaking in the large kitchen with stainless-steel appliances, granite counters, and white cabinets. "It's been fully remodeled and updated."

The house is absolutely stunning. At least the downstairs is. But maybe it's a bargain because the upstairs is a hot mess with blue carpet. Maybe someone died here? That's always a possibility and a reason for a reduced rental rate. No one wants to live somewhere a person's been murdered.

"Did someone die here?" I ask, unable to hold the grim thought to myself.

"No. Of course not," Ms. Monroe answers quickly, giving me a look like I'm insane.

"Well, okay," I mumble as Jett's thumb brushes the strap of my tank top, reminding me he's still touching me.

"We'd like to see the upstairs," he tells her.

"Sure." She smiles and starts to move toward the staircase. Her phone rings, and as soon as she fishes it from her pocket and looks at the screen, she says, "I need to take this." After a tick of her chin, we take off up the stairs, leaving Ms. Monroe to take her phone call.

"You don't have to hold me, Jett. I'm not going to run," I tell him as we walk up the stairs, his arm still around me.

"I know you're not, but—" he peers down at me, his mouth tipping up at one side "—my dick still hurts, and you're helping me walk."

I almost trip over the next step when he talks about his dick, but somehow, I stay upright and don't tumble to my knees. "So, I'm a crutch?" I ask quickly, pretending I didn't almost face-plant into the stairs.

"Never."

I turn to face him, letting his hand fall away from me. Needing his hand to fall away from me. We're too close, and since we're not an *us* and will never be an *us,* it doesn't feel appropriate to stay connected longer than we need to. "Want me to take a look?"

"No," he blurts out, almost paling. "It's fine."

"Is it still big?"

Jett raises an eyebrow, smirking. "Is it ever small?"

I'm moving right past that question. "I mean is it still swollen?"

"Not as much as yesterday."

"That's good. You're healing. You'll be back in action soon and be able to resume normal activities." I smile, not finding the fact that we're talking about his penis odd at all.

It should be, though. We're not talking about a finger being swollen, but his manhood. I don't remember another time I've ever spent this much time talking to a man about his body, and I pray I never will again.

"So." Jett clears his throat, sliding his gaze away from me. "I thought you could take the master bedroom. There's an amazing attached bathroom with a huge soaking tub."

I blink, wondering where the hell this guy came from. "You want me to take the master because of the tub?"

He nods, rubbing a spot on the back of his neck. "Of course. It makes the most sense, and I'm sure you'd get more use out of that bathroom than I would."

"It doesn't seem fair," I whisper, watching his arm flex with each movement, itching to feel if he's as hard as he looks.

"I insist," he says, ticking his chin toward the room behind me. "Go look and tell me what you think."

I turn my head, staring into the open space, unsure if I should look because, what if I like the room? I don't want to like this house. I don't want to like being in this house with Jett. It's like playing house with a man you've always lusted after but could never have.

"Go on." He gives me a light push when I don't move. "I know you're going to love it."

I move away from him, needing a little space and a Jett break. The room's plain but stunning without furniture. There's plenty of natural light, dark hardwood floors, and a window seat at the far end, perfect for curling up with a good book. I step farther into the room, my eyes landing on the bathroom, and I fall instantly in love. On one side, there's a giant soaking tub, just as Jett had told me, with a large window above it and a view of the Gulf.

"Wow."

"I knew you'd love it," he calls out from the hallway.

I lean over and smile out at him, but he's not looking at me. He's staring at the floor, talking to himself. Maybe he's questioning this entire thing too, regretting bringing me here and making me fall in love with it.

"I can totally see myself in that tub."

His face tightens along with the muscles on his arms. "Me too," he says, still not looking at me.

Could I do this? Live with him without any chance of a relationship? This room alone is enough to draw me in, but living with Jett is a complication I never thought I'd face.

"This place is perfect for us."

There it is again. Us. I should correct him, but I don't and I can't. I like how it sounds coming out of his mouth even if he doesn't mean it the way I wish he did.

"Yeah," I mumble, gaping again at the bathroom, wanting

nothing more than to soak in that tub after a long day at work.

"You want to see the best part?"

I peek my head into the closet, my eyes widening when I realize it's bigger than my entire dorm room was back at school. What the hell was I going to do with all this space? I don't have enough clothes to fill a quarter of the closet, let alone the whole thing. "There's something better than this?"

"Way better," he says, his voice louder and closer.

I turn, finding Jett watching me from the doorway, his eyes on my legs and not my face. "The third floor is the best."

I blink. "The third floor?"

That's when he looks at me, no longer staring at the two thin sticks holding me upright. "It's why I know you'll love this house and not be able to say no to me."

I'm pretty sure I couldn't say no to him anyway, no matter what's on the top floor. It's why I stick to myself. I have an inability to say no to everyone, and Jett's no exception. I'm a people pleaser, trying to make everyone else happy around me instead of myself. It's why I wasted three years of my life studying for a career in medicine when it was the last thing I wanted to do forever.

"Show me," I say, liking the way he smiles at me.

His arm is around me before we take the first step, Jett claiming he needs my help up the stairs, but I'm pretty sure he's lying. I know the piercing has to hurt and I know he's swollen, but Jett's a man's man.

When we get to the top, I see it. The sweeping view of the Gulf of Mexico from the sun-room and a large outdoor rooftop patio.

"I thought we could put some comfy furniture up here. You could read in the sunshine or under the stars."

"What are you going to be doing the entire time?" I ask, stepping away from his grip because, again, this is too much.

"I'll be here too."

"Well, duh." I snort, covering my face because the noise was louder and more piggish than I expected.

His smile grows, eyes twinkling. "I'm sure I'll find something to keep me busy."

I try to ignore the flashes of naked women underneath him playing through my mind. He's grown, and although he keeps saying we're an *us,* we are not. I can't expect him to be celibate if we live together. Should I bring up the topic with him? No way. Talk about awkward. I'd rather talk about his swollen penis than him sleeping with random women.

"I love the house, Jett," I whisper, staring off into the distance, watching the sunlight bounce off the rippling water. "But I can't."

"Why?" he asks, standing too close behind me.

"I don't think we can live together."

"Why?" he repeats, closer than before, the heat of his front against my back unmistakable.

My nose tickles as I try to erase the pictures of me living here, reading in this very spot. "I'm not the right roommate for you."

"You're perfect, Lily."

God, how I wish he meant those words. Not just as a roommate, but something more. Something bigger. But this is me, and he's him. The nerd and the player. An impossible combination in living and love.

"I'm really boring, Jett." My voice is small, but I say what needs to be said. "You don't want to live with someone like me."

He places his hands on my shoulders, the grip strong yet soft. "There's no one else," he whispers.

The tickle in my nose grows, and my vision blurs.

"Please say yes." He sweeps his thumbs under the straps of my tank top, stroking my back so tenderly, the tears grow. "Please," he begs.

I can hear Tamara and Gigi ripping into me about being a sissy and living life for once. I promised myself after I quit school that I'd try to reach beyond my comfort zone.

"Just do it." Gigi's annoying voice fills my head.

"Yes," I say, knowing I'll regret it if I don't give in, but understanding I'll probably be miserable living with him too.

"Yes?"

"Yes," I murmur, dabbing at my eyes and blinking away the tears before he can see them. "I can't say no to you."

His chest presses into my back as his hands move to my front. He wraps his arms around me as he clasps his fingers together near my stomach, hugging me. "You've made me the happiest guy in the world, Lily."

I stop breathing, soaking in his warmth, strength, and scent. My stomach knots as his chin brushes my shoulder, his lips almost touching my skin.

"So very happy," he whispers. "I won't make you regret this."

But I know… I already do.

7

JETT

My mother blinks and then looks at me funny, forehead crinkling, eyebrows drawn down just like she used to when I did something stupid. "No."

"No?" I ask, rubbing my neck and giving the look right back to her.

She shakes her head, lips pursed. "No."

I scowl, unable to hold back my distaste at the word. "Why?"

I wasn't asking her permission. I just thought I'd let her know Lily and I had signed the lease on the house, and I'd be moving out as soon as the background check came back.

"You cannot move in with her," she tells me, moving her fingers to her temples, rubbing tiny circles against her skin. "How do you even think this is a good idea?"

"Why isn't it a good idea?"

My dad takes this moment to make his grand entrance. "What's wrong?" he asks, looking between the two of us sitting at the kitchen table. "I know that look, Sophia."

Mom throws one hand toward me, rolling her eyes. "Kayden, your genius son..." She shakes her head, not even finishing the sentence. "You tell him."

I tip my head back, staring at my father upside down. "I'm moving in with Lily."

My father's eyes widen. "Lily who?"

"Gallo." I sigh.

"Lily Gallo?" he repeats, tilting his head.

"Yeah."

"Um, no." He shakes his head, staggering a little.

What the fuck? Not only is my mother acting like I'm asking permission, but now my father's doing the same.

"I wasn't asking," I tell my dad, lifting my head upright to see my mother glaring at me.

He slides into the chair between my mother and me, holding his head. "I'd like our family line to continue."

"That's the plan, Dad. Someday—not yet, though—I'll have lots of babies."

He groans, shaking his head. "Not if you move in with Lily."

My parents aren't ones to be dramatic, but right now, they're acting like I'm hitching my wagon to Satan's daughter.

I scratch at the hair along my jaw, confused. "I don't get it. I thought you two would be happy. I'm not moving in with a party animal. She's not a drug addict or a weirdo. She's a solid girl, and you've known her family forever."

He drags his hand down his face like I'd just told him I knocked the girl up. Which I didn't...not yet, at least. "I've known her father for over twenty years, Jett. Twenty freaking years."

"And the problem is?"

"Mike is going to kill you first and then me. That's the

problem." Dad slams his fist down on the table, almost foaming at the mouth.

My head jerks back because although Mike used to be a professional fighter, he's not anymore. He's older, slower, and I'm pretty sure he'll be happy his daughter is going to be living with someone who's going to keep her safe. "Why?"

"No man, no matter how loving he seems, wants his baby girl living with another man. Especially if that man is you."

"I'm a good guy, Dad. Mike likes me. I saw him a few days ago when I went to the shop to get..." I snap my mouth closed, not wanting my parents to know about my dick. Actually, not wanting my mother to know because she'd lose her shit, and it's embarrassing as hell.

My mother glares at me. "When you went to get what?" she asks, tapping her fingernail against the table, eyes hard and lips flat.

"Nothing," I lie, giving her my best smile, the one that always makes her happy. "I talked to him. He was happy to see me."

"I'd be happy to see you too until you were going to be sleeping under the same roof as my only daughter."

"Am I so bad?" I'm opening a can of worms here, but at least they're not asking about what I had done anymore.

"Baby," Mom says, placing her hand on top of mine, "you're a wonderful person. So giving and loving." She finally smiles for the first time since I told her the news. "Sometimes too loving and with too many women. I don't know anyone in this town who doesn't know you're a slut, including Lily's father."

I touch my chest, pretending to be offended, but hell, I've been called worse. "I'm not a slut."

My mother tips her head back and laughs. "You are and

not even ashamed of it either. You're just like your father before I met him."

"There was no one before you, sweetheart," Dad tells Mom, sweeping his hand up her arm. "Never anyone else."

She touches his face, brushing her fingers over his cheek. "You're a horrible liar, baby. Our son has your genes, and if he's lucky, Mike won't murder him when he hears the news."

I lean back, scratching my stomach. "I'm not worried." I wince as my jeans push into my dick, reminding me of how this entire course of events got started.

I never meant to ask Lily to move in with me. That's not why I went to Inked. I went there for a piercing, but after talking to her, I realized she was the best person I could ask. I needed a roommate, and no one else I could think of would give me peace without being up in my face all the time. After leaving the Navy, I wanted freedom, quiet, and room to move around. Something I couldn't get at my parents' house or with anyone except Lily.

"Wait," Mom says, pulling her phone in front of her and tapping on the screen. "Let's see what Suzy says."

"She'll think it's the best idea ever. Aunt Suzy loves me." I smirk, knowing the woman is a pushover for me. She's my godmother and has been a sucker for me for as far back as I can remember. My mom and she used to be roommates and have always been best friends.

"Hello." Suzy's voice comes out of the phone and I almost fall off the chair, but somehow, I retain my composure.

I thought my mother was shitting me and not really calling her, but again, I'm wrong.

"Hey, babe. What are you guys up to tonight?" Mom asks, smiling at me, looking smug.

"We're just making some popcorn and going to settle in with the girls to watch a movie. How about you guys?"

"Not too much. I was just sitting here talking to Jett."

"Hey, Jett baby. I miss you," Aunt Suzy says in a sugary tone. "When do I get to see your pretty face?"

"Whenever you want, Auntie." I stick out my tongue at my mom because victory will be mine.

"Why don't you come to Grandma's for dinner? I'm sure they'd love to see you."

I love that Suzy calls Mrs. Gallo my grandma. She's not, of course. We have no blood in common, but that never stopped them from making me feel like part of the family whenever I was around.

"Maybe I will," I tell her, crossing my arms, smiling at my mom.

"Speaking of family..." Mom clears her throat. "Jett just signed a new lease. He's moving out already."

"Didn't he just get home?" Suzy asks my mom.

"He did a few days ago."

"Joe said he came by the shop to get..."

"Will you be my first dinner guest?" I ask Aunt Suzy, doing everything I can to change the subject. I don't mind talking about Lily, but my dick is still off-limits.

"Wait," Mom says, glaring at me. "What did he stop at Inked for?" She holds up her hand as soon as I open my mouth, and her glare turns icy cold. "I want the truth."

"Oh. Well." Aunt Suzy giggles. "Maybe you should ask him."

"Jett?" Mom asks, tilting her head, eyes narrowed.

I shrug, keeping my mouth shut because I know Aunt Suzy, and she's not going to keep my secret. She always spills.

"Oh, for fuck's sake!" Uncle Joe yells in the background. "The kid got his dick pierced."

My eyes widen, and so do my mother's.

Motherfucker.

I should've known Suzy had us on speakerphone and that Uncle Joe would rat me out.

"Lily did the piercing," he adds, making things worse.

My mother covers her face, groaning into her palms. "Lily touched his penis?" Mom whispers.

Dad gives me a fist to the shoulder, but more as a congratulations than a punishment. "Did you cry?" he asks me, earning him a dirty look from my mother over the top of her hands.

"Shut up," she mouths to him. "You're not helping."

"That's usually how it works, babe," Uncle Joe tells my mom. "Can't stick a needle through it without getting your hands dirty."

My mother leans back, one hand still in front of her face like she's mortified and horrified all at once. "Un-fucking-believable. What the hell do you need another hole in your penis for?"

I shrug. "I always thought they were cool as shit. I've wanted one for a long time but never got around to getting it done while I was in the service."

"It has nothing to do with women?" Dad asks, hitting my shoulder again, raising an eyebrow. "I hear the ladies love a little jewelry."

"You two need to shut your mouths," Mom growls, and I can tell this conversation isn't going where she wants.

I laugh softly, shaking my head. "Anything not to talk about my dick anymore with my parents."

"Son, we've seen it more times than you can count. Trust

me, we're well acquainted with it," Dad says like he's making shit better, but he's not.

My mom's nodding as if the conversation is normal, but it's fucking not. If I could crawl away and never talk about my dick again in front of my parents, I'd fucking do it, but I have a feeling this won't be the last time the topic will be discussed.

"I can't believe Mike let Lily touch Jett's penis," Suzy whispers as if she's shocked just like my mom. "How did that go down?"

I lean over the phone, staring down at the screen showing her name. "Hey, Auntie, can we talk about something else other than my junk, please?"

She giggles louder. "I've seen it too, baby. Don't be embarrassed. Every guy has one."

"Fuck me. You're all wacked out of your head," I mutter, craning my neck upward and closing my eyes.

"We babysat you all the time when you were little, Jett. Be proud, boy. You're not half bad," Uncle Joe says, and it's a dig.

Half bad?

He's out of his mind.

My cock is large.

I know it.

He knows it.

And for sure, my parents know it.

Hell, most of the city knows it, from the way the women ogle me.

Even though I'm not embarrassed by the damn thing, I still don't want to sit around and talk about it all night.

"Back to Jett moving out," Mom says, tapping her finger on the table again.

"How exciting," Suzy says, always the optimist. "I know

how nervous I was when Gigi said she was getting her own place, but honestly, it was the best thing for her."

"For us too," Joe laughs, deep and loud.

"Stop it," she chides him. "Anyway, don't panic, Sophia. He's grown now. Hell, he served in the Navy and was out to sea for months at a time. I'm sure he can handle living on his own. The man needs space to spread his wings."

"He's moving in with Lily," Mom blurts out, ripping off that Band-Aid so fucking fast.

Suzy gasps and then coughs. "He's what?"

Mom smirks at me with a total I-told-you-so look while I cross my arms, not caring.

"I don't think I heard you right. I thought you said Jett's moving in with Lily," Suzy says.

"You heard me right. They signed the lease *together* this morning."

"Oh fuck," Uncle Joe mutters in the background, eavesdropping. "Don't come for dinner tomorrow, Jett. Mike will be there, and if you want to keep breathing, you stay gone."

"What's wrong with Lily and me living together?" I ask Uncle Joe, making him part of the conversation since he's already put himself in the middle.

Joe barks out a bitter laugh. "You shittin' me with that question?"

"I'm not shitting you. I'd never shit you," I grumble. "I'm a good guy. Why wouldn't Mike want Lily to live with me?"

Joe's laughter is so loud, he's almost howling.

"Ignore him," Suzy says, but she's still giggling— softly, but she is. "Jett, you are a good guy, but..."

"I don't plan on sleeping with her. Jesus." I throw up my hands, wishing my family would give me a little credit. "You know the high school version of me, not the man I am today. Maybe I'm not the slut my mom calls me."

"Oh, honey. You were and are a slut," Aunt Suzy says, punching me in the stomach with how easily those words rolled off her tongue.

"I wouldn't let Gigi live with you, and I know you'd never touch her. She's like your sister, but I know exactly how you are. Just like your dad."

I eye my father, wondering what I don't know about him that everyone else seems to. "Dad's seriously the most boring human being ever."

"Man, you got that kid snowed," Joe replies. "Ask him about the bathroom sink."

Dad's eyes widen immediately. "Just a plumbing accident."

"Bullshit," Joe coughs.

Dad smiles, trying to hide it behind his hand.

"Lily will be safe with me. She wanted to move out, and I needed a roommate. We're killing two birds with one stone. I get a quiet roommate like I want, she gets freedom, and I can watch over her and make sure she's safe."

"But who's going to watch you to make sure you behave?" Suzy whispers.

"She could do worse than me, you know, Auntie?" I say to her.

"Lily's just so innocent, baby."

"So were you when I met you, sugar," Uncle Joe says. "Look how that turned out."

I gag a little, thinking about them having sex. Ick.

"That's what I'm saying. I was so pure, sweet, and innocent, and all it took was one bad boy to ruin me forever," Suzy tells me. "You'll ruin Lily. This, I know."

"First," Mom laughs, "you were not innocent and pure.

Let's be real here, Suz. You were a dirty girl, looking for a man who'd let you live out your fantasies. But you're right. He did ruin you and Jett could ruin Lily, but he could also end up breaking her heart."

"Lily's purer than I ever was," Suzy says. "I mean, she's never even had sex before."

There's an invisible fist that connects with my stomach, knocking all the wind out of me. *A virgin.* Lily Gallo, the sweet thing, has never had sex before? I find it hard to believe. I didn't think that was still possible in this day and age. I knew she'd had a boyfriend or two during high school, and I just assumed they'd done it.

"Sugar," Uncle Joe growls. "I don't think that was public knowledge or to be shared."

"Oh damn. You guys didn't hear that from me," she says like I can wipe that shit from my memory. "Pretend I never said it."

Nothing can wipe that knowledge from my head. Nothing. No amount of alcohol or drugs could make me forget that Lily Gallo has never been touched. Never been made love to. Never felt a man move inside her.

"Well, this has been enlightening," my mother says, eyes still narrowed on me. "I'm going to go spend a little time with my son before Mike kills him tomorrow."

"You're cute, Mom," I laugh, but she isn't.

"Good idea. And, Jett," Suzy says, waiting for me to reply.

"Yeah, Auntie?"

"Maybe rethink dinner tomorrow. Although everyone would love to see you, with Lily dropping the news on her folks, maybe it's not the right day to stop by and say hello."

"Yeah. I think you're right."

"Such a dumbass," Dad whispers. "He's going to get us both killed."

"Both?" I ask, raising an eyebrow.

"I can't let you get your ass beat by Mike and not at least stick up for you. I'm going to die because of you. I knew it would happen eventually, just never thought it would be at the hands of a Gallo."

I laugh, mocking him. But tomorrow, we'll find out if he's right.

8

LILY

WHAT THE HELL was I thinking? Clearly, I wasn't, or else I wouldn't have signed the lease agreeing to move in with Jett.

I wanted out of my parents' house. That was the only thing running through my mind as I picked up the pen and scribbled my name on the blank line just below Jett's.

I've always been an overanalyzer, thinking about things for weeks or months before acting. But not with him, and not about becoming roommates.

"You have to tell them today." Gigi stares at me, arms crossed over her chest, a bright, happy smile on her face.

She's loving this. So's Tamara. Other than the day I told my parents I was dropping out of college, I've always done everything to make them happy and stay under the radar. I was the proverbial "good girl," which in real English means boring and predictable.

I clutch my stomach, leaning over my legs to stare at the cement underneath my feet. "It can wait."

Tamara's on the chaise lounge, wearing her favorite white bikini, sunglasses pushed up over her hair. "No, it can't. You have to tell them today before they hear about it from someone else."

"No one else knows," I groan. "I can't do this. It was a huge mistake."

"Babe, my parents know," Gigi says. "Jett's parents called them last night and spilled the beans."

"Mothertrucker," I whisper into my knees, knowing Aunt Suzy can only keep a secret for so long.

I think about drowning myself in the pool that's only a few feet away to avoid telling my parents about everything. But I know not even death will keep my secret.

"You're such a pussy," Tamara laughs, shaking her head, judging me. "Your parents will be okay. They were okay about college, and you thought they'd never accept your decision."

"But that was about school, and this is about living with a boy."

Gigi giggles, covering her face as soon as I glare at her. "He's not a boy, Lily. He's all man, and from the looks of him, he has his sights set on you."

I wrinkle my nose. "He does not."

"Does too," she argues.

"Girl, that man is hot for you," Tamara adds, fanning her face with her hand. "The way he looks at you…" She shakes her head and blows out a breath. "It's scorchin'."

"You're delusional."

I've seen the way he looks at me. It's like I'm a foreign creature, a weirdo he's not sure how to handle. Sure, sometimes I think there's a spark, but as soon as the ember starts to glow, it flickers out just as fast.

Tamara pulls her sunglasses down over her eyes, lying flat to soak up the rays. "I know men, and I know lust. And that man is lusting after you pretty hard."

"Are you sure we know the same guy?" I ask, rocking back and forth on the end of Gigi's chaise lounge.

"She's clueless." Tamara sighs. "How did you hang around us all these years and never learn anything?"

I curl forward, pressing my chest against my knees, still staring at the same spot on the cement of the patio. "I learned. I just never acted on anything. I know men, too," I say defensively.

"Boys in books don't count," Tamara mutters. "They're not real."

Gigi sits up and places her hand on my back. "Let's make this interesting."

"Whatcha thinking?" Tamara says without hesitation, loving my misery.

I glance over my shoulder, shooting daggers at my cousin who used to be my favorite but is quickly losing the title.

Gigi smiles, winking at me. "If Jett doesn't kiss her or have him under her in a month, we'll fund your book habit for a year."

"You realize that's a lot of money," I tell her with a raised eyebrow. "I read a book a day."

"You need to be getting dicked every day instead of just reading about it," Tamara says like it's that freaking easy.

"I don't need to get dicked every day." I fake gag because who says things like that…my cousin.

"You so do," she adds. "Hard and deep, babe. Then you wouldn't be so uptight. You need a guy who's going to fuck the worry right out of you."

I shift in the chair, giving them each a middle finger. "You two can fuck right off."

Gigi gasps before bursting into a fit of laughter. "She definitely needs some cock."

I narrow my eyes at her. "You're supposed to be on my side."

Gigi's smile grows. "Oh, I am. That's why I agree you need a man."

"Men don't complete women. They're a complication and nothing more," I grumble, curling around my legs again. "I don't need sex either. I'm perfectly fine the way I am."

"You're going to get arthritis in your hands at an early age," Tamara says with a straight face. "You need a man to touch you so your joints can get a break."

"I don't always use my fingers. So there," I say, sticking out my tongue and instantly regretting my words.

Tamara's smile is immediate and freaking huge. "Finally put that bullet I bought you for your birthday to use, then?" She raises an eyebrow, staring at me over the rim of her sunglasses.

"I'm not talking about masturbation with you."

"You know what's hot," Tamara says, ignoring my statement. "Watching a guy pleasure himself. Fuck me. That shit is off the chain."

I gape at her, wondering how we're related when we're so different. "You seriously have issues," I mutter, rolling my eyes.

"No. I have to agree with her. There's something about the way a man's hand moves against his cock that turns me on. It's so erotic, especially when they're staring at you, knowing you're watching them."

"As opposed to what?" I gape at Gigi, surprised she's agreeing with Tamara on this one.

Both my cousins are freaks. I'm Mother Teresa compared

to them. I always knew this, but the way they freely talk about sex now kind of freaks me out. We used to gossip, wondering what it would be like, but now they have real-world experience to back it up. And, me? I'm still the untouched flower with only a few hand jobs and a failed attempt at a blow job under my belt.

"As opposed to when you're being sneaky and catch them in the act. I mean, it's still sexy, though. When they don't know you're there, watching through a crack in the door as they stroke their hard cocks," she says "cock" with extra emphasis like the very thought of a penis drives her wild.

"You're a creeper," I whisper.

"You'll see," Tamara tells me. "You're going to live with a man now. Things are bound to happen. You're telling me if you catch Jett in the act, you'll just walk away and give him privacy?"

"Of course," I blurt out.

"Sure," Gigi laughs.

"I would. I wouldn't invade his privacy that way."

"You see him spanking his monkey, and I know you'll watch. You're a freak, Lily. You're hiding within the pages of your books, but you're our cousin and you're just as filthy as us. Just as slutty as us, but you've never let your freak flag fly. I know once you have a taste, you'll be hooked like it's a drug, jumping up on that fuckstick every chance you get."

I gape at Tamara, my mouth opening and closing as I wrinkle my forehead. What is wrong with her? No one uses the word fuckstick, and I'm not a freak. Maybe she is. Who am I kidding? I know she is. But I most certainly am not.

"Kids, dinner's almost ready!" my mom yells from the sliding glass door in the back of my grandparents' house.

I grab my cover-up, pulling the soft material over my head and covering my modest one-piece swimsuit.

"We need to get you a bikini," Tamara says as she stands and stretches, showing off her hot body.

"No bikinis," I tell her, staring down at the oversized cover-up that hangs to my knees. "I already show enough skin in this."

"You should've been Amish," Gigi tells me, pulling at the thin material around my body. "You have a perfect body, and all you do is hide it."

I yank the material from her hands and stalk away from the two of them, leaving them on the patio to talk about my prudishness.

I don't even have both legs inside the house when my aunt Suzy catches my arm, pulling me off to the side. "You better tell them," she says, glancing around the room like she doesn't want anyone else to hear.

"After dinner," I tell her as a knot forms in my stomach. Every second that ticks by is a second I'm closer to having to spill the beans.

Her eyes widen. "He's here," Suzy whispers.

I tilt my head, wondering why my aunt is acting like such a weirdo. "Who?"

"Jett," she squeaks, covering her mouth quickly.

Now it's my turn for my eyes to go wide. "He can't be."

Suzy grimaces, looking like she's about to cry or maybe laugh. It can go either way with her. She's a quirky one like me. "I may have invited him," she whispers.

"What?" I screech, panic clawing at my insides.

"I didn't know you two were moving in together." Aunt Suzy whispers the last bit, her gaze sweeping around the room again. "Since he just got back, I thought the family would like to see him."

I gasp, covering my mouth, trying to stop the vomit rising up my throat. "Why would you do that?"

"We always invite him over when he comes home on leave, but you've always been at school when he's around."

"Damn," I mutter.

"Yeah," she says, and we stare at each other for a few seconds without speaking. "So, you better tell them before they find out by accident."

"Shit," I whisper, hating that there's no more time to waste. The three biggest blabbermouths in the family know, and now that Jett's here, he may slip and tell my family everything before I have a chance. I know my parents are going to go ballistic, but it's better if they hear it from me first than from someone else.

"They're in the kitchen with Grandma. Go in there and tell them now. They won't freak out too bad with her around." Somehow, she says that with a straight face and places her hands on my shoulders, turning me toward the kitchen. "Do it now. Before it's too late."

She knows exactly how my father is, especially when it comes to me. The man has always been dramatic and over the top, but throw me into the mix and he gets so weird. For as big as he is and as tough as he can be, he's sometimes such a girl.

"You can do this," she tells me when I don't move.

"I can do this," I repeat, trying to convince myself that I can, in fact, do this and come out still breathing. "I can do this."

I take my first step, my fingers tingling like they're asleep. I shake out my hands, inhale slow and deep, and close my eyes before blowing out the breath and repeating the process.

"I can do this."

"Honey," Mom says, her face lighting up as soon as she sees me. "Look who's here." She throws out her hand, pointing toward the other side of the room.

My eyes follow her movement and widen immediately.

I'm met by the beautiful blue eyes of the man who's going to be my roommate. "Hey," he says, his voice deep and smooth, washing over me.

"Hey," I squeak, moving my hand toward my face, brushing away a lock of hair as my cheeks heat.

My father clears his throat, reminding us he's in the room. "It's always good to see you, Jett. I hope today is less eventful than last time."

My mother slaps my father's chest, glaring at him. "Stop it, Michael. You're the one who insisted she learn piercing and be your apprentice. You can't expect her only to work on clients she doesn't know or that you like. It can't all be about boobs and ears."

I snort because I love my mom. She knows what an idiot my dad is sometimes, and she's always quick to come to my rescue. Even after I broke the news about medical school, she still supported me. It was my father who had the meltdown, needing time to deal with the realization I was never going to be a doctor.

"Like fuck, it can't," he grumbles.

Back in the day, my dad was a total badass. When he met my mom, he was a professional fighter and even won a national championship, which he still talks about to this day. He was used to getting his way, mostly because of his size and the fact that most people thought he would beat their ass if they didn't give him what he wanted.

But I know the other side of my dad. The loving side. The side that will bend over backward for the people he loves and is selfless and giving. That doesn't mean he isn't a dramatic man-child sometimes, but my mother knows how to handle him to help him see the light.

I swing my gaze to the side, seeing Jett's eyes locked on me. My smile is immediate and tight.

"She's going to have to touch a lot of vaginas and penises in her line of work. Just like you."

"Stop." My father covers his ears, groaning. "I don't want to talk about my daughter and penises."

My mother smiles, loving tormenting him for some reason. "Lots of penises."

If I could crawl in a hole and die right now, I would. I don't want to listen to my parents talk about vaginas and penises, especially not about my touching them.

"I'm moving in with Jett," I blurt out, figuring the conversation can't get any more awkward, and at least I won't have to hear them say penis again.

My father's body goes board straight, and my mother's head snaps to the side as they both stare at me.

"You're what?" Mom blinks at me, cocking her head like she didn't hear me right the first time.

"I'm moving in with Jett. Not moving in, moving in. Like, we're not a couple. But we're going to be roommates," I blabber, hoping I can keep talking long enough for them to calm down. Maybe if I explain, or overexplain, they'll understand and we'll both walk out of this room alive. "I've wanted to move out for a while but could never find the right place. But Jett was looking for a roommate, and he found this amazing house on the water, but he needed someone to split the rent with. He asked me, and I thought, 'Sure, why not.' So, yay, I'm moving out." I suck in a breath, spewing all those words without so much as stopping to breathe.

My father growls and takes a step forward, moving toward Jett until my mother catches his wrist with her outstretched hand. "Wait," she tells him, but she's staring at me.

My father stares over his shoulder at my mother, almost foaming at the mouth. "Wait?"

She nods, not looking in his direction. "Baby, this is kind of sudden, isn't it?" she asks me.

I shake my head, glancing at Jett, pleading for him to run without saying the words. "No, I've been looking for a month now and couldn't find anything. Gigi's apartment complex is full, and they have a waiting list. I was going to move farther south as soon as I could find someplace safe and clean."

"The house is beautiful, Mrs. Gallo. And of course, Lily will be safe because I'll be there to protect her and make sure nothing happens. She's in good hands."

"You better run, son, because I don't want my daughter in your hands, and I'll rip them off your body to stop it from happening."

I gasp, covering my mouth. "Daddy, stop it," I whisper into my palm.

"Michael Salvatore Gallo, stop your foolishness right now," Mom scolds him, tightening her fingers around his wrist.

She broke out the middle name. She means business, and she's never been afraid to put him in his place. "She's a twenty-one-year-old woman who's smart, caring, and kind. I'm sure she put a lot of thought into this before she made her decision. Our Lily wouldn't rush into something unless she really wanted it."

I don't correct her because I'm not stupid. I put a lot of thought into moving out, but not into moving in with Jett. He asked, and I couldn't say no. Not because I wondered how his mouth tasted or what he sounded like when he moaned, but because I like him, and I do feel safe around him.

"Would you rather she live far away and be alone? Imagine her walking into a dark apartment in a bad neighborhood every night. Would you rather she do that than live with him?"

My mother's being rational, but my father has never been known for possessing that quality. He's always been an act first and apologize and beg for forgiveness later kind of guy.

"I didn't mean any disrespect, sir," Jett says, trying to calm my father's fears and temper. I'm not sure Jett realizes just how close to death he really is in this moment. If he did, he would've run as soon as I dropped the bomb. "Lily and I have always been friends, and when she mentioned she was looking for a place, I figured it was perfect."

"I'm sure you did," my father growls.

We've always been friends? If gawking at him from across the room while he pretended I didn't exist was friendship, we were besties.

"I trust you, Lily," Mom says and sighs. "You've always had a good head on your shoulders, sweetheart. You trust her too, don't you, Mike?" She stares at him, holding his eyes, waiting for the big lug to come to his senses.

"I trust her, Mia. I've always trusted her judgment." My father turns his head, eyes moving from Jett's feet to his face. "It's him I don't trust."

Jett puts up his hands. "I'll be a perfect gentleman. I promise."

I snort, earning me three sets of angry eyes, and I have to backpedal. "Nothing will happen. I swear. I'm me, remember." I roll my eyes because I'm the boring girl. "I'm the responsible one of the family."

"You touch her or hurt her, and I'll make you regret the day you were born, Jett," Dad tells him, pointing his big meaty index finger toward a less-than-worried Jett Michaels. "I will rip off your body parts slowly, starting with your dick, son."

My mom chuckles as Jett pales. "Sweetheart—" Mom plasters her body against my father's arm, stroking his back "—don't worry. Jett just had a piercing. He can't even begin to think about sex for weeks, if not months."

Jett tucks his hands into his front pockets, averting his eyes. "Very true, Mrs. G," he mumbles, not looking happy about the reminder. "It's a long healing process."

"Super long." I rock back on my heels, feeling the weight of breaking news fall away. "So freaking long. Long and thick," I whisper.

"What?" my father growls, snapping his head in my direction.

My eyes widen, and I freeze. "What?"

"Michael, are you just going to stand there, or carry the heavy tray of lasagna behind you into the dining room? Everyone's waiting," Grandma says, winking at me like she knows she's saving my ass.

"Coming, Ma," he grumbles, giving me the side-eye as he turns his back, grabbing the very tray Grandma told him to.

Mom smiles at me, tipping her head. "No more surprises," she mouths, and I cover my heart, giving her my promise.

"That was close," Jett says to me as soon as my parents leave the room, but not before my father almost knocks him over with his shoulder.

"It's a good thing your penis is broken, or this could have gone very differently." I laugh, nudging him with my arm.

"Yeah," he mutters, giving me a pained smile. "Everything would be very different."

And I wonder what he means, but I don't ask. I don't want to know, really. I'd like to think he picked me to live with for more than just convenience, but I know the reality, and it makes my heart hurt.

"Hungry?" I ask, somehow keeping the smile on my face.

His eyes sweep across my features, eyes flickering as his tongue sweeps over his bottom lip. "Starving."

And just like that, I don't know if he's talking about his stomach or his penis.

9

JETT

It's been a week since we broke the news to our parents. A week since Lily's father didn't smash my face in with his fist, and in my book, that's what I call winning. Everyone, including my mother, thought for sure I'd end up dead or, at the very least, in the emergency room, but they were wrong.

"I think you should put your bed on the third floor," her father says, hoisting her queen-sized mattress on his back like it weighs nothing. "The view is better."

"Daddy, I can't sleep on the patio. Be real for a minute." She swats his arm, smiling at him so sweetly, I know why he's protective of her.

Lily's the best kind of person. She's caring when others are not. She's sweet when she doesn't need to be. There's a goodness in her that wasn't taught but is genetic. Her mother is just like her, but Mia knows how to control people too, mainly her husband.

"Mike, our daughter is not sleeping on the patio."

"It has windows," he argues, groaning as the mattress starts to slip down his back. "It's a sun-room, not a patio."

I rush toward him, wanting to help, but when his eyes meet mine and narrow, I back off. Lifting my hands, I step toward the never-ending stack of boxes.

Lily runs her hand down her ponytail, smoothing the hairs that trail down to her elbow. "I'm not giving up the master bedroom and the tub."

She looks beautiful like this. Natural, without any makeup. Tiny workout shorts, a tank top, and a workout bra, leaving very little to my imagination.

"Don't forget about the view from the tub too," Mia adds, agreeing with her daughter and pissing off Mike more.

I'm not talking. Not giving him a reason to hate me more. I get it. I'd hate me too. The smug kid who slept with half the student body when I was in high school, earning those notches on my bedpost at an early age. I wasn't the type of guy girls liked to bring home to meet their parents, because, well… the moms often wanted me just as much as their daughters.

"You got it bad, man," Pike says to me, shaking his head as I walk through the front door, carrying three boxes in my arms.

"What?" I ask, not paying any attention to him, too busy thinking about Lily in that bathtub and the view. But I'm not picturing the ocean.

He tips his head and gives me a smug smirk. "You got it bad for that girl. Does she know?"

I shake my head, pushing the boxes toward him. "I keep trying to throw hints, but so far, I'd say she doesn't."

"Hints," Pike laughs, taking the boxes from my arms without hesitation. "A girl like her needs more than hints."

I turn my head, watching her talk to her parents outside. Mike's still holding the mattress on his back, Mia's at his side smiling, and Lily… She's talking, and they're both listening, totally enthralled.

"If you like her, tell her. Don't pussyfoot around. Be direct and honest, but—" he says, waiting for me to give him back my attention. As soon as I do, he starts again. "If you use her and break her heart, you're going to have more than just Mike to answer to."

"Why does everyone think I'm going to break her heart? Maybe she'll break mine."

Pike laughs, tipping his head back, teeth sparkling behind his dark beard. "Dumbass. That girl can't hurt a fly."

I disagree, but I'm not arguing with him. Not when he's helping us move in to our new place. Lily is very much the type who could break any man's heart, even mine. That's how it is with the sweet and pure ones. It's the only reason I've steered clear of her for my entire life.

"This place is crazy," Tamara says, bounding down the steps with Mammoth right behind her. "You should've asked me to move in with you."

"Like that shit was ever going to happen," Mammoth mutters, glaring at me like I've done something wrong.

Tamara snickers, rolling her eyes. "I would've loved a bathroom like hers, and we've been friends forever, Jett. Why didn't you ask me?"

I shrug and run my hands through my hair, trying to ignore the death glare from Mammoth. "Lily wanted to move out, and it seemed perfect."

"You know what would've been perfect?" Tamara asks me.

"What?" I reply.

"My ass in that tub with that view." She smiles, ignoring

the fact that Mammoth's almost plastered against her back, teeth bared and growling.

"I'm sure Lily will let you use it sometime."

"Not the same," she groans.

In all honesty, I could never live with Tamara. Although we've been friends forever, she talks way too much for me. I can't remember ever being in a room with her without her constantly chattering about something.

"You want a house like this," Mammoth tells her, wrapping his arms around her middle. "I'll get you a house like this."

She melts into him, closing her eyes and smiling. "You get me a house like this, and I'll…"

"Move," Mike barks behind me, silencing whatever naughty shit was about to come out of Tamara's mouth.

He grunts as he passes me, barely even noticing anybody else in the room. Pike, Tamara, Mammoth, and I watch as Mike takes the steps two at a time, mattress on his back, moving like he does this shit every day.

"He's a scary bastard," Pike mutters. "He's so nice most of the time, but he can crush you like a tin can in his palm if he wanted. You better sleep with one eye open."

An hour later, everything in the house, Lily's family is kissing her goodbye like she's headed off to boot camp.

"Call us tomorrow, baby," her dad says, kissing her cheek. "Or tonight too. Let us know how it's going."

"I will, Dad," she says without a hint of annoyance in her voice. "But I'll be fine. Jett will make sure of it."

My stomach drops again as his eyes move to me, blazing with anger. "Fuckin' great," I mutter, knowing eventually Mike and I will have it out.

"I checked the lock on your bedroom door. It works

great. Use it, baby," he tells her, holding on to her arms like moving away from her is painful. "Promise me."

"I promise I'll lock my bedroom door. Happy?" She smiles, a hint of laughter to her voice.

"No," he replies, sliding his hands up her arms and enveloping her in a hug. "Not as long as you're not under my roof. I don't know why you couldn't just stay at home and live with us."

"Leave the girl be, Michael," Mia says, yanking on his tank top, trying to pry him off Lily. "Stop trying to guilt-trip her for wanting to grow up. Let her live a little."

"Not too much livin'," he says into her hair, smelling her like she's a newborn in his arms.

I don't stop what I'm doing, unpacking a box of dishes in the kitchen with a direct line of sight to the front door.

"Behave," Gigi says across from me, grabbing her purse off the counter. "Or, you know...don't."

"I'm not..."

She leans over, holding her purse in her hands, staring right at me. "Save it for someone who doesn't know you, Jett. You're crazy about that girl. But I'm telling you now." She drops her head and her voice. "If you don't act fast, you're going to lose out on the best thing you'll ever have in your life."

"Where am I losing her to?" I ask, unwrapping a dish before placing it on the counter with the others.

"A girl like Lily doesn't stay single for long, especially around here. The sharks are circling, my friend, and if you wait any longer and keep acting like a fool, they're going to be eating her instead of you." Gigi laughs at the funny she made, always so easily amused by herself.

I roll my eyes. "I like her, Gigi. I'll admit it, but I don't know if I'm the right type of guy for her. She's just so..."

"Sweet?"

I nod.

"Innocent?"

I nod.

"Pure?"

I nod.

"She's dying for someone to take those titles away from her, Jett."

I jerk my head back and almost drop the plate in my hand. "You're talking out of your ass."

Gigi stands up straight, lifting her hands. "Fine," she says, glancing toward Lily. "Don't believe me. But trust me, you're going to be kicking yourself in the dick if you don't do something."

"That's physically impossible."

"You're still an asshole," she adds, laughing at me.

"I've dropped some hints, and I get nothing back from her. I don't think she likes me, babe. Not like that anyway."

Gigi moves her hand to her face, covering her eyes. "Why are men so fucking stupid?"

By men, I know she's talking about me, and I take offense. "I'm not fucking stupid."

"You've never had trouble reading women before. Why is it so hard for you to read her?"

"I don't know many women like her. She's uncharted territory."

There's no one like Lily. In all my years away, all the women I've met, no one else compares. She doesn't understand her beauty or the pull she has over a man. She could wreck me with a single glance, and that scares the hell out of me.

"You have to make the first move with her, Jett, or shit will never happen. Men like you are foreign to her. Remember the guy from high school?"

I groan, thinking of that nerd with his cardigan sweater and khaki pants, always correcting everyone's grammar in class like he was the smartest shit on the planet. "Who can forget that asshole?" He was a few years younger than me, in Lily's grade, but everyone at our small high school knew him.

"That was Lily's first boyfriend."

I gag, pretending to vomit. "Don't tell me shit like that."

"William went after her and didn't wait for her to catch his hints."

I dig my palms into my eyes, trying to wipe away the vision of William and Lily together. "Stop. I can't."

"They only kissed," she says, like somehow that makes shit better. "But at least he had the balls to tell her how he felt."

I drop my hands, glaring at Gigi. "Stop calling me a pussy. I've never been scared around a woman."

"Uh-huh. Keep lying to yourself. You're scared shitless of telling Lily you want her."

"Am not," I argue like a child.

"Fine." She crosses her arms over her chest, tilting her head as she stares at me across the kitchen island. "We'll see." She smirks. "Lily tells me everything."

"Everything?" I raise an eyebrow.

"Yep. I'm now fully acquainted with your dick even though I've never seen it."

"She talked about my junk?"

Gigi smirks. "She seemed pretty impressed by it."

I rub the back of my neck as my face heats. "Well, I…"

"Darlin', we goin'?" Pike yells from the door, standing with Tamara and Mammoth. "We got shit to do."

"Coming!" Gigi yells without looking at them and then drops her voice again. "And I hope Lily does soon too."

I grab a piece of balled-up newspaper and throw it at her head but miss. "I'm out of commission. Remember?" I glance down, pointing at my dick.

"Doesn't mean she's broken, though," she tells me as she backs away from the counter, winking.

"Fuck my life," I grumble.

Her entire family is gone ten minutes later, and the house is quiet. The only sounds are Lily's light footsteps above me as she unpacks her suitcases, settling into her new room.

"Are you hungry?" I yell up the stairs, realizing we never ate anything the entire afternoon.

The sound of her footsteps grows louder until I see a pair of legs. Sexy legs, smooth, and tanned at the top of the staircase. "Yes. Want me to whip us up something?"

"I'll make it," I tell her, trying to ignore the shimmer of the light coming off her skin. "I'll let you know when it's ready."

"Okay." She rubs her leg with her hand, and I'm entranced, unable to take my eyes off the movement. "I'm going to jump in the shower. I feel sticky."

I bite my lip, wishing I could test her statement. *I will not get a hard-on. I will not get a hard-on.* I repeat the words, reminding myself how much pain I'll be in if I allow myself to think about her naked and wet. "Good idea," I tell her, dropping my gaze to break the spell.

"Be down in five!" she yells down the stairs as I move back toward the kitchen.

"Take your time!" I yell back, rubbing my neck and cursing myself for thinking any of this was a good idea.

On the one hand, I want to make Lily dirty, and on the other, I want to soak in her sweetness forever and protect her from other assholes like me. How does a man deal with the difference?

The only way I figure is I have to step up to the plate and take the reins. Although I've never been in a relationship, maybe Lily's the one who can change my ways. Maybe she's the girl I've been waiting for my entire life.

I'm bipolar when it comes to her, unable to make a decision. Stuck in the friend zone but wanting nothing more than to call her mine.

It's odd, really.

I've never felt this way about any woman.

The need to protect her and claim her all at once is so overwhelming, I can barely resist the urge to run up the stairs and make everything the new reality. But then I remember I can't. Not because I don't want to, but because my dick's still out of commission.

The ramen and salad are on the table when Lily strolls into the kitchen, a pair of black leggings and a thin-strapped tank top her only clothing.

"Hi," she says, smiling at me as I almost choke on my tongue.

Her nipples are hard and clearly visible through the thin material covering her breasts. "Hi," I squeak, sounding like a high school kid in the full throes of puberty.

"This looks so good."

"Completely delicious," I mumble, but I'm not talking about the food.

She pulls out a chair, sitting down, pulling one knee up to her chest, thankfully covering one breast. "You going to sit?" she asks when I don't move because I'm too busy staring at her body.

"Sorry." I smile, trying to be cool but burning inside. "Shower good?" I ask, peering down at my food instead of her damp skin as I settle into the chair across from her.

"Hot and perfect."

I peer up at her, taking in her beauty and knowing, as soon as I can, I'm going to make her mine. "I agree," I whisper.

10

LILY

"How's it going?" Gigi asks.

I have her on speakerphone as I do my makeup, not quite willing to leave my bedroom without something on my face. When I lived with my college roommate, I never cared how I looked. But then again, her opinion wasn't important to me.

"Okay, I think. Awkward."

"That's your middle name, Lily."

"It is not." I sigh, opening my eyes wider and getting closer to the mirror so I don't end up with mascara in all the wrong places. "I just want to look my best for him. I've never been like this with anyone before."

"You've always liked him. Always. I can't remember a time when you've ever liked anyone more."

I wave my hands in front of my eyes, trying to get my mascara to dry quicker. "I know, but I never thought I'd be living with the man. What in the hell was I thinking?"

"Well, I think you saw his dick, and whatever crush you had turned into something more."

"This isn't about his penis, Gigi." I roll my eyes, feeling my eyelashes touch my skin, and instantly groan. "Fuck, I suck at makeup. How come I can't put on mascara without getting it everywhere?"

"Because you're so pretty, your face doesn't want to be covered up."

I stare at the phone, even if she can't see me, and throw her all types of attitude. "You're so full of it."

"Let's get back to his 'penis,' as you say. Have you seen it again?"

"It's bad, Gigi. I never really saw the aftermath of a piercing. It's like someone took a hammer to the poor thing." I blanch, remembering how it looked when he showed it to me before we went to the party. The damn thing looked so angry.

"Maybe you should kiss it and make it better." She giggles. "I'm sure Jett would be happy to let you."

I lean over the counter, wetting my fingertip before trying to clean the mascara off the skin near my eyebrow. "Don't be ridiculous. Jett doesn't like me *that* way."

"Are you blind?"

"No," I snap.

"I always thought you were the bright one in the group, but clearly, I was mistaken. Jett likes you *that* way. He likes you every way."

"I keep thinking he's going to kiss me, but nothing happens."

"Did you talk to him about it?"

"Of course not."

"Dumb," she mutters.

"I'm not going to force myself on him." I straighten, staring at myself in the mirror, finally having my makeup just right. "Anyway, I have to go. I promised Jett I'd run a few errands with him to get some things for the house."

"Already like an old married couple."

"We are not," I tell her, taking offense at the comment. "He said he was going to buy a few things and swing by ALFA today to talk to Uncle James and Thomas about a job."

"ALFA?" she gasps. "They do some dangerous, bone-headed shit, Lily."

I grab my phone off the counter, carrying Gigi back into the bedroom to grab my shoes. "I know, but it's what he wants."

"Talk him out of it. I'm sure there's something else he can do."

I giggle, imagining me talking Jett out of anything, especially putting himself in danger. "As if it were that easy."

"Damn. It's a shame the man can't draw anything more than stick figures or else I'd ask him to work at Inked."

I slide my feet into my sandals, checking myself in the full-length mirror next to the door. "Stick figures?"

"He literally has the artistic ability of a five-year-old. It's sad, really."

"It's not like I'm Picasso or anything," I snort.

"Babe, I've seen your drawings, and you could give Pablo a run for his money with the fucked-up shit you can put on paper."

"Lily!" Jett yells from downstairs. "You ready to go?"

"Coming!" I yell back.

"I hope you are," Gigi says, giggling like an idiot. "You could really use the stress relief."

I shake my head, wishing she'd stop telling me to hook up with Jett. It's not that easy, even if she thinks it is. "Shut up. I'll call you later."

"Don't do anything I wouldn't do."

"And what would that be?" I ask, leaning into the mirror, making one final check of my makeup. "I'm pretty sure there's nothing left on the list."

"Anal."

I wrinkle my nose. "Well, at least you have some limits," I tease, while she laughs. "I wasn't sure you had any left."

"Shut your face. Text me later."

"Byeeeee," I say, drawing out the word until I tap the end button, quieting her laughter.

Jett's at the bottom of the stairs, twirling his car keys around the end of his finger. When the steps creak, he looks up. His eyes travel the length of me, taking in my knee-length shorts and tank top. He doesn't say anything as he closes his fingers, curling the keys in his palm. His silence is almost deafening as he stares at me.

"What's wrong?" I gaze down at my outfit. "Should I change?"

He shakes his head, his eyes still on me. "No," he says in a husky tone. "Don't change. You look..."

I stop moving halfway down the staircase, wondering how I look in his eyes. "I thought I'd go with something more casual for our day out, but maybe I should..." I take a step back, ready to run to my room and put on my khakis.

He blinks, looking lost for words, which I never thought would be possible for Jett. "You look absolutely beautiful, Lily," he finally says when I retreat one stair more.

His words wash over me, bathing me in warmth, and I can't stop the stupid smile from spreading across my lips. "Thank you." Somehow the words come out casual, but inside, my belly does this weird dip and flip thing like it does when I'm riding a roller coaster. "Where to first?"

"Let's hit ALFA first. I told James I'd stop by around noon. Then we'll have the rest of the day to do whatever we want."

I walk by Jett, feeling his eyes still on me as I step outside. "Are you sure about ALFA? It can be a dangerous place to work. I mean, you could get a job somewhere that doesn't involve you getting shot."

When he doesn't say anything, I turn around, catching him staring at my ass. His hungry, surprised gaze snaps to my face. "I'm sure, babe. I need work, and I don't have a ton of skills. With no college degree, finding anything worth shit isn't easy. Plus, I've known all the guys since I was little, and I'm well aware of what they do. I think I can handle it."

"Think or know?" I ask, tugging on the hem of my tank top, suddenly feeling half naked. I should've worn a polo and khakis, not letting Tamara get inside my head about my clothes.

He pulls the door closed and pushes it back, testing to make sure it's locked. "I know I can handle it. I've had my ass kicked before, and I'm pretty damn good with a gun."

I walk quickly, trying to get my ass literally out of his view. When I make it to the car, my hand on the door, waiting for him to disengage the lock, I ask, "Do you even own a gun?"

He shakes his head, standing on the other side of the car from me. "No, but I'm going to get one."

"You can use mine."

His eyes widen. "You seriously own a gun?" he whispers. "I thought you were joking."

I smile, always loving it when people find the fact that I have a gun and know how to use it shocking. "I really do, and I'm a pretty good shot too."

"Huh," he mutters, smiling. "You're full of surprises, babe. Full of surprises."

"I can teach you to shoot if you don't know how."

He laughs, shaking his head slightly. "Military, sweetheart. I know how to shoot."

I snort, knowing the Navy isn't all about marksmanship. "Maybe we can go to the range sometime," I say, sliding into the passenger seat of his brand-new pickup truck.

"You want to make it interesting?" he asks, staring at me from the driver's seat, wrist resting on the steering wheel.

I twist my fingers together as he gazes at me, looking like he's about to pounce. Do I want him to? Hell yes, but I know the aftermath of making out with Jett would be certain disaster.

I've loved the man since the moment my hormones kicked in, dreaming about him and me together, living happily ever after. But the reality? We'd never work. He's too Jett, cocky, carefree, and wild. We're total opposites in every way, but I'm so not the type to back away from a bet, especially one I know I can win.

I raise an eyebrow, gazing into his blue eyes. "What do you have in mind?"

"If my shot is better, we go on a date. Not a fake one either. I want you in a dress, some high heels."

I swallow, wondering if I want to go down this path. But then, I know. I know there's no way he's going to beat me at the range. My father had snuck me there since I was tall enough to see over the counter. "And if I win?"

He shrugs, pushing the ignition button. "You name it. Whatever you want, it's yours."

"I need time to think of something," I say, looking away from him and out the windshield. I have two choices. I can pick something lame or go big. What's bigger than going on a date with Jett? I wouldn't wager my V-card, no matter how badly I'm ready to lose it. I could also throw the match, but I've never been one to lose just to make a guy feel good about himself. My dad taught me never to let a man feel superior by downplaying my ability.

"You can have as much time as you want. Doesn't matter to me. Think big because I know at the end of it, you're going to be sitting in that seat in a dress and heels, going on a date with me."

"So cocky," I whisper.

"Not cocky when it's the truth."

I wave my hand in front of me, smiling. "Let's go, big talker. My uncles are waiting."

"Now, she's in a hurry," he mutters, lifting his arm and settling his hand on my headrest.

I turn my head, our eyes locking for a moment. I blink, my mouth dry, my body hot. The way he's been looking at me is different from how he used to. I always felt invisible around Jett, but that was five years ago when I barely had any boobs and was never this close to him. Now, I feel like he's always staring at me, but not in that creeper way—in a way that says anything is possible.

I squirm a little when he smirks, averting my eyes and facing forward again as he backs the truck out of the driveway. When he drops his hand away from my seat, his fingers brush my shoulder, and goose bumps spread across my skin.

Lord have mercy. I'm so lame. The man touched me in the most innocent way, and my body's acting like we're about to get busy and christen the front seat of his shiny, new black pickup.

"ALFA?" he asks, the air around us heavy.

I nod, staring out the window, forcing myself not to look at Jett nor trusting myself enough to speak. I can't deny Jett wants me as much as I want him, but that doesn't mean it's a good idea for either of us to act on our physical need. Even kissing will change everything, and with living together, that could spell disaster.

I will not kiss him. I will not kiss him. But God, how I want to. I wonder about the softness of his lips, the softness of his tongue. What would having sex with him be like? Would it be soft and long, or hard and fast? And then there's the piercing. I still can't wrap my head around why any man would add jewelry to his cock, even if it's supposed to be more pleasurable for a woman.

I shake my head, trying to quiet the sexual thoughts from going any deeper.

"You okay?" he asks, touching my knee.

My eyes widen as he squeezes the same knee. "Fine," I squeak, my voice breaking on the single word.

"You look flushed." He glides his thumb across the skin of my knee, making those earlier goose bumps seem like child's play.

"Nope. I couldn't be better," I blurt out, cringing because, goddamn, that sounded kind of wanton and needy.

"Good," he says, not moving his hand away, leaving it there like this is something we do every day. "Thinking about what you want if you win?"

I nod, keeping my mouth shut because, holy fuck, Jett's still touching me. I try to breathe, concentrating on inhaling and exhaling at a normal pace so I don't hyperventilate. The normally quick drive to ALFA seems to go on forever, my eyes glued to the road and my mind on Jett's hand that stays on my knee.

As soon as we're in the parking lot, I'm out of the truck, heading toward the office like I'm about to pee my pants. Jett's heavy footsteps follow, keeping pace a few feet away.

"I'll make this quick," he says from behind me.

"No rush," I say without looking at him.

As I reach for the door, he somehow maneuvers his body to get in front of me, grabbing the handle first. "Allow me," he says, being a gentleman and adding one more reason why I should give in and stop fighting my crazy attraction to him.

I peer up, biting down on my lip to stop myself from throwing my arms around this hunk of a man and begging him to take my V-card.

"Sugar," Aunt Angel says as soon as the door opens, breaking the awkward moment. "I was hoping Jett would bring your pretty face in here today."

"Auntie," I say cheerfully, pushing away the nervous energy Jett's closeness seems to instill in me. "I'm so happy you're here."

She rounds her desk, holding out her arms to me. "Come give me some loving." I practically leap into her arms as she rests her head on my shoulder, gazing at Jett. "You're next," she tells him, laughing so hard, my body shakes with her.

"Auntie," I whisper, unable to stop my smile.

"Oh, hush. I'm not going to get fresh with your man."

"He's not—" I start to say, but she pats me on the back, her way of telling me to shut up.

"Jett." Uncle Thomas's voice makes me jump because he came out of nowhere. Something he's always done, and I've never been able to figure out.

Angel backs away, letting go of me, and turns to her husband, smiling at him. "You ready for him, handsome?" she asks, batting her eyelashes.

Uncle Thomas smiles, staring at his wife in a way I can only describe as gross. I've seen that look on my father's face a million times when he stares at my mother. At what age do people stop thinking about sex? I always pictured old people with very little libido, but even judging from my grandparents, I'd say I was one hundred percent wrong.

Uncle Thomas slides his hand through his dark hair, blowing out a breath like he's trying to cool himself off. "We won't be long, Angel. You and I have a lunch date."

By the way he says lunch date and the way my aunt's blushing, I'd say there wasn't going to be an ounce of food put into their mouths.

Aunt Angel twists her red hair around the end of her finger. "I'll be waiting." She winks.

"Uh," I mutter, feeling more uncomfortable watching them than I did in the truck with Jett's hand on my knee.

"This way," Uncle Thomas says to Jett, motioning toward the long hallway leading to the offices.

Aunt Angel wraps her arm around my middle, moving me toward her desk. She already has a spare chair sitting next to hers, waiting for me. "Come sit with me while the boys talk. We need to catch up without the others around."

Jett's eyes flicker to me for a second before he follows Thomas down the hallway and disappears from sight. I pull at the scoop neck collar of my tank top, it's hot even in the air-conditioned office.

"That boy is wound tight," she tells me before my butt touches the chair.

I pause, gawking at my aunt. "Pardon?"

"He wants you something fierce."

I blink, sitting slowly. "I don't think so," I whisper. "I

mean, he's flirty. But that's Jett. I'm trying not to read too much into it."

"He always look at you like he's about to devour you?"

I nod, swallowing hard.

She grabs my hand, closing her fingers around mine. "Girl, that boy has it bad for you. Now, the question is, what are you going to do about it?"

I shrug, dropping my head forward, staring at our hands. "Nothing, Auntie. I can't."

Her soft fingertips touch my chin, forcing me to look at her. "Why not, child?"

"I've always had a thing for Jett, and if we do something and it ends badly…"

She gives me a pained smile, squeezing my hand. "Listen, baby. I may not be book smart with a degree hanging on the wall, but I know men. That man has it something awful for you. And as for if it ends badly, no one knows how anything's going to go. You can't let fear of the unknown hold you back from going after what you want."

"But what if he breaks my heart?" I whisper.

"Life is a risk. There's no certainty from one day to the next. But life is also about living. I don't want you to look back someday, wondering what could've been because you were too chickenshit to let go of that fear. You only live once, babe. You're young. Have fun, let that hair down, and go after what you want. Worry about the consequences when and if they come."

"You make it sound so easy," I mutter.

"Lily, there's nothing easier than loving someone. It's getting out of your own way that's the hard part."

11

LILY

"We need house rules," Jett says as he strolls onto the rooftop patio, shirtless. "Guidelines we both have to follow."

I go back to my book, trying to keep my gaze off his bare chest. We've been living together for five days, and nothing about the situation has been easy. "Like clothing isn't optional," I murmur behind the pages, eyes glued to the words.

The cushion dips near my feet, but I still don't look at him. "Babe, how am I supposed to work on my tan with a shirt on?"

I shrug, licking my finger, and turn to the next page without having read what was on the last. "I don't know, but you walk around here half naked most of the time and not just to sunbathe."

Jett laughs as he rests his hand across the top of my feet. "Does my body repulse you?"

"No," I blurt out, but know I have to backtrack. "Your body is fine. Not fine like it's sexy, because I don't look at you like that." Oh my God. I'm lying and doing a sucktastic job, babbling and unable to stop myself. "It's good. Shit," I groan, covering my face with my hand. "I mean, it's not repulsive."

Fuck.

I could've just said no, but I had to keep going. I have this issue every time he's around. It's as if I have no filter, and the things that come out of my mouth are usually inappropriate and so against my usual nature.

Jett's laugh shakes the chaise lounge, and he doesn't move his hands away from my feet, still holding them. "Yours isn't so bad either."

I flick my gaze over the top of the page. "Never claimed it was anything special."

His jaw ticks, and his eyes sweep up my thighs to my stomach. "Are you serious?"

"What rules do you want?" I ask, going back to my book and not wanting to talk about my body with him anymore.

I've never had body issues, but I know I'm not as beautiful as some women. My stomach isn't tight and never will be. My ass, while good, isn't high and plump. My breasts are a handful for some men, but by no means big. I am average on every level. Even if I'd had a smokin' hot body, I still wouldn't flaunt it. That's never been my style, and the last thing I want is attention for something other than my brains.

He pulls my book down, making it impossible for me to hide. "No. We're not moving on that fast. You know your body is hot as fuck, right?" he asks, eyebrows drawn inward.

"Sure." I smile, trying to lift my book back up, but failing. "It's okay. Not hot as fuck, but it's not awful."

He chews his lip, looking at me like I'm insane. "Not awful?"

I nod. "Uh. Yeah. It's okay." I poke my stomach through

my one-piece swimsuit. "It could be better, but it could also be worse."

"Fuckin' women." He shakes his head, his fingers still touching my skin. "You guys are brutal to yourselves. Do you know what I see when I look at you?"

My face heats, and I can't take his gaze, averting mine to where our bodies are connected. "Can we change the topic?" I whisper, wanting nothing more than to hide.

"No. We can't. You have to understand what a man thinks and sees when he's looking at you. Do you have any idea?"

I shrug, frowning. "I never really gave it much thought. It doesn't matter, though. I don't want someone to want me just for my body anyway."

He grazes my ankle with his fingertips, sending shock waves straight up my legs to the part of my body that hasn't been touched in far too long. "Lily, your mind is the most beautiful thing about you."

"Thanks." I smile, trying to stay still and calm even though he's stroking my skin, sending all kinds of signals he shouldn't be sending. "That's the best compliment anyone's ever given me."

"You seriously need to hang out with better guys."

I glance up and give him a halfhearted smile. "I know. I've never been any good with guys. Look at all the crazy, random shit I've said to you in the last five days since we started living together. I go stupid for some reason."

"There's nothing stupid about you, and I love all the crazy, random things you say. They're cute."

I frown. "So not cute, Jett. It's so embarrassing."

Now both his hands are holding my ankles, fingers sweeping across my skin in soft, steady strokes. "I think it's endearing."

"Old people are endearing," I mutter.

"Man, you are so harsh. I'm paying you a compliment, and somehow, you twist it around, messing it all up in your head."

I set my book down and cross my arms over my chest, feeling as if I need armor for this conversation. I don't know why I'm so defensive. Jett's never been anything but kind. Maybe too kind, but I figure it's because he doesn't want to upset my family and is just sucking up because he's always been this way…but with other people. "I did not twist your words."

"When I say you're beautiful, what do you think?"

I blink, tightening my arms against my body. "I think you're lying."

"If I said I was attracted to you, you'd say?"

"I've seen your type, Jett. You're not really picky."

He glances upward, and sunshine bathes his face. "Now she has jokes."

"No jokes. Just reality. You have a reputation."

"Had, Lily. Had. I'm not that guy anymore."

"Sure," I say sarcastically, nodding.

"I'm more selective about everything. It's no longer just about sex. I've had enough of that to last a lifetime."

My entire face scrunches like I just popped a lemon in my mouth. "Enough for a lifetime?"

He sighs but doesn't stop stroking my skin. I know I should pull away, but I can't bring myself to. I like the feeling of his skin sliding against mine too much to stop him. "I'm getting older. Priorities change over time. You're not the same person you were in high school, are you?"

I do a quick mental evaluation. I'm pretty damn close to

who I was then. Still a bookworm. Still boring. Still sexless. "No, I'm the same."

He studies me for a moment and then gives me a lopsided grin. "High school Lily wouldn't be sitting here with me, letting me touch her like this. So, I'd say you've changed."

"High school me would've let you touch her like this, if you'd ever known she existed back then."

"What?" His eyes widen. "I knew you existed. Hell, I saw you every day. How could I not?"

"You never talked to me." Damn. I sound whiny and needy, two things I never want to be.

His face twists. "Fuck, I did too. When our families were together, we talked."

"I don't remember it that way."

"Your face was always in a book. Maybe you didn't realize I was talking to you."

I chew on my bottom lip, narrowing my eyes, studying his handsome face. "Sometimes, fiction is better than reality."

"Lily."

"Jett," I throw back.

"I watched you at school. Saw you with your head tucked between the pages, never giving me the time of day."

Do I tell him the truth? Do I tell him I watched him too, seeing him with all the girls, and never once did I catch him watching me? Nope. The last thing I want is for Jett Michaels to know I had the biggest crush on him—and if I'm being honest with myself, I still do. "Don't lie now, babe." I use his favorite nickname back at him. "It's not becoming."

He shakes his head, fingers still stroking my skin. "Let's get back to now and away from then. Then was a lifetime ago, and I'd rather not rehash old times."

"I'm sure you wouldn't." I snort.

"Why do you wear a one-piece?" he asks, eyeing my suit.

I shrug. "It's comfortable."

"You have this amazing body, and you cover it up, hiding yourself in baggy shirts and loose shorts. It's like you want to disappear inside them."

"I do." I smile, nodding. "I'd rather not be noticed and just go about my day, blending in with the crowd."

"You don't blend, Lily Gallo."

"I blend," I argue, gnashing my teeth.

He lifts his arm, finally letting go of my one leg, and sweeps my hair away from my shoulder. "Your face could never blend into a crowd. Those big, round eyes and all this hair. Baby, you stick out in even the biggest, most beautiful group."

I don't have to look in a mirror to know the blush on my face is severe. "You sure know the right things to say, Jett. I'll give you that. You've always been a sweet talker."

"You seriously think I'm not attracted to you?"

"I don't."

His grip tightens on my ankle. "I thought my hard-on when you were piercing me was confirmation of that fact."

I laugh, remembering how mortified he looked. "I'm pretty sure if anyone's touching your penis, it'll get hard. I didn't think I was special."

"Do you get turned on when anyone touches you?" he throws back with a straight face.

I swallow, almost choking on my saliva. "Fuck no," I blurt out. "It doesn't work that way. Men and women are different."

"We're not that different, Lily. If your dad was touching my penis that day instead of you, I most certainly wouldn't have gotten wood."

I chuckle, picturing my dad trying to pierce him and Jett's penis stiff and upright. "He's a guy. I'm sure you wouldn't get, you know…" I waggle my eyebrows, squirming in my chair. I've never talked this openly about sex with anyone outside my family.

He grabs the ends of my hair, rubbing a few strands between his fingers. "Lily." He pauses, gazing at me with an expression I've seen before but never tried to pick apart.

"Yeah?"

"I'm going to kiss you now," he says, smirking and touching me.

Panic grips me. I can't kiss Jett. God, he's probably kissed hundreds of women and has skills I could never match or comprehend.

"No." I dip my head, sliding off the chaise lounge and scrambling to my feet. The book in my lap falls to the floor, landing next to me. "You can't."

He peers up, eyes narrowing as he studies me. "I want to," he says, pushing himself upward to stand in front of me. "Do you want to kiss me?"

I chew my lip, gawking at him.

I do.

God, I want to kiss Jett. I've always wanted to kiss Jett. But that doesn't mean it's a good idea. What if I'm horrible at kissing? What if he laughs and can never look at me again without thinking about the clumsy, awkward kiss? My fingers tingle, and my heart's pounding as panic claws at my insides.

But before I can say no, he's sliding his arms around my back, drawing me close to him. "Say yes, Lily. Say you want to kiss me." He smells so good. So masculine. His skin is hot, heated by the midday sun. The muscles in his chest and on his arms are hard and soft all at the same time.

I open my mouth and quickly snap it shut, staring into his blue eyes. Holy shit. Is this really happening? I've dreamed about this moment hundreds of times, wishing it would happen. I've wondered about how he tastes, the softness of his lips, and the smoothness of his tongue.

My legs wobble as my heart pounds in my chest, beating erratically and making me feel light-headed. "We can't," I tell him, pushing against his chest until he releases me. "We can't do this."

He drops his hands to his sides, tilting his head like I'm an oddity and he's trying to figure out what's going on in my head. "We can't?"

I shake my head, rocking back on my heels. "No. We're barely even friends yet, Jett. Kissing will ruin everything. I'm awkward enough around you, and if we kiss—" I brush my fingers across my lips, wondering if his are as soft as mine "—it'll change everything. So, add no kissing to your list of rules. Must wear clothes and absolutely no mouth-to-mouth action."

There's a low rumble coming from his throat as I step back, putting more space between us. "That's not what I meant when I said we needed rules," he groans.

"They're good rules." I square my shoulders and point at him. "Obviously, you need boundaries."

"I thought we'd talk about things like no leaving dirty dishes in the sink or putting our shoes away."

"Put those on the list too," I say, reaching down and scooping up my book off the floor.

I need to get out of here. Need to get away from him before I change my mind and hurl myself into his arms.

Nothing good can come from Jett and me kissing. I could never kiss him and then go back to the same awkwardness I've always had around him. I couldn't kiss him and then see him with other women, knowing how he tastes.

"Lily, we haven't finished talking," he says, lifting his arm like he's about to touch me.

I can't let it happen, though. When he touches me, I forget the reality, thinking he really likes me and, somehow, I'm special. But this is Jett, and I'm sure every woman he touches feels the same way, only to be left heartbroken.

"We talked," I tell him and grab the glass of water I've been sipping, trying to keep myself cool while reading the steamy novel. "I'm late for work, so I have to run."

"Come on. Just five more minutes." He steps forward, following me toward the door to the patio.

"I can't be late. I'll get fired," I say over my shoulder, forgetting we both know it isn't true. My dad's not going to fire me, but it sounded good and was the only thing I could think of in the heat of the moment.

My heart's in my throat as I grab the handle to the patio door, putting more space between us. I don't turn around as I run down the stairs and seal myself in my bedroom.

I almost kissed Jett Michaels.

I plaster my back to the door, pressing the book to my chest, and gasp for air.

Jesus.

That was close.

The last thing I need is to kiss a boy, *a man*, I've fantasized about for years. My heart couldn't take the pain of seeing him every day, knowing I could never be his.

12

JETT

"HEY, STRANGER," Charlene, a girl I slept with over five years ago, says as she slides her arm around me. "Lookin' better than ever."

I dipped my stick in that well once, and I sure as hell wasn't going back for more. I learned my lesson the last time, after the crazy bitch told everyone we were "a thing."

"Hey, Char," I mumble into my glass, not even looking at her.

"You lonely?" she asks against my ear, reeking of liquor and old cigarettes.

"Nope."

She touches my cheek with her long, thin fingernail, scraping through the stubble on my face. "You look lonely."

I tilt my head away from her touch. "While I appreciate your offer, I'm going to have to pass."

"I can make you feel good," she says, sliding her other hand across my thigh.

"Beat it, Char. He said no," Gigi says, coming out of

nowhere. I hadn't even seen her walk in, too busy downing whiskey.

"Bitch," Char hisses as her hands fall away from me. "When you're looking for a real woman, Jett, you know where to find me."

Gigi slides onto the stool next to me, scooting closer until our elbows are touching. "What are you doing?"

"Drinking," I mutter, lifting up my glass in case she missed it.

"Drinking or getting drunk?" she asks, motioning for the bartender as he walks by. "I'll have what he's having."

I stare at the wall behind the bar, ignoring my oldest and dearest friend in the world. I can't explain to her what's going on in my head. She'll think I'm crazier than she usually does.

"Does this have anything to do with Lily?" she asks.

I can feel her eyes on me, but I don't look at her. "No."

"Liar." She nudges me with her elbow. "You know I've always been able to read you. What's happened with Lily?"

"Nothing," I grumble. "Absolutely nothing."

"Ah. I figured that's why you called me to meet you."

"Yeah. Ugh," I groan, lifting the glass to my lips, drowning my bullshit in whiskey.

"Lily's no Charlene."

"Ain't that shit the truth."

Gigi shrugs, but she's smiling. "Listen." She slides her drink in front of her as soon as the bartender sets it down. "You scare Lily, so be prepared to take it slow."

I lift my eyebrows, looking at Gigi funny. "I scare her? Me?"

Gigi nods, her blue eyes twinkling. "You're intimidating for most women, especially someone as innocent as Lily."

She squeezes my arm with one hand and takes a sip of her whiskey with the other. "Do you really want to start something that might kill whatever friendship you two are developing as roommates?"

"The last thing I'm trying to do is intimidate her. She told me today I need to wear a shirt around the house, even when I'm sunbathing."

Gigi snorts, covering her mouth as soon as I glare at her. "Come on. That's funny and totally Lily."

"How am I supposed to get a tan with clothes on?"

Gigi keeps on laughing, loving my misery. "She's a different one. You have to remember she hasn't been around a lot of men in her life."

"Um, your entire family is filled with big, muscular guys."

"I'm talking about people she's not related to and someone she's definitely attracted to."

"Couldn't tell by the way she acted." God, I sound like a whiny asshole, and I suddenly hate myself. I move my gaze back to the wall behind the bar, pretending to study the bottles.

"How did she act?"

I sigh, twisting the glass of whiskey in my hands. "I told her I was going to kiss her, and she couldn't run away fast enough."

"You told her what?" Gigi gasps.

I down the rest of the whiskey in my glass, motioning for the bartender to bring me another. "I thought she wanted me to. She was looking at me like she wanted me to, at least."

"Jett," Gigi whispers, grazing my arm with her hand. "You've got to move slower, man. Men are so dumb sometimes."

I turn my head, giving her my eyes again. "I'm not dumb, babe. All the signals were there."

"What's up?" Pike says, giving me a chin lift as he comes to stand off to Gigi's side.

"Hey, man," I reply, giving him the same bullshit chin lift he gave me.

"What's wrong?" Pike asks Gigi and not me.

"Jett tried to kiss Lily, and it didn't go over so well."

Pike tenses as his eyes narrow and fists clench. "He what?"

Gigi grabs his hands, swiping her fingers across his inked skin. "Calm down, baby. Lily likes him, and Jett didn't do anything. He asked her, and she ran away like the scared little bird she is sometimes."

I rub the back of my neck, hating that I'm basically crying into my drink about Lily Gallo.

"What did we tell you?" he asks, and I know he's talking to me about the little talk he and Mammoth gave me at the party.

I hold his gaze, not showing an ounce of fear or regret about what happened. "I didn't do anything. I read a situation. I asked a question. She shot me down, ran away. End of story."

The two of them can threaten me all they want. It won't stop me from acting on something I feel is right. They could fuck right off with that macho bravado like they are her keeper.

"Baby," Gigi says softly, brushing her hand along his face. "Lily likes him. She's just scared."

"She likes him?" he asks, as if it's the craziest fucking thing in the world.

"Yes."

"And she moved in with him as friends because...?"

Gigi shrugs. "She likes to torture herself."

"Leave the bottle," I tell the bartender as he sets a new drink in front of me.

He just nods, sliding the bottle in front of me before leaving us be.

"Gonna be one of those nights, huh?" Gigi asks me, but I ignore her as I down the entire contents of the glass in one swallow. "It's probably for the best that she shot you down, Jett. Your dick's in a bad way right now, and the last thing you need is to be kissing on her."

I slam the glass back on the bar and reach for the bottle, but Gigi's faster and snatches it away from me.

"Are you listening to me?"

"Do I have a fucking choice?" I grumble, trying to pull the bottle in a low-key tug-of-war.

Gigi slaps my arm, getting my full attention. "Stop being a freaking baby, and man the fuck up."

"For real?"

"What do you like most about Lily, Jett? And don't say her tits."

"I love her quirkiness. I never know what's going to come out of her mouth. Then there's the blush that crosses her face after she says something ridiculously cute and crazy." I smile, thinking about her beautiful face, hidden behind her fallen hair.

Gigi's studying me, smiling like a loon. "Aww. I think someone's smitten with my girl."

"I'm not smitten," I growl, hating the word. "I'm a grown man, Gigi."

"Dude," Pike speaks up, entering the conversation again even though I didn't ask for his opinion—or hers, for that matter. "Just admit you have it bad for her. There's no shame in saying how you feel, but you need to make sure she knows it too. Don't hide that shit, let it build up inside, and project your misery on everyone else because she has no freaking clue. Lily doesn't understand guys like us."

"Us?" I raise an eyebrow.

"Men who are used to going after what we want and getting it."

Gigi slaps him with the back of her hand. "You're a pain in my ass, but when you go all caveman..." She hums, fluttering her eyes.

I blanch, ready to gag. I love Gigi. She's beautiful, but thinking about her and Pike having sex makes me ill. She's like a little sister to me, and if I had been here when they'd met, we would've had words.

"Do you know how long it took Lily's last boyfriend to kiss her?"

I shake my head, knowing very little about Lily's sexual past besides the agonizing fact that she's a virgin.

"Three freaking months."

I shake my head. "He wasn't a real man."

"He wore a pocket protector," Gigi adds, as if that somehow has any bearing even though it's dumb as hell. "Total nerd. I think he brushed his teeth and flossed before they kissed and again after. He had some weird germ thing."

"Again," I add, "he wasn't a real man."

"But think about it. She's used to slow men and definitely not an alpha like you. So, you have to take it slow and woo her."

"Woo?" I crinkle my forehead. "Like buy her flowers and shit?"

"Do you really want to know?" she asks me, grabbing the

bottle away from my loosened grip and refilling her glass. "I'll tell you how to win her over. But I swear to God, Jett, if you break her heart, I will end your life."

"I'm pretty sure your man and Mike would get me first." I smile, but I'm dead serious.

"If Lily doesn't get you first," Gigi says, holding the bottle out to me, giving me back the liquor I'm paying for.

I take the bottle, filling my glass all the way to the top. "Lily's a cream puff."

Gigi snorts, sounding so much like her cousin. "Trust me, Uncle Mike made sure she can kick the ass of any man, even one twice her size. Don't take her sweetness for weakness. That girl will make you hurt something fierce."

I jerk my head back, never remembering Lily as a tough girl. "Lily?" I blink, knowing she's pulling my leg. "Lily Gallo?"

Gigi nods, smirking. "She has a black belt. Did you know that?"

I swallow, my mouth suddenly dry, thinking about her kicking some ass. "That's hot."

"Yeah, well, don't piss her off, or you won't think it's so hot when she puts you on your ass."

"Maybe I like that." I wink, earning me an eye roll.

Pike laughs, shaking his head. "You want my opinion on how to handle her?"

I shrug, figuring right now I could use all the inside information I can get, even if he's basically a stranger. "Sure, man. Are you going to tell me to woo her too?"

Pike runs his hand across his beard, smiling. "Fuck no. Chicks say they dig that shit, but we know the truth. And even if Lily is a sweet, innocent little thing, she still wants to be manhandled."

Gigi's eyes widen as she snaps her head to the side, glaring at her man. "You did not just say that."

"Darlin'." Pike lifts his hand to her face, grabbing her chin, searching her eyes. "You want it soft and sweet?"

"Well, I..." Her voice drifts off, and his smirk grows.

"Didn't think so." He turns his gaze toward me, still holding her chin with his fingers. "If you want Lily, you need to make your intentions known. If she turns you away, you know where you stand. If she's interested, you be the man—but be respectful when doing it. Lily's a Gallo. She's used to strong men, and until one comes along and stakes his claim, she's gonna keep hidin'."

Pike talks in riddles, but I understand what he's saying. Fuck me. Maybe because I'm a guy and I've spent most of my life around the Gallos. The women are not meek and mild, but the men are overbearing, protective, and dominant. Lily's pocket-protector boyfriends of the past didn't cut it. That much is for sure. But I don't know if she could handle a man like me and survive.

"Got it," I tell him, my eyes drifting to Gigi as she gazes at him like he's everything. "You two done?"

Gigi smiles, moving her chin out of his grip. "He's partially right," she says, tipping her head toward Pike. "Not completely, but there's truth to his words. Lily needs to know how much you want her. And when she says she wants you too, do not let her get away."

"Sounds kind of rapey, Gigi," I mutter, lifting my whiskey to my lips. "I'm not that kind of man."

She shakes her head, punching my shoulder. "It's not rapey, asshole. I'm not saying force yourself on her. Lily's scared of everything, but she needs to learn to live, love, and enjoy life a little bit. I think you're just what she needs right now."

"Because I'll..."

"Spank her ass?" Gigi asks, raising an eyebrow and laughing. "'Cause, Jett, that shit is hot."

I blanch, trying to wipe away the image of Gigi being spanked by Pike. "Stop talking," I tell her before downing the rest of the whiskey. "You've already shared too much. I'm a friend, but that doesn't mean I want to know everything about you."

"Shiiiit. You should hear about Tamara." She smiles, leaning against Pike's chest as he toys with her hair. "Now, that girl's a freak."

"There's a perfect example," Pike adds. "The wildest one of the bunch is now the tamest."

"Tame?" I lift an eyebrow, jerking my head back. "Tamara can never be tamed."

"She kneels at that man's feet."

My mouth falls open as his words work their way through my brain. "No shit?" I whisper.

"Not shitting you. She kneels," he repeats before laughing. "Never thought I'd see the fuckin' day, but there she is. The Gallo girls don't want weak men, and from the little I know about you, you may have what it takes to bring Lily out of her shell."

I reach into my back pocket and grab my wallet. "I'm out. I got a girl waiting on me," I tell them, dipping my chin their way.

But they're not even paying attention to me anymore. Gigi waves, her mouth attached to Pike's as if he's her life support.

I don't say another word, leaving them at the bar, and head home to the one girl I can't seem to get out of my head.

It's an hour later when I walk through the door, covered in sweat. I left my car in the parking lot, not wanting to drink and drive, and decided to walk home. I needed time to think. Time to process everything Gigi and Pike said as well as everything I know about Lily Gallo.

I know I don't deserve her. What man does? She's perfect, and I'm...well, not. I never have been. I've done shit things. I've cheated. I've drunk too much. Partied too hard. And only thought about myself.

But being around Lily, around her sweetness, makes me want something more.

Something greater.

No woman has ever had my head spinning the way she does. No one has ever confused and intrigued me the way she does every moment I'm around her.

The one thing I know—I don't want to let her go.

If she were to bring another man home, I don't think I could handle listening to them, even if they were just watching television. I want her little moments, her small laughs, her sweet smiles. I'll do anything I have to in order to make them mine and mine alone.

I close the door behind me, leaving my keys in the bowl Lily put near the door so we would always know where we left them. I kick off my shoes and take the stairs two at a time, heading right toward her bedroom.

The door's cracked open, soft light streaming into the hallway from her bedroom. I walk slowly toward her door, reaching for the handle, and stopping when I see her.

Jesus Christ.

She's a vision.

Every man's wet dream.

My fuckin' wet dream come to life.

I can't move.

My hand is on the doorknob, my eyes glued to her breasts, to her fingers working her nipples. Her eyes are closed, mouth open, her lower body covered by a blanket, but her hand's moving underneath the material.

I know I shouldn't be watching. I know it's an invasion of privacy. But goddamn it, I can't stop myself.

But then her eyes open and meet mine, widening, and I know I've been caught.

I stumble backward, the liquor coursing through my veins, making my movements neither smooth nor quiet. Stepping on my sock, I tumble back, twisting my body the wrong fucking way. I howl as my jeans bunch up, wrapping around my dick.

I gasp, turning on my side, gripping my junk with tears in my eyes.

"Oh my God." Lily runs into the hallway, fastening her robe around her body. "Are you okay?" she asks, kneeling next to me.

"I'm. Fine," I grit out, barely able to breathe or speak, rocking back and forth. Sweat is dotting my brow as the pain radiates from my groin, balling in my stomach.

She slides her hands under me, lifting my head to her lap. "Jesus, Jett. You're almost as clumsy as me."

"Lily," I whisper, unable to talk any louder. Not only am I in an unbelievable amount of pain, everything's made worse by being this close to her pussy.

She smells of sex.

"Shh," she tells me, stroking my cheek with the fingers she just had on her clit.

I inhale, deep and long, memorizing the deliciousness of her scent as she pets me. This is probably the closest I'll ever get, especially after being a creep and watching her play with herself.

She smiles sweetly, leaning over me, exposing her cleavage. "Do you want me to get you some ice?"

This is payment for all the bad shit I've done. Taunt me with the most beautiful, purest creature, knowing I can never have her. Make me fuck up so badly, I'll never have a chance.

"No," I tell her, letting her rub my face as I study her expression.

She doesn't look mad. She doesn't seem embarrassed. But I know she saw me watching her, and I'd have no excuse if she asked me why either.

I close my eyes, losing myself in her softness. "I'm sorry," I tell her, holding my dick, still curled on my side. "So, so sorry."

"Are you drunk?" she asks.

Then it hits me. "Yes. So, so drunk," I slur, playing it up because this is my out and the only thing that's going to save me.

"I should be mad at you, but I think God already gave you your punishment."

I open one eye, not moving my cheek away from her lap. "You're loving this, aren't you?"

"If your penis wasn't broken before, it sure as heck is now." She snorts, enjoying my agony. "Come on, big guy. Let's get you to bed. Hopefully tomorrow, this won't even be a memory."

I don't care if I had an entire bottle of whiskey, I'll never forget what I saw.

13

LILY

I AVOID Jett in the morning, rushing out the door for work without even grabbing a cup of coffee first. I am a mix of angry, embarrassed, and more than a little curious. Angry because he watched me, embarrassed because he saw me, and curious because he only stopped when I caught him.

"How was last night?" Gigi asks, finally having some free time between her clients.

I busy myself with paperwork, unable to meet her eyes. "Good. Fine. Nothing exciting."

"Did you see Jett after he came home from the bar?"

I look up, surprised she knew where he was last night. "Were you with him?"

She leans over the front desk, arms resting on the counter, smirking. "Yep, and we had a very *interesting* conversation."

"That's nice," I tell her, pretending to read over the schedule for today, even though I have it memorized. I've been trying to get Jett off my mind all day—failing, of course—and now she wants to talk.

When I don't say anything else, she sighs. "Don't you want to know what we talked about?"

"No. I'm good. Super busy," I answer, speaking quickly. I don't look up, knowing exactly what I'll see. She's judging me, gawking at me like I have two heads.

"He has it bad for you," she tells me, not giving two shits that I said I didn't want to talk about him.

I snap my head up, eyes wide, and stop moving. Hell, I almost stop breathing too. "Shut up. He does not."

"He so does," she says in a singsong voice, resting her chin in her palm, batting her eyelashes. "Like crazy, super bad."

"He was drunk last night," I whisper, knowing he probably wasn't all with it when they had their conversation.

"I know. I was there. The man wouldn't stop going on about you. Lily this. Lily that. Lily. Lily. Lily." She rolls her eyes. "I don't think I've seen him so hung up and scared about anyone in his life."

"Scared?" I giggle. "The man didn't look scared as he creeped on me outside my bedroom."

Her eyes widen as she peels her chin away from her hand and stands up straight. "Creeped on you outside your bedroom?"

God, this is so embarrassing. I've never talked to anyone about pleasuring myself. It's not something I've ever been comfortable discussing, unlike my cousins, who talk about everything sex, including self-pleasure. "I may have been... you know..." I glance down, waggling my eyebrows, unable to say the words.

"Oh. My. God." She covers her mouth and gasps. "And?"

"And he saw me," I groan, covering my eyes with my hands as my face heats. "So freaking embarrassing."

She slaps her hand down on the desk, eyes sparkling, no doubt. "Girl…"

"Yeah," I mutter into my palms.

"No." She touches my hands, prying them away from my face. "Don't you remember what we said about watching a guy touching himself?"

"That it was hot?"

"One of the hottest things ever." She nods, a smirk playing on her lips. "It's the same for a guy when he watches you."

Even if it is hot, I didn't invite him to watch. I wasn't engaging in some kinky foreplay with the man. I thought I was alone, and I was enjoying my evening, fantasizing about Jett while doing it. But that's beside the point. "Should I be pissed at him, Gigi?"

She shrugs, picking at her fingernails like we're talking about the weather. "Eh," she mumbles. "When did he stop watching you?"

"When I caught him."

Her eyes widen, and her mouth falls open. "He saw you watching him, watching you?"

I nod slowly, almost ready to cry.

"Then what happened?" She's smiling like she's enjoying my misery, and a small part of me hates her.

"Then he fell down and hurt himself. I had to go into the hallway and help him because he was almost in tears."

She barks out a laugh, tipping her head back, almost hysterical. "Wait." She gasps, putting her hand up. "He fell down?"

I smirk. "He deserved the pain. It's what he gets for watching me without permission."

Her laughter doesn't die as she shakes her head, gasping for air. "What did you do?"

"Well…" I lick my lips, remembering how nice it felt to have his head in my lap even if I wanted to punch him. "I sat with him for a minute so he could catch his breath."

"Was he lying on the floor?"

"Curled into a ball, holding himself, almost in tears."

She laughs louder. "And you helped him? After he invaded your privacy?"

"Well, duh. I couldn't just leave him in the hallway like a wounded animal."

"You so like him." She points at me, and I bat her hand away.

"I do not."

She narrows her eyes, twisting her lips, knowing me just as well as I know myself.

"Okay. Okay." I throw my hands up. "Maybe a little."

She blinks, face frozen, calling my bullshit.

"Fine. I like him. Happy?"

Her smile is immediate. "Now let's talk about how you're going to make him pay and finally land the guy of your dreams."

"He's not the man of my dreams," I argue.

"Lily." She places her hand over mine, leveling me with her beautiful blue eyes. "You've been pining over the man for most of your life. I think you can finally admit, at least to me, he's the one you've been saving yourself for."

"He is not. We'd never work."

"Yeah, he is, and you'd be perfect together."

"I'm saving myself for my husband, and I don't think Jett's ever going to settle down."

The corners of her mouth lift. "Every man changes."

"I'm not marrying Jett Michaels, Gigi. We haven't even kissed, and he's never been a one-woman man."

"Because he's been waiting for the right one, Lily, and that is you."

I wave her off, knowing she's full of shit.

"I'm being serious," she says as she grabs my hand, forcing my arm down. "I've never seen him so in knots. If that's not a man in love, I don't know what is."

"Jett does not love me."

"Do you believe the lies you tell yourself?" she asks, raising an eyebrow.

I shrug, yanking my hand away from her. "I'm not lying. The man may want me, I'll admit that. He's curious and wants to take a walk on the nerd side. But love…" I chuckle sardonically. "You're way off base."

"Do you want to lose your V-card?"

I hold my breath, filling my cheeks with air. Am I ready to lose my V-card? I think so. I always told myself I would save my first time for the man I'd spend the rest of my life with. But with each passing year, I know it's probably a childish notion. Most likely, any man I marry will have had more than a handful of partners and be light-years ahead of me in the experience department. Am I cheating myself by waiting? The older I get, the more I think I am. "I don't know, Gigi. I honestly don't know."

"I wish I'd given mine to a friend or at least to someone who knew what the hell they were doing."

"But you were in college and older."

"He was an awful lay. Seriously bad."

"But you didn't know that at the time," I say, remembering how excited and happy she was after they finally did it. I was almost jealous of her. She didn't have her virginity hanging over her. At some point, it's no longer a badge of honor, but more of a scarlet letter, especially in today's sexually free society.

She goes back to resting her chin in her hand, elbow propped on the desk. "I know it now, though." She sighs, her shoulders sagging. "After being with Pike, knowing real pleasure and a selfless partner, I now know how shitty of a fuck Erik really was. Do you want to go through life never knowing how good it's supposed to be? Imagine if I'd married Erik." Gigi blanches, shaking her head as she fake gags. "I mean, how depressing is that to think about?"

"So depressing," I mumble, but my situation is more depressing than hers ever was.

At least she had a long-term boyfriend in college, someone she decided to give her virginity to because she thought they were in love.

But me? I was too busy with my head buried in my books, knee-deep in lecture notes. I didn't have time to date. Not with my hectic and full schedule for the three years I attended college. I had a full-ride scholarship, and in order to keep it, I had to maintain my grades. I knew if I had a boyfriend, someone I wanted to spend all my time with, I'd screw everything up.

Now, I have all the time in the world. There are no exams hanging over my head. I'm free as a bird, with nothing but time on my hands.

"How long until his dick is healed?" she asks me, snapping me out of my woe-is-me spiral.

"A few more weeks."

She smirks, shifting on her feet. "Then we have time to make a plan. First, we're going to have a little fun. But in the end…we'll have him eating out of your hand, begging to be your first."

I cover my face, shaking my head. "I can't do that, Gigi."

"You want to make him suffer for watching? Make him pant with need? You'll have him wound so tight. He's going to rock your fuckin' world. You're going to need to wear a hard hat to protect your head from the headboard." She giggles.

"You doing construction?" my dad asks, stalking out of the back room like he's a ninja.

I jump, grabbing at my chest. "Shit. I didn't even hear you. You scared the shit out of me."

"Fuck, Uncle Mike. Make some noise when you move. A man as big as you should sound like an earthquake coming."

"Hire more women," he mutters. "It's just what the shop needs." He scrubs his big hand down his face, talking to himself. "Bunch of lies."

"We were talking about some work Lily needs to get done."

He drops his hand, raising an eyebrow. "I'm more than willing to get my hands dirty."

I give Gigi the side-eye, and she's laughing her ass off, trying to hide her face in her palm, staring down at the front desk. I swallow, trying not to die of embarrassment as I look at my father. "No, Dad. I got this."

"Jett's there, and I'm sure he's more than happy to lend Lily a hand, Uncle Mike."

I glare at my cousin, wanting to wring her neck or smack her smile right off her beautiful face. "Shut up," I mouth, wishing I could disappear.

Dad places his hand on my shoulder and leans over, kissing

the top of my head. "Whatever you want, sweetheart. I'm sure Jett's more than capable." His voice is strained as if even the mention of Jett's name is painful to him. "But that doesn't mean you can't ask dear old dad for some help when you need it."

"You're the best, Daddy," I tell him, curling into his massive chest, still glaring at Gigi because she's eating this shit up. "Have I told you that lately?"

He wraps his arms around me, hugging me tight. "I know, baby. I know," he says, still full of himself after all these years.

"We'll talk later," Gigi tells me. "We have plans to make." She winks at me even as I shoo her away.

Dad pulls back, gazing down at me. "Everything okay at home?"

"Perfect." I smile. "Couldn't be better, in fact."

"You watch out for that boy," he tells me, studying my face, always able to read me. "You hear me? He's no good."

"Dad," I groan, shaking my head. "Jett's fine. He's been nothing but a gentleman." I'm lying, but hell, I know my dad would straight up murder Jett if he knew what happened, and my uncles would have no problem helping him hide his body either. "And anyway, Jett is a good guy."

"He's a womanizer."

"Um." I giggle, tilting my head at my father's serious face. "I'm pretty sure Mom says the same thing about you before you met her."

"I love your mother. She changed me. Made me a better man."

"See?" I say, touching his chest again. "Everyone has the ability to change."

"Lily," he warns, his tone dark and dangerous. "If he so much as..."

"I'm grown, Daddy, and if he does something wrong, I'll

use that one move you taught me. You know the one?" I smirk. "And right now, I'm pretty sure it would lead to him losing the ability to make babies for the rest of his life."

"It's a good move. Use it if you need to because if you don't and I find out he touched you, I will."

"Don't you have something you need to do?" I ask him, totally uncomfortable with this conversation, especially with him.

He nods, brushing his warm lips against my temple. "I have a few things to do in the office. Call me when my next appointment gets here."

"I'll do it," I tell him, glancing down at the appointment book again, seeing Cherise written next to the word "hood." Yippee. Nothing like having someone spread-eagled on my table before lunch to get the day started right. "She'll probably be more comfortable with me doing it anyway."

"Call me if you run into trouble."

I nod, pushing him out of the waiting room. "Now, go. I've got this covered."

He smiles down at me, looking every bit the proud papa. "I'm so happy you're here, baby. Never thought I'd see the day you'd work at Inked, but walking in here, seeing your pretty face every afternoon, makes me excited to come to work."

"I love you, Daddy," I tell him as my nose tickles, the big lug always saying things to give me all the feels.

"Love you too, sweetheart."

The phone on the desk rings, breaking up the sweetness of the moment.

"Holler if you need me," he says, walking away as I turn toward the phone, lifting the receiver to my ear.

"Inked. This is Lily. How can I help you?"

"God, I thought he was never going to leave," Gigi says on the other end of the call. "I figured out what we're going to do."

I turn around, making sure I'm really alone. "*We're* going to do?" I whisper, glancing in the back but not seeing Gigi. "Where the hell are you?"

"Out back, so no one can hear me," she whispers, the sound of traffic in the background.

"Then why are you whispering?"

"Fuck if I know," she whispers again. "I'll text you the plan. Step one starts tonight."

"Gigi, I don't think—" I start to say, but the line goes dead.

I gawk at the phone, blinking. "Asshole," I mumble, hating when she hangs up on me.

My phone vibrates, the screen flashing Gigi the Great, the name she put in herself. I swipe my finger, wincing as the text comes up, scared to read what she has in store for me.

Gigi the Great: Step One – Make him miserable.

I raise my head and look over my shoulder, chewing my lip. Shit. I don't know if I can do whatever she's about to tell me. Clearly, she's forgetting this is me we're talking about. Besides some kissing and the time Leland, the guy with the sexy pocket protector, put his hand up my shirt, I have little experience with men.

Before working at Inked, I'd never even touched a penis before, and lucky for me, the first time was in front of my father, with a perfect stranger waiting for me to jam a needle through his shaft.

Ugh.

Things need to change in my life. I'd been so busy studying, I could only watch as the people around me enjoyed themselves, doing things I'd always wished I could do.

Every day that ticks by is a lost chance, a missed moment, a little piece of happiness I can never get back.

I am ready for the change.

I am ready to move on.

I am ready to be free.

Me: I'm in.

14

JETT

Lily hasn't come out of her room for an hour. She walked through the front door and ran upstairs without even saying hello.

Last night was a clusterfuck. Out of all the dumb shit I could've done, she caught me watching her as she touched herself. Nothing in my life compared to the vision of her spread-eagled, hands working over her skin in perfect harmony. As high as that moment made me, when she looked at me and I stumbled, falling backward…that was the lowest of the low.

I claimed to be drunk, but I wasn't. A few shots weren't enough to erase the glorious memory. I texted her a few times today, feeling her out to see how pissed she was at me. She seemed like the sweet Lily I knew before I was a peeping Tom.

My phone vibrates next to me, pulling my thoughts away from Lily's naked body and the mindless television show playing on the big screen.

Gigi: Man the fuck up tonight.

I blink, staring at the screen in utter confusion. Man up? What the hell did I have to man up about? I glance around the room, finding only myself.

Me: ?

Gigi: Tonight's your chance to either go after what you want or possibly lose it forever.

I peer over my shoulder toward the staircase, finding it empty, wondering what the hell Gigi's talking about. I know she's referring to Lily, but since she's virtually locked herself in her bedroom, I'd say my chances are slim to none.

Me: Still not following you.

Gigi: Pay attention.

Me: Are you drunk?

Clearly, she's hitting the sauce pretty hard. She's making no sense and being more combative than she usually is.

Gigi: No, moron. Sober as can be.

Me: Then WTF are you talking about?

Gigi: Stop staring at your phone and pay attention.

I growl, ready to throw my phone across the room. Chicks are impossible and confusing, but Gigi Gallo can be downright frustrating. It's like she's speaking in code, trying to fuck with my head.

Me: Stop texting me, and to what?

Gigi: Lily, oh dumb one. Lily.

Again, I glance over my shoulder, tipping my head up, listening for movement from Lily's room, but I hear only silence.

Me: I think she's asleep.

Gigi: Nope. She's just giving herself a pep talk. I'm texting her too.

I scratch my head, grimacing. A pep talk?

Me: I think she's mad about what happened last night.

Gigi: She thinks you were too drunk to remember, but I know better.

I laugh to myself, shaking my head. I have no defense, and even if I did, Gigi wouldn't buy it.

Me: It was a good cover. I got lucky.

Gigi: Nope, but you're about to if you get your head out of your ass.

I blink as I part my lips, and the familiar knot of lust forms in the pit of my stomach.

Me: My head is never in my ass. I'm not that bendy. If I were, I would've learned to suck my own cock a long time ago.

Gigi: You're not amusing.

Me: I'm very amusing and handsome too.

Gigi: <eye roll> Don't fuck this up. I'm banking on you.

She's banking on me? I never thought she'd be in my corner, especially when it comes to Lily. Tamara, maybe. She's the wildcat of the Gallo cousins. She was the tiger chasing the boys, going after exactly what she wanted.

Me: Is this your idea of a sex pep talk?

Gigi: Yes, Jett. I know your dick's broken, but if you give that girl an ounce of what I think you can still deliver, you're going to have her begging for more.

I smirk, loving the idea of Lily begging for more of me. But at the same time, her naïveté and inexperience when it comes to sex scare the shit out of me too.

Being a girl's first is a big responsibility. I've slept with virgins, but that was back in high school. Teenage me didn't really give two shits or put much thought into the reality of what it meant to be the first time for a girl. Older me…fuck, it's a weighty responsibility.

Me: She'll want aboard the Jett Express?

Gigi: You did not just call yourself that. You are SO lame.

Me: Am not.

Gigi: OMG. She's coming. Prepare yourself. Act natural. Pretend to be surprised.

The door to Lily's bedroom creaks open, and I freeze, sucking in a deep breath like someone's punched me.

Me: ...

I'm in the middle of typing my reply, saying...what? Hell if I know. I look over at the stairs, seeing Lily's bare feet patter down the steps. I drop my phone, leaving the message unsent, and hold my breath as I direct my eyes back to the television.

Act normal. Those were Gigi's words. I don't have a normal around Lily. I've always been a chill guy, filled with swagger and throwing off pussy like there was an endless supply.

But with Lily, I'm another person. A better version of myself, always looking to please her before me.

"You hungry?" Lily asks from my side, standing somewhere near the staircase, but for a moment, I'm too chickenshit to look.

"I could eat." I stare straight ahead, as if the television show I'm watching is the most interesting thing in the world. "What are you making?"

She doesn't answer.

I suck in a breath, clenching my fists on my knees as I turn, readying myself. But what I see, I'm nowhere near prepared to take in.

She's standing at the bottom of the staircase, only a few feet away, wearing white boy shorts and a thin white tank top, showing off her breasts and nipples. A complete vision and the total package of a supersexy angel.

The air I'd just taken in evaporates from my lungs, leaving me breathless and more than a little speechless. Lily never wears so little clothing, especially around the house. The girl has more pairs of full-body pajamas in her dresser than anyone I've ever known.

She peers down at the floor as she slides her hand along the railing as if she's about to bolt. I gape at her, still in shock, still not moving. Is she offering herself to me? Could it really be that easy? I feel like there's a catch I'm missing, and any minute now, someone's about to beat my ass for what I did yesterday.

"I'm just going to..." She inches backward, eyes still cast down.

"Don't," I whisper, unable to find my full voice.

She lifts her head, locking eyes with me. "Don't?" she whispers back as she stops her ascent.

Man up.

Those were Gigi's words.

They come back to me and slam into my chest, kick-starting my heart. I'm on my feet, moving toward Lily so fast, she rocks back.

"Don't go," I tell her, lifting my hand to cradle her cheek as soon as I'm close enough.

She blinks up at me, lips parted, eyes big. "This is a mistake," she whispers. "I should go."

I shake my head as my breathing becomes shallower and more labored. "Don't leave," I beg, sounding needier than I ever have in my entire life. "I want you." I tighten my hold on her face, sweeping my thumb across her cheek.

Her lips part as she melts into my palm, closing her eyes.

"What if..."

"Do you want this?" I ask her, my heart pounding in my chest, making me feel more alive than I have in years. Is it fear? "Are you sure you want me?"

Shit. I sound like I'm trying to talk her out of it, but I'm not. I want her to be one hundred percent sure she's thought this through, because the last thing I want is to be her mistake.

Her eyelids flutter open as she stares up at me with fiery blue eyes. "I've never wanted anything more," she admits, sweeping what little control and self-doubt I have right away.

"I can't..." My voice trails off as my cock grows, reminding me I'm not healed enough to please her in all the ways I want to. It's the universe's way of playing a cruel, sick joke on me.

"We could maybe kiss." She bites her bottom lip, face reddening. "But we totally don't have to if you—" I don't let her get the rest of the words out.

I slam my mouth down on hers, taking what she's offering without remorse. Her lips are as soft and sweet as I'd always imagined. And God knows, I've thought about them for years, dreaming of this moment.

She touches my arm as I sweep my hand to the back of her neck, tilting her head back. Wrapping my other arm around her back, I pull her flush against me, leaving no space between us.

Her scent envelops me. The sounds of her sweet moans fill my ears, sending shock waves through my system and a warning shot straight to my dick.

I groan, both from pleasure and pain, wishing the timing were different but not caring if tonight's about her and not me. I've never been a completely selfish lover, but never am I selfless. Even tonight, giving her whatever she wants and needs, it's about more than just her pleasure. This is about a foundation. Tearing down the tension that's been building between us and piecing together what could be a very interesting future.

"Jett," she murmurs against my lips.

"Shh, baby. I got you," I tell her between kisses, tangling my fingers in the hair at the base of her neck. "Let me please you."

She moans again, leaning forward, pressing her breasts against my chest as she opens her lips, letting me in. I sweep my tongue inside, taking in her sweetness and warmth, memorizing the way she feels in my arms. I kiss her deeper, moving one hand from her back to her ass, squeezing her cheek roughly.

Control.

It's something I've never had much of, but I need it in a moment like this. Lily isn't a party girl. She barely has any experience, and the little she's gotten hasn't been with real men with rabid sexual appetites like me.

"Baby, I want you so bad," I tell her, whispering softly, my voice filled with need. "So bad, I hurt." I'm not lying. My cock is killing me, a constant reminder that not only has she touched me before, but no matter how much I want to sink into her, I can't.

"I've never…" She moans as I squeeze her ass again, not wanting her to admit what I already know.

I pull back, gazing into her blue eyes, searching for and seeing how much she wants this, wants me. "It doesn't matter. I'll go slow. This is about you, not me."

She nods, running her tongue along her bottom lip,

driving me crazy. Any control I had is gone in that moment. I dip my head, covering her mouth with mine again. Sliding my hand down her back, I grope her ass with both hands, lifting her bare feet off the floor. She wraps her legs around my body, sliding her arms around my neck and anchoring herself to me.

It's so natural, it's like we've done this a million times. Maybe it's because we've known each other forever, even if it's the first time we've ever really touched. At least touched in the way I've always wanted but never actually tried.

She hooks her ankles behind my back, pressing her warmth to my stomach as I lift her higher, careful of my cock. I step toward the couch, moving on memory and instinct, loving kissing her too much to stop.

I groan when my toes smack into the coffee table, and I push away the pain like I'm a man possessed. And I am. I'm taken over by my need to kiss, touch, and someday, if I'm lucky, be the first man to be inside Lily.

Quickly turning, I fall onto the couch, bringing Lily with me. She lands on my legs, sparing my cock from any more misery, already having been through enough. She straddles my legs, feet dangling over the floor, arms still around my neck, kissing me deeply.

My hands are everywhere, slipping and sliding over the soft cotton of her tank, feeling the dip of her ribs and the swell of her breasts.

Her fingers are soft and unsure as they move over my shoulders to my biceps. My bare skin tingles like I've never been touched before, sending another round of shock waves through my system.

I move my hand up her back, shoving my fingers into her hair to pull her head back, exposing her neck. My lips are quick, sliding from her mouth, down to her jaw, and not stopping until they're on her neck.

She pushes her pussy against my stomach, dropping her hands to my forearms and gripping me tight. I lick her skin, tasting her and moaning like she's the most delectable thing I've ever tasted.

I hit the spot, the one that makes most girls go wild, near her shoulder, and she quivers in my arms, gasping. By her response, I'd say no man has ever touched her there with their mouth, and the very thought spurs me on, making me want to please her now more than ever.

As I slide my hand up her stomach, brushing my fingertips across her nipple, she tenses. I glance up, praying to God she's not about to change her mind and call the entire thing off.

"More," she says, begging for me to touch her in all the dirty ways a man usually can only dream about.

Her words are like a punch to the chest, sucking every bit of air out of my body, but in the best possible way. I don't speak, burying my face in her neck as I move my fingers to her shoulder, sliding the strap of her tank down her arms.

I want to pull away and look at her naked skin, but I don't dare. Not now anyway. I cover her breast with my hand, sliding my thumb over her bare nipple, wanting her moans and gasps again. She squirms at the sensation, moving in my lap, pushing her breasts into my touch.

I ignore the intense, burning ache in my pants, putting my dick and the piercing out of my mind as I suck on her neck and play with her breasts. Each pass of my fingers earns me a small moan and a shift of her body. She's almost dry-humping my pelvis, working her body against me like she did with her fingers.

Any other girl and I'd already have her underwear off, but not Lily. This is about slow. This is about making it good. I know she's never had sex before, but I don't know exactly how far she's gone. Has anyone touched her pussy? Has a man ever given her an orgasm? I'm pretty sure pocket-protector guy didn't have the skills to get her off, but I'm going to do everything in my power to make sure she comes.

I move my mouth back to hers, kissing her hard and deeper than before. Keeping one hand on her breast, I slide the other down her back, to her stomach, and skim over her boy shorts hard enough for her to feel my touch.

She gasps into my mouth, and I groan, wishing I were healed enough to hear the sound she'd make as I slid my dick into her.

What a cruel fucking joke.

I break the kiss, gazing into her eyes, watching as hers flutter open and try to focus. My hand never stops, rubbing her softly through the cotton. "Has anyone ever touched you here?" I press harder, making sure my fingers are over her clit.

"N...No," she stutters, shivering. "Only you."

"Want me to stop?" I ask her again, never wanting to do anything she doesn't want me to. We have a connection, and no matter how much I want her, I don't want to ruin whatever this is we have.

"No," she breathes, spreading her legs for me. "Don't stop, Jett. Please don't stop."

I wish she were naked, but I'm not going to be picky or ruin the moment to have her undress. I do what any red-blooded man would do, pull her boy shorts to the side, finally touching her silky softness. She's bare. No hair. Only smooth, wet skin in need of my attention after a lifetime of neglect.

Holy mother of God.

Her hands are back around my neck, fingers playing with my hair just above my neck as I flatten my palm against her slickness.

It takes everything in me to remain composed. If my dick weren't in a bad way, I'd probably come in my pants like a dumb-ass teenager.

She rocks against my hand, slow and steady, but this isn't what I want. I want to be the one to get her off. She's done it to herself a million times. Now it's my turn to do it and let her lie back and enjoy herself.

I close my fingers around her nipple, pinching hard enough to make her jolt. "Fuck," she gasps, and God, do I wish I could.

"Baby, stop moving so much. Just enjoy this," I tell her, soothing her skin with my fingertip.

"I was," she says, her eyes fiery and fierce. "Until you..."

I smirk, knowing that look. Being able to spot it anywhere on any girl. Need. "You liked it."

Her eyes widen, blazing with both embarrassment and lust, but I don't give her a chance to reply before my lips are on hers again.

I close my fingertips on her nipple again, this time not as hard but enough to cause her to jolt and quake in my arms.

That's my bad girl.

There is so much I want to do to her, so much I want to explore. She's lived a sheltered sexual life, and I'm the right man to make all her fantasies a reality.

I slide my fingers through her wetness, coating them as I go, readying myself as much as I am her. When I sweep two fingers over her clit, she convulses like she's coming from the simple movement.

She digs her fingernails into the skin at my neck, holding on to me like she's afraid if she doesn't, she'll fall.

"I got you," I whisper against her mouth, sliding my hand away from her breast to hold her back.

Moving my legs apart, I spread her wider, knowing it's now or never. She's dripping with need, ready for more. After a few swipes of my fingers, circling her clit with each pass, I press one finger to her opening, gently pushing the length inside.

She moans, stiffening for a moment as I still, letting her body adjust to the invasion. I loosen my grip on her back, letting her lean into my touch as I slide my mouth from her face to her chest. Taking her nipple between my lips, I close my mouth around her hardened nub and suck.

Her pussy constricts around my finger, sucking it deeper, wanting more. A moment later, with my thumb against her clit, I pull my finger out and thrust it back in, careful not to be too rough. She drops her head back, mouth open, gasping for air with every stroke. I'm in a wicked mix of heaven and hell, loving the way she responds and knowing I can't feel the same pleasure.

Within moments, she's rocking against my hand, pushing her pussy down over my finger, riding me. When she cries out, I suck hard on her breast, stroking her deeper and harder.

When she finally goes limp, my finger still buried deep inside her, I can't stop the smile from spreading across my lips.

If she wasn't mine before, she is now. I'll make damn sure of it.

15

LILY

Two Weeks Later

"Lily!" Jett yells from his bedroom as I run out the front door, doing my best to avoid him.

It's been two weeks since *the* night. Fourteen days since I made out with Jett. From the moment it happened, I've done everything I can to steer clear of him, even going as far as sneaking out of the house before he wakes up.

I'm acting childish, but it's the only way I can guard myself against the feelings swirling around in my head.

I know Jett. I've known him my entire life even if we've never been close friends. He's never been a one-woman man, and no matter how much I'd like to think I'll be the one to change him, I know it's a lie.

My phone vibrates in my hand as I slide into the front seat of my car, staring out the windshield, making sure he's not following me. I glance down at the screen, my eyes widening when I see the message is from him.

Jett: We need to talk.

I blink, breathing heavily, frozen for a second as I think

of a reply. Turning on the ignition, I know the time to ignore Jett is coming to an end. Eventually, I'll have to face him and what we've done, effectively altering our living arrangements.

Me: Late for work. We can talk later.

How can I honestly stay in the house with him, rolling back our relationship to where it was when we first moved in together? I was perfectly happy with the awkwardness we had, but no, I had to mess everything up by basically throwing myself at him.

Fucking Gigi.

I've let my cousins talk me into some dumb shit, but that was beyond compare. Not only did I get a taste of how good sex could be, I put my heart on the line for someone who is and always will be unavailable.

Jett: I'll meet you for lunch.

My eyes widen, panic crawling up my spine. Lunch? I can't meet him for lunch or any other meal, for that matter. My hand trembles as I type out a reply, heading off the catastrophe before it begins.

Me: No time. Fully booked. Maybe we'll talk tonight if I don't get home too late.

Jett: I'll wait up. I'll wait all night if I have to.

I groan, falling forward until my head hits the steering wheel. *Why me?* Tossing my phone onto the seat next to me, I back out of the drive and speed toward Inked, driving faster than my normal, old-lady pace.

The parking lot's empty except for Gigi's truck, always the first one to the shop, taking over the role from our parents.

"Hey, hooker," she says between bites of a bagel as soon as I stalk through the front door.

I glare at her, throwing my purse down on a waiting room seat and plopping myself into the one next to it. "I hate you," I mutter, ready to crawl out of my skin.

She slaps her hands together, forgoing a napkin. A shitty habit she's picked up from Pike and certainly didn't learn from her parents. "What did I do now?"

"Jett." I frown, unable to stop my lips from pulling down at the corners. "I can't believe I let you talk me into kissing him."

"You did a little more than kissing." She waggles her eyebrows, giving me a smug grin.

I growl, my top lip curling as I narrow my gaze at my beautiful cousin who's always felt comfortable in her own skin. "It's your fault this happened."

She touches her chest, the grin still firmly planted on her face. "My fault? I didn't throw you in his lap and tell you to let him finger-fuck you."

I cringe when she says that, remembering she only told me to kiss him, feel him out a little to see if he felt the same way. It was me who let things get out of control, going further than I'd ever planned. "It just happened," I argue, feeling defensive.

She chuckles, shaking her pretty little head. "It was about damn time too."

I give her my middle finger, going slack in the chair to stare up at the ceiling. "Sex complicates everything."

"You haven't had sex with him yet," she argues, her voice coming closer as she moves my way. Her face fills my vision, blocking out the white ceiling tiles.

"There is no *yet*," I tell her, pushing her to the side with my legs. "There will be no yet either."

She looms over me, hands on her hips, staring at me like

I'm an alien or at least a chickenshit. "It's been two weeks, Lily. I think it's time to take the next step."

I kick her leg, knocking her to the side, but not over. "There is no next step, big jerk. I haven't talked to him since…"

She rights herself, hands back on her lips, eyes wide as saucers. "You still haven't talked to him?"

She's judging me. Hell, I'm judging myself. I'm such a freaking coward. I place my arms over my chest, hugging myself. "I can't," I whisper as flashes of that night and how I rode his hand like a cat in heat play through my mind. "It's too embarrassing."

She grabs my purse off the chair, placing it on the table before sitting down next to me. "Babe, there's nothing to be embarrassed about."

I close my eyes, remembering the way I moaned as the orgasm ripped through me and almost knocked me off his lap. "I did unspeakable things."

"Did you shit on him when you came?"

I turn my head, gawking at her. Where the hell does she come up with the weirdest shit? "What?" I gasp, jerking my head back. "Be serious, Gigi. Fuck. I didn't shit on him."

"Piss on his hand?"

"No!"

"Cry out another man's name?"

"Be serious," I chide her, rolling my eyes. "None of that happened. You're a sick and twisted individual."

She laughs, placing her hand on my shoulder. "Babe, you didn't do anything wrong. What happened that was so awful?"

I gape at her, blinking a few times, swallowing down the fear of telling her everything. I told her we kissed and he gave me an orgasm, but I didn't go into more detail. "I... Uh..." I squeeze my eyes shut, not able to look at her when I speak. "I rode his hand."

She doesn't move or speak, just sits there in silence. Probably just as shocked as I am about what happened, and no doubt embarrassed for me. After what feels like forever, I open one eye, glancing at my cousin. "I told you," I whisper.

Her lips are flat, head tilted a smidge to the side. "Are you for fuckin' real with this bullshit?"

"Does that statement require two swear words?" I throw back, feeling assaulted.

"I should have used three, but I wasn't feeling so creative."

My arms tighten around my body, wishing I could go back two weeks and get a do-over. "I am for fuckin' real with this bullshit. God, I was so embarrassed afterward. I mean, who does what I did?"

Gigi's laughter fills the room as she slaps her knee. "Lily." She gasps between her fit of giggles, not bothering to hide how funny my life is to her. "You haven't lived until you've ridden a man's face."

I gape at her, shocked. "You've ridden a man's face?"

She nods, smugness back in her expression. "Not just once, babe. All the damn time. I'm pretty sure someone's ridden Jett's face sometime in his past too, so I wouldn't be so embarrassed about ridin' his hand."

I jerk my head back like her words are a punch to my face. "Don't talk about him with other women," I whisper as my stomach knots, the unfamiliar pang of jealousy overcoming me.

She raises an eyebrow, studying me. "Jealous?"

"No," I lie. "I just don't like it."

"Because you're jealous," she tells me, growing giddier

with every miserable second. "You like him so much you can't picture him with another woman without feeling sick. Am I right?"

"No." My answer is too quick to be convincing, even to me.

I've never been the jealous type, but then again, I never really had a boyfriend who would bring that out in me. My last one, didn't have ladies throwing themselves at him... repeatedly. I didn't have to watch for three years as women did everything they could to get his attention and in his pants like I did with Jett in high school.

"Wait," Gigi says, pulling her phone from the back pocket of her jeans and tapping the screen.

"Heyyyyy." Tamara's voice comes from the phone, and I already want to slide off the chair and slink back to my car.

"Don't," I whisper, trying to pull the phone from Gigi's hand. "Don't do this to me."

Gigi yanks the phone away, standing quickly and moving out of reach. "Lemme ask you something, hooker. How many guys' hands have you ridden?"

"Hands?" Tamara asks, and I can hear her surprise at the question without having to see her face. "How am I supposed to remember that kind of shit?"

"Hence why I called you hooker." Gigi laughs as I throw my arm over my face, hiding. "How many faces have you ridden, then?"

"Gigi, come on. Ask me something I really know the answer to."

"Give me a ballpark figure, sluttastic."

"I was never slutty. I was just an equal opportunity orgasmer."

"I'm going to put that on a T-shirt for you and give it to

you for your birthday," Gigi replies, her laughter drowning out my miserable groan.

"I'd wear that shit all day long. Mammoth may not like it, especially when he's not around, but I'll deal with him."

"Sweetheart, let's be honest. Mammoth handles you and not the other way around."

I stare at my cousin from the relative safety underneath my arm. Who are these two? I remember when the three of us played Barbies in my bedroom, talking about how we were going to meet and marry royalty. Now, I have two cousins, both in love with dirty bikers who are the furthest thing possible from princes.

"Whatever, bitch. Lemme think here." There's a long pause, and Gigi glances my way, shrugging. "I don't know. Maybe ten guys, and there was this one time with a chick, but I was drunk, so it doesn't count."

My eyes widen.

"It counts, dumbass. You don't get a pass because you were drunk."

"I do get a pass, and no, it doesn't count."

"This one over here." Gigi tilts her head at me like Tamara can see me, but she can't. "She rode Jett's hand one time, and now she thinks her world's coming to an end."

"Flip the camera around," Tamara tells her.

I gasp, jumping up from the chair, looking for an out.

"Don't you move," Gigi says, pushing me back down and climbing on top of me. "You're not getting away so easy. I'm not Jett, sweetheart. You're going to face this before you get too lost in that pretty little head of yours."

I try to push her off me, but she locks her knees against my thighs, squeezing me roughly. "I'm going to bruise," I warn her, struggling to get away.

"Then stop moving," she tells me, holding the phone up in my face. "There she is."

"Lily! Baby," Tamara squeals. "I miss your face."

I stop moving, finally giving in. Might as well get this over with because neither of them is going to stop until they get the answers they want. "Hey, Tam," I say through clenched teeth, trying to sound happy but failing.

"So. Did you do it?"

"It?" I ask as Gigi laughs.

"Fuck Jett?"

I shake my head, eyes wide. "No way. We just..."

"They kissed, he finger-banged her, and she rode his hand."

"That's it?" Tamara asks.

Gigi nods like Tamara can see her. "That's it. Now the girl's mortified that she rode his hand all the way to orgasm."

"Get it, girl," Tamara says in a singsong voice. "But why haven't you slept with him?"

"Broken dick, remember," Gigi replies before I can speak.

"Ah. Damn. That's right. He has to be about healed by now, though, yeah?"

"I'm sure he's good enough to go right now if she'd only ask him."

"Oh my God. Lily, you've totally got to bang him," Tamara says, as if it's that easy.

"I'm not sleeping with him." I roll my eyes at the stupidity of the entire conversation.

"Was he bad? I mean, was he a sloppy kisser and fumbled around with that pussy like he didn't have a clue?"

I feel my face heat, and I can't look at the phone or in Gigi's eyes. "No. He's a really good kisser and..." I can't finish the sentence.

"She liked it," Gigi tells Tamara, her gaze sweeping over my face, no doubt all red and splotchy from embarrassment. "Liked it a lot. She's also dodging him."

"What?" Tamara gasps. "Why?"

I push the phone out of my face, done with them both.

"Because she's a coward."

"I am not," I argue. "It's complicated."

"She likes him," Tamara says. "Oh my God, you really like him?"

I sigh. "I do, and now I've made a fool of myself."

"Girl, just bang his brains out, and he'll forget all about anything that happened before."

"I can't do that," I tell her, finally pushing Gigi off my lap. "It's not that easy either, Tamara. You know I've never *done it.*"

"That's why Jett is perfect."

Gigi nods as Tamara speaks, following me around the customer waiting area of the shop.

"No girl should have her first time be with a bumbling idiot. You've already said you want to give up your V-card, and there's no better person to do it with than Jett."

"Tamara, I want my first time to be special." I blow out a breath and shake my head. "I don't want to wait until I'm married anymore, but I also want to be memorable to the guy I give it to in some way. You know?" I shrug, knowing I sound like a moron. "I know it's stupid, but I'm going to give him something special, and I want it to mean at least a little something to him too."

"First," Gigi says, not giving Tamara a chance to answer. "It would be special with Jett. No guy takes a girl's V-card and doesn't feel a sense of pride. I guarantee he'd remember the moment for the rest of his life. I don't know why you think Jett doesn't like or care for you. The man has been stupid over you since the day he came back to town."

The shop telephone rings, and I jump, nearly smacking my hip on the edge of the counter. I glance at the caller ID, recognizing the number and gasping. "It's him," I whisper like he can hear me.

Gigi rushes to the phone, grabbing the receiver before I can swat her hands away. "Inked. This is Gigi," she says like she doesn't know who's on the other end. She lifts her finger to her lips, signaling for Tamara to keep her trap shut as I gape at her.

She smiles, listening to him talk for a second. "Hey," she greets him, sounding way too excited. "Wait, let me put you on speakerphone. I'm trying to get a few things done before anyone shows up." She taps the speaker button and places the receiver back on the cradle.

"Lily's not there yet?" Jett asks, his velvety smooth voice filling the shop.

"Nope. She texted me a few minutes ago, saying she had to make a quick stop somewhere. So, you have about five minutes before she walks through the door." Gigi smiles at me like I'm supposed to be happy about any of this, which I'm not.

"I need your advice, Gigi. I need it bad," he tells her.

Gigi shakes her cell phone, signaling for me to take it from her hands. I do, staring at Tamara, who's smiling like an idiot on the other end of the video chat.

"Whatever you need, I'm your girl," Gigi tells him, almost choking when I look at her funny. "I mean, I'm not *your* girl, but I'll give you whatever advice I can. What's wrong? Is it Lily?"

He blows out a shaky breath, and I stand there, staring at

the phone on the counter, unable to breathe. "I think I fucked up. She hasn't talked to me in weeks. Every time I try to get her attention, she runs out of the house, acting like her ass is on fire."

"You know Lily," Gigi tells him, to which I give her a middle finger.

"That's just it. I don't," he admits. "I thought I did. I thought something was happening between us. I thought she liked me. I thought so many things, and then..."

I suck in a breath, feeling his words and the emotion behind them. He thought I liked him? God, I more than like him.

"Until you kissed her?" Gigi finishes the sentence for him.

"She told you?"

"Yeah. She tells me everything." Gigi smirks, and I want to punch her, but I can't because he'll know I'm here. The bitch is using that to her advantage, throwing me right under the bus.

"Everything?" he asks, his voice dropping low and deep.

"Everything." Gigi leans over the counter, resting her chin in her palm as she sighs. "Listen, Jett, Lily isn't like other girls—"

"I know," he says, interrupting her. "Fuck me. I know. We've talked about this. You know how I feel, but I need you to tell me how she feels. Do I chase her or back off, giving her space?"

They've talked about me? When? Why? What the hell were they saying, and how did I not know that they'd spoken about me behind my back?

Wait. He wants to chase me?

My eyes widen.

Oh. My. God.

Gigi smirks, nodding at me because she can see my shock and panic. "She thinks she did something wrong and that now you think badly about her."

"What? No fuckin' way."

I throw the first thing I can grab at her, trying to smack her in her betraying mouth, but she ducks, coming out unscathed.

"That night—" he clears his throat and swallows so loud, we can all hear him "—was the hottest thing that's ever happened in my life."

I blink, staring at the phone where his voice is coming from, as if somehow, I heard him wrong.

"I told you," Tamara whispers at me. "Man is crazy stupid over you."

"Shut up," I whisper back without looking down at her. I'm too busy staring at the phone on the desk.

"I want more of her, Gigi. I want all of her. Not just sexually. Fuck," he hisses. "What am I saying? I'm an idiot to think a girl as classy and smart as Lily would want a guy like me."

Jett thinks I'm too good for him? I blink rapidly, dumbfounded for one of the first times in my life.

"She's scared, babe. She likes you. Trust me. The girl has been stupid crazy for you since high school." Gigi smiles at me like she's helping, and I cringe.

"What? No way."

"Way. She used to stare at you for hours."

"Hey," I call out, finally speaking up because I need to stop her from embarrassing me anymore. "Sorry I'm late."

There's a click, and the phone goes dead.

"Nice going, asshole. Now he hung up."

"You said enough." I point my finger at her, glaring. "Why did you tell him that?"

"So he'll chase. Now, you've just got to let him catch you."

"I can't!" I cry out, shaking my head. "He's going to break my heart, Gigi. Don't you get that? Jett's not a relationship guy. He never has been. I already like him much more than I should."

"Did you hear a damn word?"

"Oh lord," Tamara adds. "Wish I were there for this one, but I'm late for class. You bitches duke it out and let me know what the verdict is," she says before disappearing from the screen, leaving only Gigi and me to have it out.

"He said he wanted *all* of you. All. Of. You. Lily," she repeats as if I needed to be told more than once.

"All of me?" I whisper, not really realizing what that means.

"Yes, babe." She walks over to me and grabs my shoulders, filling my line of sight. "Now, you need to decide if you're going to risk heartbreak for the boy you've always wanted or if you're going to throw away your chance at happiness and be a coward."

"But he'll break me."

Gigi tilts her head, her eyes searching my face. "There's not a person on the planet who hasn't had their heart broken. It's part of life. Even if you'd stayed with Jeremy."

"George," I correct her.

"Whoever pocket-protector guy was doesn't matter. He still could've broken your heart. There're no guarantees in life, but we have to live for the moment, holding on to whatever good we can find because it can all be over in a second."

"I know," I groan, hating that I have to agree with her on anything right now.

"Do you still like him?"

I nod.

"Do you want him?"

I nod.

"Then stop being ridiculous. Let the man chase you, woo you a little, even. And when it's time, give yourself to him freely and let yourself fall."

"Fall?" I whisper.

She nods and smiles. "You deserve to be happy, Lily." She squeezes my shoulders again. "Allow yourself to live without worrying and planning for the worst. Give in. Be free. And for the love of God, enjoy yourself. Take everything that man has to offer and run with it."

"Hey," Dad says, looking between Gigi and me. "What's wrong?" His forehead wrinkles as his eyes drop down to her hands on my shoulders.

"Nothing, Uncle Mike. Just having a girl talk."

His eyes narrow, eyebrows up. "About?"

"You're not a girl, silly. We can't tell you." She giggles, finally releasing her hold on me.

"Hey, Daddy." I walk up to him, popping up on my tippy toes, barely able to reach his cheek. "You're here early."

"Baby girl," he whispers, wrapping a giant arm around me, lifting me off the floor. "You sure you're okay?"

I stare up at his handsome face, soaking in his blue eyes, the same ones that have always made me feel secure. "I couldn't be better, Daddy."

And for the first time in a long time, I'm not lying.

16

JETT

GIGI LOOKS up from the counter, her eyes going wide. "Jett?"

I shake my head, placing my finger over my lips. "Shh. Where is she?"

Gigi pitches her thumb over her shoulder, pointing toward the back. "In the piercing room."

Drastic times call for drastic measures. With Lily avoiding me, ducking away every time I'm near, I figured the only way to corner her was to come to her work. I knew she was here; the phone call proved it. I wasn't about to sit at home, waiting for hours to say what I needed to say.

"She have someone back there with her?"

"Nope." She smiles.

"When's her next appointment?" I ask, leaning to the right and peering into the back area, but I see no one.

"In an hour."

"Her dad?"

"At dinner," she tells me, her smile growing wider. "What are you going to do?"

"I have a situation to correct. Just make sure no one interrupts us."

She throws a wink at me. "Eager little beaver, aren't you?"

"I'm sick of playing games," I tell her, stalking toward the back and leaving Gigi in the waiting room.

I don't knock.

I don't call out Lily's name.

I pull open the door and march inside, finding Lily with her back to me. She turns, eyes moving slowly from my legs to my face before she stiffens.

"Jett?" she whispers, eyes wider than Gigi's were when I walked into Inked. "What are you doing here?"

"We need to talk." I push the door closed, blocking her exit. Knowing Lily, she's already plotting to run. "I'm sick of waiting for you to come to your senses, so I'm bringing you a reality check."

"A reality check?" She wrinkles her cute little nose at me like she doesn't understand what I'm talking about, even though she does.

Lily's a smart girl. Maybe the smartest I've ever known when it comes to bookish things. But, as for real life, not so much. And men? Not a fucking clue.

"Yeah, baby. You need to face reality about what this is—" I wave my hand toward her before bringing it back to me "—and where we're going from here."

"What this is?" She waves her hand, motioning the exact same way as I did as she climbs to her feet. "What exactly is it?"

I stalk toward her, and she backs up, only stopping when her back hits the wall behind her. Lifting my hand, I brush away a few strands of hair that have fallen near her face, wanting to see her blue eyes more than anything. She needs to see how I feel and not just hear. "Lily Gallo, you're the most frustrating human being I've ever met."

She's breathing hard, almost hyperventilating, as my body pushes into hers, leaving no space between us. "I-I…" she stutters, craning her neck back and peering up at me. "I am not."

I cover her jaw with my palm, swiping my thumb just under her lip. "You are, baby. You so are. And I'm okay with you being frustrating to a point, but when you keep running, not getting out of that pretty little head long enough to figure us out, then I have an issue." I lean forward, pressing my mouth to hers, tasting her for the first time in weeks.

She kisses me back, her fingers finding the hem of my T-shirt, slipping under the cotton and resting on my skin. She moans when I gently bite her lip, digging those nails into my skin like she's trying to anchor herself to me.

She wants me.

I knew she wanted me.

That night on the couch wasn't a fluke.

Lily overthinks everything, never acting without considering the consequences. But what happened after we made out, the way she froze me out entirely, has never made sense to me.

I pull away, gazing at her face, her eyes closed, lips still puckered. "Tell me what you want," I growl, knowing what I want is right in front of me and not willing to stop until she tells me to. "Use all those fancy words you know, Lily."

Her eyes snap open, blazing with fire and need. "I want you, Jett. I've always wanted you," she admits. "It's always been you and only you."

I slide my hand around the back of her head, grasping her hair in my fingers. She stares up at me, mouth open, looking so fucking hot with her lips bee-stung from our kiss. "Then what the hell, babe? Every time I try to talk to you, you run away."

She squeezes her eyes shut. "I'm scared," she admits, pain marring her beautiful features. "Scared of this."

I loosen my grip, careful not to hurt her and definitely never wanting to make her afraid. "Of me? Baby, I'd never hurt you," I promise truthfully. I'd cut off my own arm before I'd ever let anyone, including me, hurt Lily.

"I know," she whispers, finally opening her eyes again. "I know you'd never hurt me."

"Then, what? Tell me how to make you feel safe," I beg her, wanting nothing more than for her to open up to me.

"I've never felt this way about anyone before, Jett. I've never worried about someone breaking my heart. I've never been afraid that I wasn't good enough for them or that they'd find someone else they wanted more."

I release her hair completely, moving my hand to her face, gripping her chin gently. I force her eyes to stay on me, knowing she needs to look at me when I say what I'm about to say. "I want you to listen and listen good."

"Okay."

"Don't interrupt."

I smirk as she draws her bottom lip between her teeth like she's trying to lock herself down. "I won't," she says, the words coming out garbled and almost unintelligible.

I shake my head, holding back the laugh because, goddamn, she's cute as fuck. "I know you think of me a certain way. You know my history better than anyone. But —" I suck in a breath, never having spoken these words to anyone before "—I've never felt this way about anyone else either. I've never allowed myself to feel much of anything for anyone. I made that choice, knowing I wasn't ready to fall in love and never wanting to do so with the wrong girl."

Her fingers press into my sides and her eyes widen, but she doesn't speak. I'd call that progress.

"You're the type of sweetness that could wreck a man like me. I know you don't have any experience when it comes to sex, but none of that matters to me. I want the silly, clumsy girl who wears pajamas to bed and still has a teddy bear on her pillow. I'm happy you're a virgin. Fuck, I'm thrilled."

"You are?" she whispers, sealing her mouth shut again as soon as the words slip out.

I lean forward, brushing my lips against hers for only a moment. "I am. I want to be your first. I like that this girl I have feelings for hasn't been with another man. I love that she's waited, keeping that special gift for someone she trusts. It's an honor, Lily. One I'm not entirely sure I deserve."

"You do."

"I keep going around and around in my head, wondering if I should back off, let you be free. But then I think about you with another man, and my blood boils, my skin crawls, and all I want to do is beat the shit out of the imaginary guy."

She smiles up at me, sliding her hands to my back, splaying her fingers against my skin. "Don't back off. I don't want anyone else. I don't want freedom."

"Neither do I," I tell her, sweeping my eyes over her full lips before going back to her eyes. "I want whatever's been happening between us to grow. I know when you're not around, I find myself thinking about you, wondering what you're doing or if you're okay. I've never worried about anyone but myself. This is as new to me as it is to you. I'm scared, Lily, and that's some hard shit to admit for a guy like me."

"I won't break your heart."

"You already did," I tell her, referring to the last two weeks when she shut me out. "What was that about?"

Her eyes soften, and her fingertips press into my back like she's holding me. "I was embarrassed. So, so, so embarrassed."

I crinkle my forehead at the absurdity of her statement. "About what?"

"What I did."

"Again, babe. What did you do that was embarrassing? We kissed, I touched you in a way you'd never been touched, and you came."

"I know," she whispers, closing her eyes. "I remember every second of it."

"And the embarrassing part?"

She swallows, opening her eyes slowly and peering up at me. "How I moved against your hand."

I level her with my gaze, sliding my hand back around her head, gripping her hair. "Babe, that shit was hot. I'm not talking a warm summer breeze. I'm talking so fucking hot, you have to run across the sand so you don't get burned."

"You liked it?" She blinks rapidly.

"I fucking loved it. Only thing hotter would be to look up and find you riding my cock that way with your tits in my hands, watching you come apart because I'm buried so deep in you, you can't fuckin' breathe."

The blush that covers her face is darker than I've ever seen. Her mouth opens and closes, but she says nothing. The one thing she does do is dig those damn fingernails into my skin the same way I'd want her to if I were inside her.

"You..." She swallows hard, blinking slowly. "I..." Her

breasts move closer to my face as she leans into me, tempting me. "You…"

Clearly what I said has scrambled her brain, and if I'm being honest, mine is too. The very thought of Lily Gallo sends my body into overdrive.

"Would you like that, Lily?" I ask, needing her words and confirmation.

She nods, sliding her hands lower on my back but stopping when her fingertips touch the top of my pants. "Yes, but promise me you'll go slow."

"Baby, we can take as long as you want."

"How's your…" Her gaze dips down. "Is it okay?"

"Say the word, Lily."

She bites her lip, eyes snapping back to mine. "How's your penis?"

"No, sweetheart. Say 'cock,'" I breathe against her lips, wanting to hear all the dirty things from her.

"Is your cock healed?"

I nod, my dick getting harder when the filthy words slip from her lips. "As healed as I need to be." I smirk, wishing I could bury myself in her now.

There's a pounding at the door, followed by the sound of footsteps. Not one set either. "Lily," Izzy says from the other side. "We brought you back some food. Come eat, baby girl."

"Coming!" Lily yells out.

I pull her hair, bending her head back, giving me a full view of her neck. "You will be," I murmur as I lean forward, pressing my mouth to her skin.

Her pulse quickens under my lips as her fingernails dig back into my skin, liking what I'm doing to her.

"Can you sneak out of here when I go out?"

I lift my gaze, staring at her as I straighten. "Why?"

"My dad," she whispers. "If he finds you in here, he'll..."

"Are you going to tell him about us?"

Her eyes widen again. "Not yet," she tells me.

"You're going to have to tell him sometime. You won't be able to hide what we have forever."

"I will. I swear."

"Sometime I'd like to come by, bring my girl dinner, spend a little time with her. I can't do that if her family doesn't know we're more than just roommates."

"I'd like that." She smiles, pulling that lip between her teeth again. "I'd like that a lot."

I release my grip on her, needing some space and a moment to get myself and my dick together before I even try to leave this room. "Go," I tell her, motioning toward the door with my head. "I just need a minute."

She peers down, no doubt spotting the wood I'm sporting through my jeans. "Looks like you are all healed." She giggles softly.

"There's only one real way to find out." I waggle my eyebrows as she stares at my dick.

She blushes again. "Wait up for me?"

I want to tell her to crawl into bed with me, but I don't want to do anything to scare her off. I'm not fucking her tonight. Not yet. I will not rush her or this, whatever it is and will be. For the first time ever, I want to make sure everything is perfect, leaving no room for her to be embarrassed again.

"I'd wait an eternity for you, Lily Gallo."

Her face brightens as if my words are exactly what she needed to hear. "Stay here one minute and then go," she tells me, pushing me to the side so she can get to the door. "You're no good to me if my father gets his hands around your neck."

"I'm not worried about your pops." I wave her off. "I think he'll be happy you found yourself a real man and not the type who wears a pocket protector."

"He really liked George."

"Of course he would," I mutter, knowing if she were my kid, I'd want her with someone who's not threatening in any way possible, especially sexually. "Go, Lily, before I make you stay."

She giggles again as she leans over, kissing my cheek. "Bye, baby," she whispers, calling me by the term for the first time.

I force myself to keep my hands at my sides, not grabbing her and hauling her back against me. "Until later," I say, promise lacing my voice.

She's gone a moment later, leaving me in the room with my cock still hard and the taste of her on my lips. The door opens again, and I turn, seeing Gigi staring at me.

"You good?"

I nod.

"She good?"

I nod.

She smiles. "Perfect," she whispers before her gaze locks in on my pants and the tent I've no doubt popped. "Looks like it went better than good."

"Get out of here," I tell her, pushing the door closed before she can say something else.

I wait five minutes, hearing footsteps move past the room before I turn the handle, poking my head out. There's no one around, but I can hear the murmur of their conversation.

"How's it going with Jett?" Izzy asks.

"Oh, good," Lily replies, and I take a step toward the waiting area, knowing it's not my place to listen.

"Just good?" Gigi asks. "You sure about that?"

"Shut up," Lily tells her. "It's just good."

"What's good?" Lily's father asks, and that's when I hurry my steps, not wanting to get my ass jacked before I have a chance to really make Lily mine.

17

LILY

THE EVENING DRAGGED on for what felt like forever after Jett left. There was an endless line of people looking to get new holes in their bodies, keeping us busy until we locked the front door.

"Breathe," I repeat to myself as I sit in my car, staring up at the house. "You can do this."

I inhale through my nose and close my eyes before blowing out the breath slowly, emptying my lungs. My fingers tingle, the sensation I've felt a million times in my past when I've been stressed about a big test.

I pull down the visor, staring at myself in the mirror, and fix my makeup before I dare to walk inside. Whatever happens, I want tonight to be as perfect as possible.

"You got this," I whisper, forcing a nervous smile on to my face.

The front door opens, and the outline of Jett's body is a dark shadow in the warm light. He leans against the frame, arms crossed, looking every bit as magnificent as he did when we were younger. I open the car door, unfolding my body and somehow finding my footing without falling on my face.

"I was getting worried," he says as I shake out my hands, taking careful steps toward the house as my knees wobble.

"About what?" I ask, managing to keep my voice from shaking.

"That you'd run away."

A nervous laugh bubbles out of me as I move closer to him. "Don't be silly. I'd never do that." It's a lie. I thought about turning the car around and staying at Gigi's tonight dozens of times during the short ride. But I knew she'd push me out and tell me to stop being a chickenshit.

A smile slides across Jett's lips as he holds out his hand to me when we're close enough to touch. "I made you a snack and opened a bottle of wine."

"You did?" I gape at him as I set my palm in his.

He closes his fingers around my hand, helping me inside. "Can't have my girl hungry or stressed."

A shiver runs through me with his words. *My girl.* I waited years to hear those words, but never did I imagine it would feel this way.

My heart races as he releases my hand, moving to slide the strap of my purse off my shoulder. "You want to change into something more comfortable?"

My eyes widen, flashes of every sexy movie I've ever seen running through my head. "Um, sure," I whisper, tucking a lock of my hair behind my ear, unable to look at him.

I don't own many sexy things. At least, nothing a man of Jett's caliber would find titillating. He's wearing nothing but a pair of gray sweatpants and somehow looks delicious. It's almost unfair how easily sexiness comes off the man.

"Babe, I'm talking about getting comfortable in a pair of sweats or shorts, not a nightie."

I giggle, loving that he seems to read my mind, especially when I'm panicked. "Oh."

"If you're comfortable in that—" his gaze moves away from my face, traveling down my body ever so slowly "—then I'm happy to look at you wearing it. Happy to remember having you up against the wall at Inked wearing it too."

The blush I feel spreading across my face is immediate and deep as my nervous laughter dies. "I'm super comfortable," I say, my voice husky and needy, remembering him having me up against the wall at Inked too.

"Good, baby," he murmurs, helping me to the couch.

There's a tray of fruit, some cheese cut into perfect cubes, two wineglasses, and an open bottle of white on the coffee table. Candles flicker around the room, setting the romantic mood I only thought happened in those sexy Hollywood movies.

I watch him, unable to tear my eyes away as he grabs a glass off the table, filling it with wine. His muscles move, the ridges shadowed in the dim lighting, looking every bit as luscious as the food laid out before me. I realize now, my shirt requirement around the house is utterly ridiculous and almost criminal.

"How was your day?" I ask, feeling the need to fill the silence as he hands me the glass and starts to fill his own.

"Good. Stopped by ALFA after I left the shop. Got shit in order to start tomorrow."

"Tomorrow? I thought maybe you'd change your mind. Are you sure you want to do this? It's so dangerous."

He sits, turning his body so he's facing me, leg bent and

on the couch. "I didn't change my mind, babe. The paperwork finally came in and I passed my background check, but that's not surprising. James said I could start when I want. I'm getting bored playing the housewife around here, so I told him I'd start right away."

My gaze slides to the clock on the wall. "It's late, Jett. Maybe you should be asleep already so you're fresh for work tomorrow. The first day is the most important."

Jett smirks, studying my face. "I learned to survive on very little sleep. The military does that to you. I only need a few hours a night to make do."

"But still," I argue, lifting the glass to my lips, "you should be in bed already since it's after midnight."

He shakes his head, eyes never leaving mine. "The only way I'm going up to my bed right now is if you're coming with me, sweetheart."

I almost choke on the wine sliding down my throat, his words catching me off guard. Pounding on my chest, I gasp for air, fighting back the tears filling my eyes. "The couch is good," I barely get out as my knee starts to bounce uncontrollably.

Jett moves his hand to my knee, holding me still. "Calm down, Lily. Just breathe, baby."

"I'm trying," I groan, not even bothering to hide the fact that I'm freaking the fuck out. "I'm really, really trying."

He tightens his fingers against my skin, smiling softly. "Nothing's going to happen tonight unless you want it to. I'll never force myself on you or make you do anything you don't want. If you want to kiss, we kiss. If you want to make out like we did the other night, we make out. I'm in no hurry. I'm not going anywhere, and neither are you. We have all the time in the world, baby, and we're taking this at your speed."

I blink, holding the glass in front of my lips, staring at this patient and kind man sitting next to me. I knew Jett was a good guy, but he's being so understanding, while I'm being a nervous twit. "You don't want to do it tonight?"

He smiles, shaking his head as he places his wineglass down on the side table next to him. "Of course I do. There's nothing I want more. But when it happens, I want it to be natural and something you want. The last thing I need is for you to be nervous and force yourself into doing something just to make me happy."

"Thank you," I whisper, feeling some of the nervous energy in my body melt away.

"I'd be happy if you crawled up in my lap, kissed me like you did a few weeks ago, and let me give you a couple orgasms in the process."

My mouth falls open, my pussy pulsating at the very reminder of coming on his hand. "Well, I..." I swallow, the wine doing nothing to help with my unquenchable thirst. I take another gulp, draining half the glass in the process, before placing the goblet on the table.

Jett's eyes are glued to me, silently watching me as I move toward him, crawling the few feet separating us and kicking off my shoes.

"I'd like that too," I say, finally finding my words and my balls.

"The kissing or the orgasms?" he asks, a hint of laughter on his lips as he wraps an arm around my back, pulling me on top of him.

"Both." I smirk, remembering how I loved the way he kissed me and how amazing it was to come without having to touch myself.

I settle into his lap, straddling his hips with my knees and my pussy pressed against his very hard and well-endowed cock. Our eyes are locked on each other, our breathing shallow as the thick air crackles around us.

"Kiss me, babe," he tells me, sliding his hand from my back to my ass. "I've been waiting hours to taste you."

I lean forward, hands on his shoulders, and give him what he wants. It's what I want too, having spent the entire evening fantasizing about being in this very position, mouths fused, hands roaming each other's bodies.

His kiss is harder and more demanding than the last time. I'm swept up in the moment, wrapped up in him, opening my mouth and sliding my tongue between his lips. I moan when I taste him again, the wine mixing with the sweetness that's pure Jett.

There's nothing soft or sweet about the moment. Nothing like the last time. Any embarrassment I felt before is gone, wiped away by his words and the hard-on pressing into me.

He moves me with his hands, grinding against me as his mouth takes my lips hard and hungrily. I gasp at the sensation, our chests pressed together, his body sliding under me. It feels so lush and naughty, wonderful and sexy, and everything I thought it would feel like to have a real man against me.

I'm panting against his lips, wanting and needing more of the pleasure radiating from my core. His hand slips under my shirt, sliding up my ribs until his fingertips find my nipple. And, goddamn, the fire raging between my legs burns out of control.

I take over, moving my hips faster, rubbing our bodies together harder, humping him like I've never humped anyone before. Which I haven't. Not even my prudish boyfriends would do this with me, and while it's not something men in their twenties probably love, I'm totally getting off on it.

Jett grips my ass harder before sliding his hands to my waist, stopping my movement. He breaks our kiss, pulling away slightly and panting. "Wait," he gasps. "I want to taste you."

"You are," I say breathlessly, still trying to move my hips.

His eyes blaze with desire, holding me still. "No, Lily. I want to taste you," he repeats.

My eyes widen, and my entire body tingles at the realization that he wants to put his mouth on me. No one's ever done that. I've heard Gigi and Tamara, along with every other girl I know, rave about the feeling of a man's mouth between their legs. I was always envious each of them had a man, and even more that he was willing to pleasure her with his mouth.

He leans forward, pushing me backward into the couch and hovering above me. "Are you okay with this?"

I blink, barely able to breathe and not sure if I can speak loud enough for him to hear, but I try anyway. "Yes. I want this," I tell him, running my fingers over the scruff on his jaw.

The smile that slides across his face is nothing short of sinful. He moves down my body, finger dipping into the waistband of my pants and taking them, along with my panties, all the way down to my ankles.

I freeze, resisting the urge to cover myself because no one's ever seen that part of me. I feel the heat creep across my face, and I close my eyes, pushing away any fear.

"Relax, baby," he whispers. "You're beautiful."

There's something about the way he says the words that

makes me feel like I am just what he says...beautiful. No one's ever made me feel as pretty as him or as wanted.

I relax into the cushions, concentrating on my breathing as he pulls my clothing off my ankles and drops it to the floor. When he touches my legs, I close my eyes, knowing I can't watch him.

He spreads my legs, and cool air rushes over my warm body. I hold my breath, curling my fingers into the material of the couch, bracing myself for his touch. A moment later, the featherlight caress of his lips against the most sensitive part of my body makes me convulse in a way I never thought possible. He loops his arms around my legs, holding me still and spreading me wider.

Oh sweet Jesus. He's barely touched me, and I'm already about to come apart at the seams. The girls told me it was amazing, but I never imagined something could be so deliciously dirty.

The softness of his lips is followed by a wet warmth sliding across my skin. I rock my hips into him, wanting more of his mouth on me. And dear lord, when he closes his lips around my skin, practically devouring me in a single bite, I gasp.

I open my eyes, peering down at the mess of brown hair between my legs, Jett eating me like he's a starved man. Just when I think it can't get any better, he sucks my skin into his mouth, and I arch my bottom off the couch, wanting more.

Fuck. This is good.

No, that's not right. This is fantastic.

The best thing I've ever experienced. I've read about oral sex, but I never believed until right now, with Jett's mouth against me, exactly how great it really is.

And watching him do it is beyond words. Far sexier than

anything I ever could have imagined or read. I tangle my fingers in his hair as I roll my eyes back, the pleasure too much for me to see straight.

After a few flicks of his tongue, my toes curl and my back bows as the orgasm crashes over me. Wave after wave flows, and he never lets up, feasting on me as I scream "Fuck!" repeatedly as if it's a word I use every damn day.

"Baby, just when I think you couldn't get any hotter," Jett says from between my legs, bringing me back to my senses.

I open my eyes, peering down my body, taking in his handsome face and the sexy smirk on his lips. I smile, too drunk off the orgasm to speak, too foggy-headed to form real words or trust myself to even try.

"Want to try for two?"

I widen my eyes, and I blink. "Two?" I whisper.

He nods, not waiting for a reply before his mouth is back on me, giving me everything he has.

18

JETT

"JETT," Lily whispers in my dreams.

I moan, too tired to talk and too comfortable to move.

Fingers stroke my bicep, back and forth, back and forth, in a slow, steady movement.

"Jett," she whispers again.

"Lily," I whisper back, still dreaming.

I've become so obsessed with the girl, I can't stop thinking about her, not even in my dreams.

Her fingers slide up my arms, over my shoulders, running down the middle of my chest. The touch is light and sweet, sending goose bumps across my skin.

"I want to do it," she says softly as her hand slides down the planes of my stomach, finding my happy trail. I moan again, liking where this dream is going, wanting nothing more than to have everything Lily's willing to offer...even if I'm only dreaming.

"Whatever you want, baby, it's yours," I say.

Please don't let me wake up.

Fingertips touch the head of my cock, bumping my piercing, and a very real and different sensation goes through me, causing me to shoot straight up.

I suck in a breath, sweat covering my body, my heart pounding, sitting in the darkness.

"I'm sorry," she says.

I widen my eyes as I turn my head, realizing I wasn't dreaming. Lily's next to me, lying on her side, arm out and next to my hip.

"I didn't mean to hurt you." She bites her lip, her face aglow in the dim light of the television at the end of my bed. "I had a bad dream, and I didn't know what else to do."

Do not blow this, dumbass.

I collapse backward, my heart still racing, and reach an arm out, pulling her to my side. "Do you want to talk about it?"

She shakes her head against my shoulder as her fingers go back to my chest. "I'm better now that I'm here."

"I'm better now that you're here too." I work my fingers through her hair, finding the bare skin of her back. "You didn't hurt me, Lily. Just surprised me," I tell her, never wanting her to feel uncomfortable, even if she took me by surprise.

Then it hits me. She was about to touch my dick, and I ruined the entire thing by sitting up like an idiot.

She gazes up at me with soft eyes. "I feel bad about last night."

"Why? There's nothing to feel bad about. It was a great night."

Not only did I finally get a taste of her, but I took more than one until she could barely form a sentence. I did that. I gave her as many orgasms as she could handle until she practically passed out. The one thing I didn't do was fuck her. I don't know why. The moment didn't feel right, or maybe I wasn't entirely convinced Lily was ready.

Her hand on my chest drifts to my stomach, sending warning signals to my brain and dick. "I didn't get to give you anything in return."

"I didn't need anything," I lie, feeling my cock harden underneath the sheet.

The most difficult part about the piercing isn't the pain; it's going over a month without an orgasm. I don't think I've gone that long since the moment I realized my dick was more than an organ for pissing. From the very second I figured out how to pleasure myself, I never stopped, just like every other red-blooded man in the world.

"I want to give you what you gave me."

I trace the line of her spine with my fingers, stroking her skin softly, trying to keep my shit under control. "You don't have to do that, baby. I was happy to give you what you wanted last night."

"Jett," she whispers, her hand slipping lower and sliding under the sheet. "I want to."

I hold my breath, waiting for the moment her hand touches my cock. Any air I had in my lungs quickly evaporates. Her skin's warm, her touch light as her fingers find my shaft, thankfully missing the head this time.

"Lily. I want you to be..." The words die on my lips as her fingers curl around my length and she starts to stroke me.

If the heavens could part and the angels sing, this would be the moment. Lily's touching me for the first time of her own free will and not because she's required to for work. I thought I'd lose it when I was in the chair at Inked. But now, with her in my bed, touching me, there's no way I can keep my need for her contained.

I bend my neck, searching her eyes for any hesitation or fear, but there's none. She looks sure of herself, so comfortable tucked against my side, touching me. As if she was always meant to be there and has been many times before.

"Kiss me," she says, her hand moving faster, her fingers tightening around me.

I smile as I lean forward, closing the space between us, pressing my lips to hers. At first, the kiss is gentle, sleep still clouding my thoughts, and the shock of waking up to find her in my bed hasn't worn off. But when she opens her mouth, sliding her tongue between my lips, the animal that's been hibernating inside me is finally unleashed.

With my hand on her back, I pull her upper body toward me, careful not to stop her from touching my cock. For a virgin, she's pretty fucking fantastic at the way she's stroking with just the right amount of pressure.

She moans as I kiss her deeper, tangling my tongue around hers. I slide my other hand under her arm, wanting to touch her body, needing to feel the warmth of her skin and make her feel as good as she's making me.

When my hand finds her thigh, I move my fingers upward, pausing when I realize she's not wearing any panties. The one thing I know about Lily is the girl always has on underwear. Always. And not the sexy type most women her age wear. She's all about the comfortable cotton ones. But tonight, in my bed, wearing nothing but a thin, soft nightie, she's otherwise naked.

This isn't by chance.

She didn't just wander into my bedroom after a bad dream.

She planned this.

The underwear is a dead giveaway, especially since I

woke up to her trying to touch me. She wants this, and there's no doubt in my mind she came in here fully intending to follow through. I don't need to ask her anymore if she's sure. I don't need to repeat the question, trying to make the consequences easier on my conscience. Lily tiptoed into my room for more than comfort.

I inch my fingertips higher, sliding over the soft, wet skin of her pussy, earning me a squeeze to my cock and a moan against my lips. She lifts her leg, resting her knee on my thigh, giving me complete access to her body.

I don't pause.

I don't think.

I just do what she needs and what I want.

I graze her clit, moving my fingers against her pussy in the way I know she likes. The way that makes her moan, rubbing her body against my hand like she can't get enough.

I'm already turned on beyond comprehension, feeling like a teenage boy being touched for the first time. Add in the sounds she's making as I touch her most private area, and I'm ready to explode. If I'm not careful, the entire thing will be over before we can even start.

She whines when my hand drifts from between her legs, and I break our kiss. Moving into a sitting position, I bring her with me, instantly regretting the moment her hand unlatches from around my cock.

Without saying a word, I slip my fingers under the straps of her nightie, wanting to feel all of her flesh on mine. I want no barriers, nothing separating us the first time we're really and truly together.

Her eyes sparkle in the soft glow from the television, her eyes holding mine as she raises her arms, allowing me to slip the gown over her head. Her breasts are perfect. Not too big and not too small, but the perfect handful, as if they were made for me.

"You're so beautiful," I whisper, my gaze roaming over her bare flesh. She's the most beautiful woman I've ever been with, and not just physically but inside too. There's no ugly side to Lily. She's kind, sweet, and caring all the way to her core.

"No talking," she tells me, her cheeks stained pink. "I want this, Jett. You don't need to lavish compliments on me to get me to sleep with you. I'm here and now." She swallows and sucks in a quick breath. "I'm naked. I'm ready for this. I want this. I want this with you."

I toss her nightie to the floor at the side of the bed, not caring where it lands because she isn't going to need it anymore. "I'm not lavishing compliments on you. I'm telling you what I see, wanting you to know how I feel because I've never felt this way before. This is as new to me as it is to you."

I've never been good at sharing my feelings, always too worried a girl would become too clingy. But with Lily, I need to be honest. She deserves as much. I've always seen her. Not just as the bookworm avoiding eye contact, but as a beautiful, shy thing, scared of being who she truly is. She always had her nose buried in a book, living her life through others instead of for herself.

But when she told me she dropped out of school, I realized she wasn't the same person I knew in high school. She wasn't the dutiful daughter, always looking to please her parents. She'd finally found a part of herself she'd always been missing. This moment, with her in my bed, naked and waiting, is another step on her journey of self-discovery.

I push her back, resting my body on top of hers, caging

her head in with my arms. Lifting up on my elbows, I gaze at her for another moment before pressing my mouth to hers again. I don't stay long, knowing I need to make her wet so the entire experience is as painless as possible.

Sliding down her body, I drag my lips across her skin, tasting her everywhere I can. Her legs fall to the sides, no longer pressing against me, granting me access to every inch of her body. I pepper her upper body with gentle kisses, moving my mouth to her breasts before finally closing my lips around her nipple.

She arches her back, pushing her breasts into my face as I suck her nipple into my mouth, flicking the hard tip with my tongue. She rocks into me, grinding her wet pussy against my impossibly hard cock. I moan, wanting to slide into her, feel her bare.

"Are you on the pill?" I murmur against her breast, peering up at her.

"No." She pouts for only a second, her mouth going slack when I suck again.

"Damn," I whisper, knowing skin on skin would be all kinds of wrong. "Get on that, baby."

"I never needed to be," she says, reminding me she's untouched and has never been fucked before. "Do you have a condom?"

If I had any doubt at all, which I didn't, about her wanting to follow through, it's gone. I nod, tracing her nipple with my tongue. "When you're ready, I'll get it."

Her fingers slide across my shoulders and settle near my neck. "I'm ready," she whispers.

I shake my head. No matter how badly I want to bury myself inside her, she's not ready. "Not yet, baby."

She lets out a small growl. "I am," she argues.

I place my hand between us, running my fingers between her legs. She's wet for sure, but taking a finger is quite different from taking a cock, especially one as big as mine. I push a finger slowly inside her, careful to keep my lips around her nipple, giving her pleasure.

Her nails dig into my skin as she arches her back and spreads her legs. After thrusting in and out of her a few times, I run my second finger through her wetness and start to push inside. Slowly, ever so fucking slow, I stretch her pussy around my fingers as she holds her breath and stiffens.

"Relax, Lily. I got you," I tell her, swiping my thumb across her clit.

She exhales as the pleasure shoots through her, and I touch her in the way I know she loves to be touched. Her body is responsive, quick to climb, easy to get off. Untouched and unspoiled by anyone before me.

She rocks into my hand, her breasts still pushed high, and I don't waste the moment, sucking and laving at her nipples as my fingers ready her for my cock. Her pussy adjusts, almost pulling my fingers inside her as her body races toward the orgasm she's always so eager to get.

It doesn't take long before she's shaking underneath me, gasping for air as the orgasm crashes over her. Her nails bite into my shoulders as I thrust my fingers in and out of her through each wave, giving her as much pleasure as possible. She twists and moans until my hand slows and her body goes limp.

I reach over, opening the drawer of my nightstand, feeling around for the condoms I have there just in case. Not that I ever planned on fucking Lily, but a man always has to be prepared for anything and everything, including a pussy so sweet you'd give your last breath to be inside.

I gaze down at Lily as I lift the wrapper to my lips. Her eyes are closed and she's breathing heavy, coming off the orgasm I know just rocked her world. Her eyes fly open as I tear the wrapper with my teeth. She gives me a lazy smile, watching in sheer fascination as I pluck the latex from the packaging.

I lean back as she slides her hands along my body and give her a full view of my body and my cock. Her gaze drifts down my chest, eyes widening like she's never seen my dick before.

"Jesus," she whispers, her mouth hanging open. "I don't think…"

"It'll fit, baby. Trust me. It'll fit," I say, almost begging because right now, I'm so fucking worked up, I know I'll come in record time.

"Go slow," she pleads, chewing on her bottom lip. "Promise me you'll go slow."

"I'll be gentle," I promise, wanting this to be as good for her as it's going to be for me.

I peer down, staring at my piercing, trying to figure out how the fuck to position the condom around the damn thing. It only takes me a minute to work the latex around the metal, rolling over the head, and down my shaft.

When I lean back over her, dick between her legs, body craving for her touch, she drops her knees to the bed. "I'm ready," she whispers. "I want this."

I gaze into her eyes, studying her face, knowing she's speaking the truth. "I've never wanted anything more."

She pulls my face to hers, taking my mouth in a hard kiss as I fist my cock, rubbing the tip against her warmth. I hate condoms. They kill the sensation, dulling the pleasure. Even though the end result is the same, nothing else about the experience is.

"I want you bare, Lily," I whisper against her lips between kisses. "I want to feel all of you."

She moans her agreement, hands moving along my arms. At first, there's a twinge of pain, the piercing being pulled and squished in a way I hadn't experienced yet. I don't let the different feeling stop me as I slowly push my head inside her.

Her knees come off the bed, pressing into my hips. I kiss her deeper, trying to distract her from the nervousness I know is coursing through her. At first, she's tense, her body barely moving except her hands, which have touched every inch of my shoulders and back.

I push inside another inch, waiting for her body to get used to the invasion and giving myself time to adjust to her tightness and the new addition to my body. If something could feel like heaven, it would be being inside her.

I pull back, peering down at her, studying her face. "You okay, baby?" I ask softly, barely getting the words out because hell, I'm not sure if I'm okay.

This is a religious experience. I'm not much of a believer in a higher power, but hell if I'm not at least partially converted, pushing inside her. The only way this could be better is if there were no barriers between us. Skin on skin.

She exhales and swallows, nodding, her eyes locked on mine. "I'm okay," she says, her voice cracking on the last word.

I lean forward, moving my head down her body, and take her nipple into my mouth. This girl loves having her nipples sucked, and I know the pleasure will help her relax, making the entire experience better.

Her back bows as her eyes flutter closed and her lips part.

I push deeper, forcing myself an inch closer to being completely inside her, but careful not to hurt her. It's a test of will and self-control.

One final thrust and I'm fully inside her. I stop moving my hips, licking her nipples, giving myself this moment. I'm her first. The only person to touch her this way, to be this deep.

It's not lost on me. The importance of what she's giving me. The trust she's put in my hands and how, no matter what happens between us, she'll never forget me.

Pulling out slowly, I suck her nipple harder and thrust inside again, still gentle, still careful. It only takes a few minutes for Lily to relax and her body to move with mine. Only then do I lift my head, giving her my lips and taking her until there's nothing more to give.

19

LILY

"So, are you guys officially a thing now?" Tamara asks, gazing up at me, searching my face like she can read all my dirty thoughts if she stares hard enough.

I shrug, twisting around to get a glimpse of Jett shaking hands with Uncle Joe. "We haven't discussed the true nature of our relationship yet."

Tamara blinks at me like I'm an alien. "Is he sleeping with anyone else?"

I shake my head.

"Are you seeing anyone else?"

I shake my head.

"Then you're a couple, and by the blush on your face and the fact that you didn't correct my statement, I'd say someone's not a virgin anymore."

Gigi's eyes widen, and the straw between her lips falls back into the glass as her mouth hangs open. "You finally did it?" she asks.

I smile, unable to hold back my excitement. We've always

shared everything. Sometimes more than I wanted to know, but this time, it's me with the big news and not them.

"We did," I whisper, not wanting anyone else to hear.

Gigi and Tamara squeal, rising from their chairs to envelop me in a group hug.

"This is huge. Are you okay?" Tamara asks, surprising me because I figured she'd ask about the size of his cock before anything else.

"I'm good." I pause, my smile getting wider. "Great, actually."

Gigi holds my hand, staring at Jett over my shoulder. "Do your parents know?"

"About us having sex?" I blink.

"About you two dating, dumb-dumb." She snorts, shaking her head.

"Oh my God. No. My dad would probably..." I turn my head, catching my dad talking with James, but he's staring at me. "Shit. I should probably tell them before they figure it out."

"Normally, I'd say truth is the best way, but with Uncle Mike, I'm not sure," Gigi says, moving to my side and glancing at my father. "He's kind of a hothead."

"Kind of?" Tamara snorts. "The man can be scary."

Gigi waves her hand toward our uncles and fathers. "Which one of them isn't? They're all ridiculous."

"What are you three doing?" Pike asks, walking up behind us and catching us completely off guard.

"Jesus, make some noise next time," Tamara mutters.

"Thought our boots would be enough, but you're too consumed by...what?" Mammoth asks.

Tamara snuggles into Mammoth's chest, peering up at

him. "Just talking about Jett and if Lily should tell her dad that they're more than living together."

"That's a negative, babe." Mammoth's gray eyes swing to me. "Keep that shit on lockdown as long as you can. Understand?"

"Um, no," I mutter, tucking a lock of hair behind my ear.

I like Mammoth. I like him a lot. He's great for Tamara. But sometimes, like now, he's confusing. Why should I hide my relationship with Jett when no one else in the family does?

Mammoth gives me a lopsided smile. "Doll, you're living with the man, and while you two may be bumping uglies, I think it's best if your parents think otherwise."

I blanch at his crassness, shaking my head at just how wrong he is. "It's not like that. It's been beautiful."

Mammoth levels me with his gaze. "I swear to fuck, don't tell them. Not yet. They're still getting used to you living with a friend who's male, let alone sleeping with him."

Tamara and Gigi are nodding, totally agreeing with Mammoth, but Pike's quiet, standing behind Gigi, eyes on Jett.

"And you?" I ask Pike, valuing his opinion.

Pike ticks his head toward Mammoth. "I'm with him. Wait a little longer to be sure."

"I thought honesty was always the best policy." I cross my arms, glaring at the four of them. "I can't believe you all want me to lie."

"No—" Pike puts up his hand "—don't lie. If they ask, then answer honestly, but don't blurt it out just to make yourself feel better."

"Let's go out after this. Celebrate a little, yeah?" Tamara

asks, wrapping her arms around Mammoth's middle. "It's been a while since we've been out together."

"Don't you have school tomorrow?" I ask Tamara.

She shakes her head. "Holiday."

"Fucker," I whisper.

I miss holidays. The shop never closes except for something like five holidays out of the year, along with every Sunday. I miss the easy schedule of college with endless holidays, spring break, winter break, and anything else they can use as an excuse not to have to work.

Gigi glances down, taking in her surf shorts and flip-flops. "I need to run home and change, so let's say eight at Duff's."

"Got it," I say, staring at Jett as he stalks my way.

There's a smile on his face, and it grows wider the closer he gets. "Hey, sweetheart. Talkin' about me?"

I blush, fluttering my eyelashes like a love-sick teenager. "Maybe a little."

"Are we telling everyone?" he asks, keeping his hands off me for the first time in days.

"Not yet. They—" I wave my hand toward my cousins and their men "—think it's best to wait a little while."

Jett lets out a long, relieved exhale as he touches his chest. "I get to live another day."

"Truth, brother," Pike tells Jett, earning the stink eye from me.

"Seriously, my dad is no worse than Joe, and you're still breathing," I tell him, rolling my eyes.

"We're going out tonight, Jett. Want to come? We're celebrating you two finally..." Tamara waggles her eyebrows. "You know."

Jett blushes, something I wasn't sure he could ever do,

under any circumstances. "I'm not sure that's a reason to celebrate, especially with your family."

"It's only us, silly," Tamara says, smacking Jett's shoulder. "We're celebrating that you two are a couple, not that you finally did it."

"What they'd do?" Uncle James asks, coming up behind Jett, who's now frozen like a statue.

"They've officially unpacked every box," Gigi replies, thinking quick on her feet and totally lying.

James rubs his forehead, staring at us like we're all insane. "You guys are celebrating that? I just don't understand kids today."

Gigi giggles behind her hand, having the worst poker face out of everyone. "Something like that, Uncle," she says.

"Well, you're going to have to party without Jett. We need him tonight for a case."

I swing my gaze to Jett, and he's staring at my uncle with a smile. "You're finally putting me to work?"

James nods. "This one requires someone younger than me, or I'd be going in as bait."

I swallow, replaying the word *bait* in my mind. They're going to use Jett as bait. Nothing about what Uncle James said sounds even remotely good or safe. I know my uncles and the fact that they've put themselves in danger more times than I can count. They are used to risking their lives, but I'm not sure how I feel about them using Jett in the same way.

"Bait?" Tamara asks, pushing herself away from Mammoth. "How dangerous are we talking?"

James laughs. "No danger, babe. Just need someone who's a looker and younger to attract some different eyes."

Tamara giggles. "You're using him as sex bait?"

"No. No. Of course not," James argues, shaking his head a little too quickly. "We're not like that."

"What's wrong?" Thomas asks, coming up behind James as he sweeps his eyes over us.

"Nothing, man." James rubs the back of his neck, trying not to look us in the eye. "Just talking about Jett and tonight."

"Ah," Thomas replies, placing his hand on Jett's shoulder. "He's just perfect for this project."

"What is it?" I ask, unable to keep totally silent.

"Can't say, sweetheart. You know we can't discuss cases."

"Is it dangerous?" I ask, hoping he'll give me something…anything.

Thomas shakes his head. "Not dangerous. This is a domestic issue and not criminal."

I've been around them long enough to know that is code for an affair. Someone, probably the wife since they're using Jett, is sleeping around on her husband, and they're using him as the worm, dangling his pretty face and hot body in front of her.

"Well, that's good. Right, Lily?" Tamara asks me.

I stare at the ground, kicking at the cement, and shrug. "Yeah. That's good." The words may come out calmly, but I don't feel that way. I don't like the idea of Jett being used as bait, even if it's only to catch a cheating wife.

"Give us a minute," Jett says to everyone around us, including my uncles, who are the last to leave, but I don't dare look up at them.

I keep my gaze pinned to the ground, feeling foolish about being upset over something so stupid. This is his job after all. He'll probably have to do something like this again. He'll probably have to do things I haven't and can't imagine.

Jett takes my hand, leading me away from the living room

and toward the staircase, heading to the upstairs of my grandparents' house. I don't say anything, not wanting to draw attention to ourselves as we slip away.

He pulls me into the first room, closing the door behind us. "We need to talk," he says, not releasing his grip on my hand.

"About what?" I ask, pretending not to be affected or jealous that someone else may touch him tonight.

His fingers are at my chin, forcing my gaze upward to meet his. "About us. About tonight. About boundaries and my inability to always keep them."

"What?" I ask, confused.

"Lily, sometimes work may have me do things I don't want to do. Just like tonight. I don't want to do this assignment, but I don't have a choice. I need to have this woman at least kiss me or else the evening is for shit."

"Kiss you?" I repeat his words, still shocked and confused.

"Yeah, baby. She has to kiss me. But just know, I'm going to hate every minute of it."

I blink, suddenly feeling sick. "I don't—"

He places his finger against my lips, staring at me with pained eyes. "I won't like it, Lily, and I know you won't either. Just like I don't love the idea of you touching other men's junk at work all day."

I roll my eyes. "I don't touch their *junk* all day."

"But you do touch dicks that aren't mine."

I nod, because he's right. I can't be a hypocrite, but there're things which are nonnegotiable. "But I'm not kissing them."

"But you're holding their dicks, babe. If tonight goes down the way it's supposed to, I'll kiss her for ten seconds max, and then I'll be out the door and on the way home to you." He slides his hand up my jaw, cupping my cheek. "Just know I don't want to kiss her. The only person my lips want is you."

I force a smile on my face and try to tamp down the jealousy I've never felt with anyone before. "I know."

"If you'd rather me tell everyone we're a couple and my lips are off-limits, I will. It's the only way out of it."

"No." She places her hand over my mouth. "Don't tell them. Not yet."

"Is everything okay in here?" The door opens, my aunt Izzy popping her head inside as soon as Jett drops his hand.

"We're good. Just talking," he says, not taking his eyes off me.

"Can I have a minute with my niece?" she asks Jett, looking between us with her auntie spidey senses no doubt going off.

"Sure." Jett gives me a small smile. "If Lily's okay with it."

"Go," I tell him, doing everything I can to stop my eyes from rolling. If she didn't know anything was going on before, she sure as hell does now.

Her gaze is pinned on me as Jett steps back and walks around her before leaving.

"So," she says, studying me, knowing me better than anyone besides my parents. "How long have you two been a thing?"

"A thing?" I play stupid, but by the way her shoulder's raised and she's tapping her foot, she knows I'm lying.

"Kid, I've known you since the moment you came out of your mama's womb. I've seen the subtle changes in you over the last month after moving in with Jett."

"Auntie, you have to promise not to tell anyone," I beg and reach for her hand. "Say it."

She stares at me, a smile on her face. "I won't say a thing to anyone. It's your news to share, not mine. Are you doing okay? Is he treating you right? I know how Jett is."

I shake my head, gripping her hands tighter. "He's different now. He's not the same man he was when he left town years ago. He's treated me so good, Auntie. He's going with Uncle James and Thomas tonight, and they're expecting him to kiss some woman who's the center of their case."

"Ah," she says, clicking her tongue. "The first time is always the hardest."

My eyes widen. "The first time?" I whisper and swallow, looking at my aunt in an entirely new light. "Uncle James has kissed someone else?"

"Lily." She pulls me toward the bed, sitting on the edge and patting the comforter with her palm. "Our men have a job which sometimes requires them to step outside their real lives. They have to put themselves in danger, do things that aren't always completely legal, and occasionally have to use themselves as bait, but that's usually only in the most extreme circumstances."

"So, Uncle James has kissed someone else?" I repeat because she didn't answer the first time.

"Fuck no. He knows I'd murder him."

I snort, loving the hell out of my aunt.

20

JETT

LYING IS something I've never been comfortable with. Sure, I've skated around the truth sometimes, but only when it was completely necessary, and even then, I hated it. But sitting here, surrounded by Gallos, lying my ass off about Lily and me, has been the absolute worst.

"So, Jett," Joe asks, forkful of spaghetti in front of his face. "How are things working out with you and Lily?"

I thought I'd be happy to be away from the kids' table and for the first time ever be sitting with the adults in the family, but that single question alone kills any happiness I felt. "Great. Just great."

Joe's gaze moves to Lily, who's busy shoving the long noodles into her mouth with wide eyes. "And you, Lily? How are things with Jett?"

Lily points at her full mouth, chewing slowly and wasting time because she doesn't want to answer the question. Knowing her, she'd say something ridiculously cute and let the news slip that we are more than roommates. She tosses him the okay sign, pinching her thumb and index finger together.

"Are you dating anyone?" Mia, Lily's mother, asks me.

"Yes, ma'am," I say as Lily shovels more pasta into her mouth, acting like she's never eaten before.

"Is it serious?" Suzy asks, studying my face and always being a little nosy, just like my mother. I'm sure she's been recruited to report back with any intel she's able to gather about me.

I've been tight-lipped with everyone in my life. Everyone besides Lily's cousins. Other than that, people are on a need-to-know basis, and Lily hasn't found a reason for any of them to know just yet. I'm more than happy to let it be known she's my girl, but she isn't ready to take that step. And while I hate it, I'm going to give her a little more time before we make the announcement.

"Very serious." I squeeze Lily's thigh under the table.

She flinches, knocking her knee against the wood, causing all the plates and cups to jump. "They're very, very serious," she mumbles with her mouth full, placing her hand in front of her lips. "She's really great."

I gawk at her, surprised by how easily she lied. She didn't even blink or say something wacky like she's done so many times in the past.

But when I look around, I see I'm not the only one staring at Lily. Her little stunt with the knee was enough to turn a few heads.

"Just great," she mutters again after swallowing down the pasta and twirling more around her fork.

Mike runs his fingers across his chin, studying his daughter closely. "And you two are settled in now?"

"Oh, yeah. They've done it," James says, repeating our words from earlier.

My eyes snap to his, finding a smug grin on his face. He knows we weren't talking about boxes. The man isn't stupid, even if he let us get away with the stupid cover-up. But now, in front of everyone, he's throwing me under the bus. Is this a test to see if I can handle the pressure or if I'll crack under the watchful eye of the Gallos?

"You've done it?" Lily's father asks, holding his water glass in front of his lips, blinking down at me like he's trying to decide if he's going to murder me or not.

Lily laughs nervously, patting her dad's arm. "We've finally finished unpacking every box, Dad. I've told you this."

He stares at Lily. "Is that what you've done?"

She nods, giving him a big smile. "Of course. You'll have to come over and see what we've done with the place. You're going to love it."

He grunts, mumbling something under his breath about me.

"As long as you're safe and happy, baby, we're happy," Lily's mom says, answering for her husband, who's too busy fuming to respond with actual words. "Your father and I didn't like the idea of you living alone." Mia's eyes move to me, a smile spreading across her lips. "We like knowing someone's there for you in case something happens. It's always nice to have a man around to make you feel safe."

"Sweetheart," Mike interrupts, sliding his big, meaty palm over her arm. "Lily's tough. She doesn't need a man around to be safe. She has Statham and all the moves I taught her over the years."

"Statham?" I ask, confused.

"My 9mm Glock," Lily tells me as if I should know this, but I don't. "I told you about him."

"Your gun is a him?"

She nods, smirking. "Always."

"And Statham?"

"She named it after Jason Statham. Lily's always had a thing for that man," Gigi tells me and the entire family about Lily's Hollywood crush.

Lily rests her fork on her plate, leaning back in her chair to stare down her cousin. "What's wrong with Jason? He's hot."

I turn my head, looking at Lily in a whole new light. Not only does she carry a Glock, when I assumed she was more of a .38 Revolver or a .42 since they'd both fit easily inside any of her purses.

"He's not hard on the eyes," Gigi argues. "But I'll take Momoa any day."

Lily tips her head back and laughs. "Momoa is a pretty boy. But when shit gets real, you need a guy like Statham to have your back."

"Ridiculous," Tamara says, finally joining the conversation. "You are both wrong. The Rock is the one you want when bad things happen."

Gigi and Lily roll their eyes. "We'll never agree on this," Lily tells Tamara. "Anyway, my baby isn't a Rock. He's more of a Statham."

"You're such a weirdo," Tamara tells her, smiling at Lily. "That's why I love you so damn much."

"You know," Mike says, thankfully interrupting the conversation about hot men. "Maybe you can have Lily teach you some of the moves I taught her."

I blink, swiveling my head back to her father when I

realize he's talking to me. I laugh. I can't help myself. He wants his daughter to teach me how to fight? "You're talking to me?" I ask, touching my chest.

He nods. "She's damn good."

"I'm sure, but I don't think I need a girl—" And that's where I fuck up. Every female in the room turns, glaring at me as if I've said the worst thing ever, insulting them all at once. "I didn't mean that the way it sounded. I'm sorry. I just meant..." I swallow, the words dying in my throat.

"Oh sweet Jesus," Pike mutters, covering his face with his hand. "Dumbass."

Mammoth's the only one laughing, finding my faux pas wildly hilarious. The other men at the table, including Joe, are gawking at me like I'm about to burst into flames. But the women, they look like they're about to lunge out of their seats, wrap their hands around my neck, and choke me out.

"I really didn't mean it that way. I swear," I argue, trying to save my life.

"Then..." Mike crosses his arms in front of his massive chest, leaning back in his chair, "I'm sure you won't mind if Lily showed you some moves. I'd feel better about her living with someone if I knew he could fight too."

"I know how to fight," I tell him, placing my fork back on my plate, staring him down. "I may not have a title, but I know how to throw a punch. I fought in the service all the time."

"Not the same," Mike says. "If you have a problem learning from a woman, stop by the gym, and I'll teach you a few moves."

Lily moves her hand to my leg, squeezing. "Do it," she whispers, because she's not the one who's going to get punched in the face.

I'm sure when her father trained her, he was gentle. She's his daughter after all. But me? He's going to beat me to a bloody pulp, showing off his ability and making it clear which one of us is tougher.

"It'll be good for you to get a few lessons before we send you out on too many assignments," Thomas says, adding to my misery.

"Fine. Fine. Lily can teach me," I say because there's no way I'm going toe-to-toe with a retired professional fighter and the man whose daughter I'm currently sleeping with.

"I'll do it," Lily says, smiling. "I could use the practice anyway."

"You can use the gym. I can schedule some time for you two in the ring," Mike offers.

Lily shakes her head. "We'll do it at home, Dad. The sand is just as soft and more private. I'd hate for anyone else to be around when I kick Jett's ass." She giggles, sounding so sure of herself for the first time.

I chuckle, but a small part of me wonders if she can, in fact, kick my ass. "I can't wait to see you try, baby."

Size doesn't matter. That's a mistake so many people make when deciding if their opponent has the power to bring them to their knees. And with Lily, I'm at a total disadvantage. I can't hit her. I can't hurt her. I wouldn't be able to live with myself. So, I'm going to be stuck on the defensive, trying not to get my ass beat by a chick, and powerless to fight back.

There's silence around the room, all eyes on me. "What?" I ask, throwing out my arms, wondering why they're all gaping at me.

"Baby?" Mike raises an eyebrow.

I blink and freeze. "Um."

"We all call Lily baby, Uncle Mike," Gigi tells him, trying to save my life and the dining room from turning into a fighting ring. "You know this."

Mike eyes me cautiously, not completely buying Gigi's excuse, even if it was a good one. "It came off his lips a little too easy."

"I call everyone baby, Mr. Gallo, even Gigi." I smile nervously, hoping Gigi keeps rolling with me and doesn't throw me under the bus.

"It's all the rage right now. The kids are all using it. I think it's sweet," Izzy adds, because she knows.

Dear fucking God, Lily cracked upstairs and spilled her guts to her aunt. The only person in the family I'm more fearful of than Mike is Isabella Gallo. The woman is a ball-buster, soul-crusher, and man-killer. Not literally, of course. But she, like her mother, is in charge in this family. Upset her, and your time is over, card punched, tossed out like trash.

"It's dumb," Mike growls.

"Jett, I made your favorite," Mrs. Gallo, the grandma and boss of the family, says.

"Why?" Mike asks, being the asshole he is and always has been.

"Shush it," she tells him, bringing her sweet gaze back to me. "I was so happy you were coming back this week, I went all out for you and made my banana split sheet cake."

My already full stomach rumbles at those words. "You didn't have to do that, Mrs. Gallo, but I can never turn down your dessert."

"Smart man," Lily's grandfather says at the end of the table, having been unusually quiet throughout the meal. "I'm sure you missed home-cooked meals like this when you were on deployment."

"I missed home-cooked meals like this my entire time in the service, sir. No one cooks like Mrs. G."

I get an appreciative nod from the family patriarch. "Did you see anything interesting when you were deployed? Have a favorite place you visited?"

"Dubai was interesting," I say, and just like that, the mood in the room changes along with the conversation.

THREE LONG HOURS LATER, I'm prepping for my first case with the ALFA team. The door to my bedroom creaks open, and Lily walks in, finding a spot on the end of my bed.

"Be careful tonight," she says, staring up at me as she fiddles with the hem of her skirt. "I have a bad feeling about this."

I move away from the mirror, kneeling in front of Lily and taking her hand in mine. "I'll be fine. The guys will make sure I'm protected and won't put me in any unnecessary danger."

"Do you want to take Statham?" she asks so sweetly, as if we're talking about a guard dog and not her gun.

"No, sweetheart. I'll be okay." I move a lock of hair away from her face, tucking it behind her ear. "I promise."

"Okay," she whispers.

I cup her face as she lowers her gaze. "What else is bothering you, Lily?"

She lifts a shoulder, dropping it quickly. "I know you may have to kiss someone else tonight." She raises her eyes to mine, and they're swimming in emotion. "I want you to know I'm okay with it."

"I'd never cheat on you. I'm going to do everything in my power to avoid her lips too."

"I know," she replies, moving her cheek into my hand. "I do, and I know you may have to do things sometimes that will make me uncomfortable, but I'll deal with them as they happen."

"It's hard to wiggle out of this one without telling your family that we're a couple. I could've maybe played that card if you'd have told them."

She shakes her head.

"No one means anything to me except you. I've never felt the way I feel about you for anyone else ever, Lily."

"I have feelings for you, Jett," she whispers. "And that scares me."

I lean forward, bringing my face close to hers, gazing into her beautiful blue eyes. "I have feelings for you too, and I'd be lying if I didn't admit saying those words terrifies me too."

She throws her arms around me, clinging to me. "Thank you for being so sweet to me."

I wrap my arms around her, holding her tight, rubbing her back. "Why wouldn't I be sweet, baby? All I want is to see you happy."

"You've made me happy. I was so nervous last night, creeping into your room. I thought you'd turn me away."

I pull back, a smile on my face. This girl. She's crazy if she thought I'd turn her away when all I've wanted is to be with her. "You offered me the most precious gift, Lily. I could never turn you away for putting yourself out there and telling me what you wanted."

"Promise me you won't sleep with anyone else? Promise me I'm enough," she begs as my smile falters.

"You're everything. There's no one else and can never be anyone else to fill your shoes. I'm head over heels, hopelessly gone for you, baby."

"I believe you," she whispers.

"There's no one as beautiful, inside and out, as you. No one as silly and sweet as you. No one I can be myself with, never having to pretend to be someone I'm not. I love that about you. I love that about us," I tell her. "And I love everything you are. The crazy things you say, how easily you blush, how shy you can be, and the tiger you turn into."

Her eyes widen. "I'm not a tiger."

"Baby, crawling into my bed last night, touching me, you were." I kiss the corner of her mouth as she snaps it shut. "Loved that shit so much. Hotter than the sun."

"Crawl into bed with me tonight when you get home?" she asks against my mouth.

"Count on it," I tell her before pressing my lips to hers, sealing that promise with a long, deep kiss.

21

LILY

I'M CURLED UNDER A BLANKET, the stars dotting the sky above me, reading my cousin Bianca's newest book, when the doorbell rings. I check the security camera because I'm too comfortable to move, and at this hour, I'm not answering without knowing who's here first.

Gigi's standing there, a tall man behind her, his back to the camera. The man isn't Pike, based on his build—wide shoulders and nearly a foot taller than Gigi. "Bitch, open the door," she says like she knows I'm watching. "I have a surprise for you." She pushes against the man's back, keeping him facing away from the camera on purpose.

I set down the book, lifting the phone closer to my face to try to get a better look at the stranger. "It's late, Gigi. I'm not really in the mood for company."

"Trust me, you want to see this person." She smiles, moving her face closer to the camera outside the front door, blocking out everything except her mug. "I can just pick the lock."

"Don't you dare," I hiss, knowing full well she could, and

probably would, jimmy her way into the house. "I'm coming down."

"Good," she says as the smile spreads across her face, and she backs away, covering the camera with her hand. "She's coming."

The man grunts, leaving his identity a complete unknown as I throw back the blanket and abandon the peaceful sanctuary Jett has built for me on the rooftop deck. I toss my phone aside, leaving it next to the book I had been devouring until I was rudely interrupted.

After walking slowly down the stairs, I throw open the door with a scowl on my face. "Who's so important you had to come over at this hour?"

Gigi's smile widens as she taps the man's back with her knuckles. "Wipe that sourpuss look off your face, princess, because I'm about to blow your mind."

Then the tall, broad-shouldered man turns around, facing me. "Nick?" I gasp, covering my mouth with my hand, my eyes wide.

He blinks, gawking at me like he doesn't recognize me. "Lily?" he whispers, his gaze moving over my face and down my body. "What happened to you?"

"What happened to me?" I ask, studying him. "What the hell happened to you?"

My cousin Nick, Thomas and Angel's son, has been away at boarding school for the last year. He didn't even bother coming home for summer break, spending it backpacking across Europe instead. Something my parents never would've let me do while still in high school. But Angel and Thomas...they treated him like he was a god who could do no wrong in their eyes.

"Grew up. Filled out. Became a man," he mutters, a cocky

smirk playing on his lips. He's eighteen, and even though he's inches taller than the last time I saw him, he's still just as arrogant.

I chuckle, shaking my head. *Became a man.* I hate to burst his self-confidence bubble, but he is not and has not become a man.

"He's clearly still the same asshole, though," Gigi says, reading my mind about our smug little cousin.

"It's part of his DNA," I mumble, knowing he's every bit a Gallo man. "But what the hell are you doing here?"

It's October, and school's in full swing. It's his senior year, and he's not supposed to come home until Christmas break. Uncle Thomas wanted him to get a leg up on the competition, meaning other boys his age, so he could attend West Point and someday be an officer in the military.

Nick swipes his massive palm over his face and lifts a shoulder. "School and I didn't agree anymore."

Gigi slaps him with the back of her hand, shaking her head. "He got kicked out."

My eyes widen. "You got kicked out?" I whisper.

I'd never seen Uncle Thomas completely lose his shit. Not like his brothers, including my father, had in the past. But if there were something that would drive him over the edge, this would be it.

Nick nods, the cocky grin faltering for only a second. "Shit happens."

"How are you still alive?" I ask, blinking at the impossibility of it all.

Gigi pushes past me, opening the door and kicking off her shoes as she wanders inside. "Get in here. We have a lot to talk about," she says, motioning for us to follow her as I peer over my shoulder.

"Come on," I tell him, tipping my head back toward the foyer.

I think Nick's going to step around me and walk inside, but he doesn't. Instead, my little cousin—well, younger is the right word—grabs me, wrapping me in a giant bear hug. "I missed you most of all, Lily," he says, his voice too deep for his age.

I'm helpless, my arms plastered to my sides and my feet dangling off the ground. "Missed you too," I bite out, struggling for breath in his freakishly large arms.

He steps forward, me still in his arms, and kicks the door closed before setting me on the floor. "Swanky joint," he says before whistling. "Better than the shithole she lives in."

"I take offense to that statement. My apartment is the best in the city," she tells him, collapsing onto the very large sectional in the living room.

"Do your parents know you're here?" I ask, running my hand along my ribs, which he, no doubt, bruised with the way he manhandled me.

He shakes his head. "Not yet, but they will tomorrow."

"Well, shit," I mutter, knowing things are about to get interesting.

"Sit, Nicholas." Gigi pats the spot next to her. "You have a lot of explaining to do."

I follow him to the couch and take the spot next to him, both of us caging him in on the sides. "Spill the beans," I tell him, folding my leg underneath me. "What the hell happened?"

He collapses back, letting out a long-exasperated exhale. "I was running a side hustle and got caught. Simple as that."

Naturally, my cousin had a hustle. All the kids at boarding school had one, according to him, but he was the lucky one who was actually caught and reprimanded for his actions.

"I guess making and selling fake IDs is not only against school policy, but also against the law. I begged for mercy and leniency, but they told me to fuck off." He shrugs one shoulder, his lips snarling. "Especially after Malcolm Harrison was found drunk and passed out, my well-crafted ID in his pocket. The asshole was told to either give up his supplier or get kicked out. The rat sang like a canary, I got the boot, and he's recovering in his fancy-ass room back in North Carolina."

My mouth's hanging open, my eyes sweeping over my cousin's face as the reality of his words wash over me. "You sold fake IDs?"

He grins, running his hand through his thick, dark, messy hair. "Made them too."

I roll my eyes, annoyed at his cockiness, but not surprised he's proud of the fact either. "Your dad is going to straight up murder you."

He waves off my comment. "He'll be pissed for a minute, but he'll get over it."

Gigi tips her head back, laughing. "You're so dead, Nick. So, so dead."

"Nah. My parents aren't going to kill me. Who would carry on the family name?"

I cock my head, raising an eyebrow. "The other Gallo boys."

"There're only two others, Lily. Stone, Asher, and me. We're the only ones who carry the Gallo last name and have the ability to procreate."

"Um," I mumble, pulling at my bottom lip, trying to hold

back my giggle. "I'm pretty sure the two of us—" I wave my hand toward Gigi "—can procreate too, dumbass."

"But your baby daddy would want his child to carry his name, so the weight of the family rests on my shoulders."

I roll my eyes, trying to remind myself I'm dealing with a smug, self-centered high school senior. Reality doesn't always mix with whatever's going on inside his brain.

"Just because my imaginary baby daddy would *want* his child to carry his name doesn't mean it would happen," Gigi tells him, smacking him in the shoulder. "I know you think men run the world, but I hate to burst your bubble, little cousin. They don't."

Nick places his hand on my knee, smiling his beautiful white smile. "Want to grab me a beer, babe?"

I blink, gawking at this kid sitting on my couch, pretending he's a man, looking pretty damn comfortable too. "Uh, sweetheart, you can have Coke, because there's no way in hell I'm giving a beer to an underage kid."

"Kid?" He laughs, patting my leg. "I haven't been a kid in years, and anyway, I drank my weight in Europe over the summer."

I pat his leg, mimicking his movements. "Well, you're not in Europe anymore, kid. Time for you to come back down to reality with the rest of us simpletons."

He blows out a breath, running his fingers through his hair again like he's obsessed. Which he probably is, because Nick always has been. He's good-looking. Even as his cousin, I can appreciate his handsome face, looking every bit like Uncle Thomas. "I'll be high school royalty here, cousin. Don't ever mistake me for anything less."

I roll my eyes, pushing myself off the couch using my hands instead of smacking him across his pretty face. "Three

Cokes it is, then," I mutter, leaving him and Gigi on the couch.

"Between you and Austin, the girls in this town aren't going to know what hit them."

"Austin?" Nick asks her.

"My boyfriend's brother," she tells him. "He moved here from Tennessee to finish his senior year. So far, he's big man on campus."

"He's about to lose his title."

I chuckle, shaking my head, thankful I'm no longer in high school. Not because the men are any more mature at my age, but at least I don't have to deal with the hierarchy, the backstabbing bitches, and the drama. Oh, the high school drama.

"That's if you survive," Gigi snickers. "We'll see after tomorrow if you're still breathing."

"Lily," Nick calls out as I fish three cans of Coke out of the fridge. "Can I crash here tonight?"

"Uh, sure," I blurt out, not thinking about asking Jett first or talking anything over with Gigi.

"Fuckin' kick-ass. You got a hot tub around here?" he asks, looking around, spotting the lanai in the backyard.

"It's closed for the season," I lie, holding out a can to him, shaking it when he just gawks at me.

"Closed for the season?" He lifts an eyebrow, taking the can from my hand. "Do people believe your lies?"

"Do they believe yours?" I throw back at him, handing the other Coke to Gigi. "Anyway, there's no time for lounging in the hot tub. You're not having friends over. You can crash on the couch, and in the morning, I'll drive you home."

"Fuckin' great," he mutters, popping the top of the can without a hint of a smile on his face anymore.

"Jett still gone?" Gigi asks, looking around the room.

"Yeah, the guys said it would be a late night."

Nick is about to take a swig, placing the can against his lips before he pauses. "Wait." His gaze swings to me, and his head tilts. "Jett Michaels?"

I nod, smiling. "We're roommates," I tell him.

"Roommates?" Gigi laughs, bumping Nick's shoulder. "They're way more than roommates."

He blinks, gawking at me. "Uncle Mike's letting you live in sin?"

"He doesn't know," Gigi whispers. "He thinks they are, in fact, only roommates."

His smug grin is back, and he's judging me. I can feel it in the way he looks at me. "You're lying to your parents?"

I shake my head, glaring at my big-mouthed cousin. "No."

"Omitting a fact is still a lie, Lily," Gigi tells me, giving me a know-it-all grin.

"It just happened," I groan. "It's not like we've been having wild monkey sex for months and hiding it from them."

Nick gags a little. "I can't talk sex with you two. It's gross."

"Gross?" My lip curls. "You're seriously going to sit here, after all the shit we've had to hear from you over the last two years, and tell us we're gross?"

He nods, lifting the can to his lips. "Mm-hm," he mumbles against the rim of the can before taking a swig. "And seriously…Jett Michaels?"

"What's wrong with Jett?" I ask defensively.

"Nothing." He lifts his shoulders, resting the can against his knee. "Just never pictured you with someone like him. I figured you more for a Bill Nye type."

I pinch the bridge of my nose, groaning. "You're a tool."

"She was the Bill Nye type herself until Jett came along,

offered her this place—" Gigi waves her hand around the living room "—and swept her right off her feet."

"How the hell did that happen, exactly? Wait." Nick blinks, lifting the Coke back to his lips and pausing. "Why the hell aren't you at college?"

"She dropped out," Gigi tells him just as he tips his head back, filling his mouth.

His body lurches and he coughs, pounding on his chest, trying to clear his throat. "She what?"

"I realized I wasn't living my best life."

"Okay, Deepak Chopra," Gigi says, always busting my chops about everything. "She's working at Inked now. That's how she hooked up with Jett."

Nick coughs again, still trying to work the liquid out of his throat. "You're at Inked forever now?"

I shrug. "Forever's a long time, but for now, I'm there."

"She's doing piercing."

"And Jett came in to get…?" Nick asks.

"His dick pierced," Gigi answers for me.

Nick gags again, throwing up a hand. "Whatever floats his boat."

"Gigi and Tamara are dating bikers who are in an MC," I blurt out, feeling the weight of Nick's stare.

"Pike is not and has never been in an MC," she argues, placing her can on the coffee table and turning to face me. "We've been over this a million times."

"Well," I say, doing the same and crossing my arms. "You were almost killed not that long ago because of him."

"Wait, what?" Nick shakes his head. "How?"

"It's not important," she tells him, placing her hand on his forearm. "There was an issue, but it's been resolved."

"And Tamara?" I lift an eyebrow.

"Well..." Gigi smiles. "She *is* dating a biker in an MC, but he won't be there for long. She said he's moving here as soon as she's done with school."

I roll my eyes, something I'm doing way too often with these two around. "Of course, he'd tell her that. Do you think he's really going to do it?"

Gigi nods. "I do. Mammoth is a man of his word."

"Mammoth. Pike. Jett?" Nick asks, his eyes swinging between the two of us. "I see you ladies have been busy since the last time I saw you. I'm impressed, really. Didn't think you had it in you."

It's funny how Nick somehow thinks he's our equal. He's three years younger than me, which in the grand scheme of things isn't much, but as a teenager, it's worlds away. He's spent the last three years away at boarding school, only visiting on holidays and in the summer. It's as if he's been away at college like the three of us were, but he was attending a fancy and very strict high school.

"I see you're still the same egotistical asshole you were the last time I saw you," I tell him. "We'll see how cocky you are tomorrow after your daddy gets his hands on you."

"It'll be fine." Nick doesn't even flinch. "I'm not worried."

"I'm pretty sure your fancy-ass school cost more than my college tuition. If I were you, I'd kiss my ass goodbye along with any social life because Uncle Thomas is about to put you on house arrest."

"Nah." Nick waves off Gigi's comment. "He'll be pissed, for sure, but once he calms down, he'll be happy I'm home."

"Sure, it's going to be that easy." I chuckle and shake my head. "I only wish it were Sunday."

The front door swings open, the wood smashing into the

wall behind. Jett limps in, arm slung around Uncle Thomas's shoulder like he can't walk on his own two feet.

I'm on the move immediately, forgetting Nick and Gigi on the couch, and rushing toward the door, grabbing hold of Jett's waist. "Oh my God, what happened?"

"Shit went south. Took a few licks, but Jett here took the brunt of them after someone drugged his drink," Uncle Thomas says, still not seeing Nick on the couch. "He'll be fine after some rest."

"You look..." My voice drifts off as Jett winces, leaning on me a little more than Uncle Thomas.

"What. The. Fuck?" Uncle Thomas hisses, finally lifting his eyes, spotting Nick frozen on the couch. "Am I seeing shit, or is my kid in your living room?" The steely glare on my uncle's face is nothing short of scary.

"I can explain," Nick says, scrambling to his feet, almost knocking over the coffee table in the process.

"Hey," Jett whispers to me, giving me a lopsided, bloody grin as I try to take some of his weight. "You're looking sexy."

"Shut up," I tell him, smiling like an idiot because, drugged or not, I love his compliments.

"Get your ass in the car," Uncle Thomas growls, squaring his shoulders, staring at his son. "I don't want to have this talk in mixed company."

"Catch y'all later," Nick says, throwing up his hand as he marches toward the door.

"Bye, Nicky," Gigi calls out, trying to hide her smile behind her hand. "Don't die!"

Uncle Thomas grunts, not even bothering to move so Nick can slide past him. "You're going to wish for death."

I grimace as my eyes meet Gigi's. "Sucks to be him," I mouth.

"Jett's going to be acting weird for a few hours. Probably talking nonsense if you don't put his ass to bed. He's been rambling on and on in the back seat for over an hour."

"My ass," Jett says, laughing.

Uncle Thomas scrubs his hand down his face, muttering a slew of curse words. "As if I don't have enough shit to deal with, this goddamn kid shows up out of nowhere."

"Love you, Uncle Thomas," Gigi calls out before he has a chance to follow Nick out the door.

"Bye, cupcake." Thomas winks at her. "Your dad is so lucky to have girls."

"He'd disagree," she tells him, blowing him a kiss before he disappears into the night.

"Now what?" Gigi asks, gawking at Jett as he hangs on my shoulder, finally finding his footing.

"Threesome?" he asks, a sloppy grin on his face.

I stop moving, dropping my arm from his body as he sways. "I'm going to let that one slide because you're drunk, but the next dumb thing that comes out of your mouth is going to make you wish you—"

"Baby, I love you," Jett murmurs, gazing at me but not entirely focusing.

"He's drugged," Gigi reminds me, still planted on the couch. "Ignore his stupidity. Want help getting him upstairs?"

I shake my head, knowing full well I can handle the man on my own. "He can sleep down here."

"The couch has always been our favorite spot." He grins.

She shoots up, staring down at the couch like the cushions are contagious. "And you let me sit there?"

"Oh, shut up," I tell her. "It's not like you and Pike haven't done it on every surface in your place. If we were going by those standards, I'm pretty sure I couldn't even sit on your floor."

She giggles and then sobers when her gaze moves to Jett. My eyes follow, watching as he props himself up against a wall, fishing in his pocket for something.

"Well, I see you have your hands full, so I'm going to head home. You should put him to bed."

"Bed," he mutters and throws me a wink. "Been waiting all day to hear that word."

"No nookie for you, mister," I say, wrapping my arm around his middle again. "You need some sleep."

"Cuddle with me?" he asks so sweetly, I freeze.

"Cuddle?" I blink.

He nods. "I want to hold you tonight, baby."

"I'm out!" Gigi moves toward the door, tossing a wave over her shoulder. "You two kids have fun."

"I hate you," I grumble toward her.

"Don't hate me," he whispers, brushing his lips against my temple.

"I don't," I tell him, knowing it's going to be a long, long night. "Come on, big guy. It's bedtime."

He stands a little straighter as we make our way to the first stair. "Lily."

I glance up, my shoulder under his arm, trying to take most of his body weight for the trip up the stairs. "Yeah?"

"I love you more than anyone else in the world," he whispers, making my heart skip a beat.

22

JETT

I CRACK ONE EYE OPEN, and the light streaming through the bedroom window is so intense, I shut it immediately. Lavender fills my nostrils, and warmth radiates across my skin as the body lying next to me stretches.

I stiffen as the woman beside me curls into me, and sporadic memories of last night come back.

Oh God. Please let this be Lily.

I didn't drink much last night, but what exactly happened isn't clear. I only had two drinks while chatting with the woman who's the subject of our investigation, and then things started moving in slow motion, warping and stretching like I'd been drugged.

"Jett," Lily says as I hold my breath, panic coursing through me. "You okay?"

I exhale, relaxing into the mattress, and tighten my arm around her. "Fine, babe. Totally fine," I mutter, feeling completely relieved I didn't somehow fuck everything up and sleep with someone else.

I force my eyes open, wincing as the sun hits me in the

face, momentarily blinding me. "What the hell happened?"

She moves her hand over my bare chest, tilting her face upward. "You don't remember?"

I shake my head, regretting the move as pain shoots through my skull. "Not much. Certainly not coming home and what happened afterward." My hand slides along her bare back until my thumb catches in the strap of her cami. For a moment, I'm relieved we didn't have sex, especially since I don't remember a damn thing.

"You were pretty messed up. Uncle Thomas said you were drugged."

I blink up at the ceiling, wondering why someone would drug me and how they did it. "Everything's fuzzy. Did we..."

"No." Lily snuggles closer, tracing my pec with her fingertip. "You were a perfect gentleman and way too messed up to walk on your own, let alone do anything more."

I breathe a sigh of relief, happy I didn't have sex with her when I was fucked up beyond belief. "I don't know what happened."

"Me either, but I'm sure my uncles will fill you in on everything since Uncle Thomas brought you home."

I turn my head, yawning through the haze and not wanting to breathe my morning breath all over my pretty girl. "I feel like I have cotton in my mouth," I tell her, moving my tongue around my mouth.

"I could use some coffee. How about you?"

I gaze down, smiling at the beautiful angel at my side, and nod.

"Meet me downstairs in five. I'll get a pot started," she tells me and leans forward. I watch in sheer fascination as she places her lips against my chest, kissing my skin.

"I can do it," I tell her, wanting to wait on her and not the other way around. I'm usually up before Lily, used to early mornings from being in the military.

"No. Rest a few more minutes. Get your bearings."

I don't argue, my head pounding and still fuzzy from whatever the hell someone gave me last night. I blink a few times, trying to clear my mind as the bed dips and Lily's warmth disappears.

She rolls to the edge, climbing to her feet and stretching. Her cami rides up, exposing the soft, perfect skin of her stomach. I stare at her as her body shakes and she yawns. "It's too early to be awake," she groans, dropping her arms, "and functioning."

I nod, unable to take my eyes off her as she stands off to the side, barely dressed. She has on a pair of boy shorts and a thin, revealing tank, showing off more of her body than she normally does.

"What time is it?" I ask, unable to focus or move.

"Eight." She slides her arms into her robe, tying the material tightly around her body.

I push myself up, regretting the sudden movement when the pain inside my head grows. "Shit, I'm going to be late if I don't get my ass in gear."

"What time do you have to be at ALFA?"

"Ten."

"Go shower and meet me downstairs," she says, walking toward the doorway, her sweet ass cheeks tempting me from under the robe. "Take your time." She smiles over her shoulder, catching me gawking at her.

"Be down in ten," I tell her, winking.

I collapse backward as soon as she's gone, trying to remember what the hell happened. I was at the bar, talking to the target—a pretty, older woman whose husband thought she was cheating—and then I woke up here. There are glimpses of other moments, but they're distant and foggy, as if I wasn't the one who lived them.

I climb out of bed, strip off my pants, and head to the shower, needing to wash away last night. I make it quick, wanting to be with Lily this morning before I head to the office and try to piece together what happened.

"Jett!" Lily yells from downstairs as I dress. "Jett!"

I pull on my jeans and grab a shirt and shoes, rushing from the bathroom and running down the steps. Lily's standing in the foyer, arms covering her chest, staring at a man.

"Michaels," the guy says, drawing my attention away from Lily. "So fucking good to see you, man."

I blink, shaking my head because I know the guy, but I have no idea what he's doing here. "Marcus?" I ask, still blinking and confused.

He drops his pack from his shoulder with a loud thud. "Thanks for saying I could crash here."

Lily glances at me, and I smile, clearly having missed something. I rub the back of my neck, wishing I could remember everything from last night.

I haven't seen Marcus since I left the Navy a year ago, leaving San Diego behind. He's been my best friend for the last three years, but I never thought I'd see him so soon, and I definitely don't remember talking to him lately.

"Didn't know you had such a pretty roommate," he says, stepping toward Lily, gawking at her like she's the most delicious thing in the world.

I move quickly, going to Lily's side and sliding my arm around her back. "Marcus, this is my girlfriend, Lily."

His eyes widen in recognition.

Fuck.

"*The* Lily?" he asks, a smile moving across his face.

She tips her face up toward me. "The Lily?"

I smile nervously and swing my gaze back to Marcus. "This is *the* Lily. My Lily." I tighten my arm around her middle, and she melts into me.

"I just made some coffee. Would you like some?" she asks him.

He smiles. "There's nothing I'd love more right now."

"I was just pouring you a cup," she says to me, touching my cheek to get my attention because I'm too busy staring at Marcus.

I knew he'd be getting leave soon, and although we talked about him coming to Florida to visit, I never really thought he'd follow through.

"Thanks, sweetheart," I whisper, bending my neck and brushing my lips against hers for a brief moment.

She peels away from me, sauntering toward the kitchen, leaving Marcus and me in the foyer.

"Did we talk?" I ask.

He nods, looking at me funny. "Dude, last night."

"Fuck." I rub my forehead, wishing I didn't have holes in my memories. "I went out on a case and was drugged. Everything's fuzzy or gone."

"Someone roofied you?" He gapes at me.

"Seems like it." I shrug, hoping the guys at ALFA can fill me in on what I missed. "I don't even remember coming home last night." I motion toward the kitchen, knowing Lily's going to become impatient. "But I'm hoping the memories come back to me."

Marcus follows me, leaving his big pack near the door. "Don't count on that shit, man. At least you made it home and were with people you know and trust. That drug has some serious power."

Lily smiles when she sees us. "Cream or sugar?" she asks Marcus, already knowing how I like mine.

"Black, ma'am."

Her smile widens. "Black, it is," she says, sliding the coffee mug across the island to him. "So, how long have you known Jett?" she asks him, leaning over, holding her own mug.

He blows out a breath, wrapping his fingers around the pink mug with a unicorn on the front that she'd given him. "Three years. We were both stationed in San Diego, but I reenlisted, while this fucker chose to leave."

"I bet you could tell me lots of stories about him." She raises an eyebrow.

"No stories, sweetheart," I say quickly, throwing Marcus a warning glare.

"Stories?" he mumbles against the mug. "He lived the life of a priest, so there's not much to tell."

She rolls her eyes. "Lies."

"You're much prettier than your picture," Marcus says, and my eyes widen, my body stiffening.

She blinks at me before swinging her gaze to Marcus. "You've seen my photo?"

He nods, smirking.

"How long are you here for?" I ask, trying like hell to change the subject.

"Just a few days, then I'm headed to my new post in Key West."

"Sounds like a hard life," I laugh. "Key West is nothing like San Diego."

"I'm counting on that," Marcus replies.

"So, back to this picture," Lily says, not forgetting his

words even though we've moved on. "When did you see a picture of me?"

I groan, plopping down onto a stool, knowing Marcus is going to spill my secret and there's nothing I can do to stop him.

"This one—" he motions toward me "—had this photo of you above his rack. He looked at it every night until it basically crumbled into a million pieces."

She moves her gaze to me, and she blinks, lips parted. "You kept a photo of me by your bed?"

I nod, knowing I can't deny it because Marcus has loose lips. "I did."

She smiles and touches her chest. "Of me?" she asks again as if she can't believe what he just told her.

"Yeah. Of you," I repeat.

"How?" She bites her bottom lip, face turning a light shade of pink.

"Aunt Suzy would send me photos a few times a year. And you were so pretty in one, I pulled it to the side, keeping it close."

"Which one was it?"

I focus on my coffee, turning the mug in my hands. "I think she said it was taken at your high school graduation party. You were wearing..."

"A pink sundress with spaghetti straps," she finishes my statement.

I nod, wishing I could punch Marcus right in his traitorous face. "You looked so happy in that photo. I'd never seen you in much more than your khaki pants and polos. I couldn't take my eyes off the photo, and I carried it in my pack for years."

"So fucking hot," Marcus adds, earning him a death glare from me, but Lily doesn't even blink.

"You thought I was pretty?"

"I've always thought you were and are pretty, Lily."

"A hot chick who doesn't know she's hot," Marcus mutters into his mug. "Totally unbelievable."

"I just can't believe you would keep a picture of me by your bed," she whispers. "God, I didn't even think you realized I existed sometimes."

"Oh, he knew," Marcus says, almost choking on his coffee when I swing my glare his way.

"I told you I always saw you, Lily. I told you I always had a thing for you."

"You never really spoke to me, though."

"Anytime I tried, you'd run away."

She giggles so sweetly, the sound makes my heart flutter. "Well, you're Jett, the cool kid with the line of girls a mile long waiting for your attention. And I'm…"

"Hot as fuck," I tell her. "Smart. Sweet. Quiet. But always hot as fuck."

"I second that," Marcus adds.

"Dude, shut it," I tell him, making my way around the island to stand next to my girl.

He throws up his hand, dipping his head. "I'm just going to enjoy this delicious coffee."

"Don't be so mean, Jett Michaels. I'm happy your friend told me. I never would've believed you had a thing for me."

I run my finger across her bare shoulder, wishing we were alone and had time to spend together this morning. "I told you I always had it bad for you, but you never believed me." I smile, staring her straight in her beautiful blue eyes. "It took this fool to utter my secrets, and suddenly, now you're a believer."

"Want to know something about me?" she asks, tipping her head back and placing her hand on my chest.

"I want to know everything about you."

"I had a picture of you on my nightstand too."

"You two are like a gross Hallmark movie," Marcus whispers, but neither of us looks at him.

I smile, loving that she had a thing for me too. Maybe somewhere in the back of her mind, she was always saving herself for me. At least, I like to think she has been, not giving her body to anyone before now.

"We were meant to be, Lily Gallo," I whisper before bending my neck and taking her lips with mine. The kiss is sweet and short since we have an audience. "Are you working late tonight?"

She nods, groaning. "I'll be back around midnight."

"I'll wait up for you," I tell her, tightening my hold around her back.

"Okay," she says softly, pressing her body into me.

"I'll take Marcus with me so you can have some time to yourself this morning."

"I'm exhausted after taking the red-eye. Maybe I can just crash here while you go wherever you're going."

I level him with my gaze. "You've done more on less sleep. You're coming with me. There's no way I'm leaving you here with my girl."

"I'm trustworthy," he argues.

"Still not happening." I can't trust him to keep from saying anything else, spilling every secret I have or telling her everything I ever said to him about her.

"Fine," he grumbles, which causes Lily to giggle.

I kiss Lily goodbye, forcing Marcus to his feet and out of the house.

"You got it so fucking bad for her, man," he says, following me down the sidewalk outside the house. "Never thought I'd see the day, but I never should've doubted your ability to make shit happen."

"Didn't think I'd be living with her, but the timing was perfect and things just worked out."

"Some people have the best dumb luck." He slides into the truck next to me. "You going to put a ring on her?" he asks.

"We're not there yet."

"Sounded like you were to me." He shrugs.

"Don't worry. I'm going to lock that shit down as soon as the time is right."

"Don't wait too long, or else you could end up messing up the best thing to ever happen to you."

"It's only been a few weeks. I don't want to scare her away. She's never been with a guy like me before."

"You mean an asshole?" Marcus laughs.

"Takes one to know one, man."

But Marcus is right. It's not time to propose to Lily, but I need to tell her how I feel.

23

LILY

THE LIGHTS ARE on in the kitchen when I walk in. There are no voices, no low murmur of the television like on most nights when I get home late.

"Jett?" I call out, kicking off my sandals and dropping my purse near the door.

"Marcus," Marcus hollers back from the kitchen. "Jett got called out on a case."

My shoulders slump, exhaustion and disappointment overcoming me. I was really looking forward to coming home, curling up with Jett, and getting some much-needed sleep.

Marcus stalks out of the kitchen, drying his hands with a towel, wearing entirely too little clothing. "He said he'd be late and not to wait up."

"Oh. Okay." I glance up the stairs, feeling a bit awkward with his half-dressed friend I barely know. I'm annoyed Jett didn't so much as text me, telling me he was leaving Marcus, a man I didn't know, alone in our house. He and I will have words about that later, but for now, I put aside my feelings and try to be a good host. I smile, mustering all my mental strength to be nice and courteous. "I'm going to head to bed. Do you need anything before I crash?"

"Did you eat?" Marcus throws the towel over his naked shoulder and moves his hands to his hips. "I made something, and I can't eat it all myself."

My stomach rumbles, betraying me. "Eh, I don't think it's…"

Marcus laughs, motioning for me to follow him. "Eat a little something before you go to bed. It's never good to sleep on an empty stomach." He takes a step back, but I don't move. "Come on, Lily. I won't bite."

There's something about the smirk on his face that makes me want to run up the stairs and hide away in my room. But this is also Jett's friend, and I've always been taught to welcome guests, even ones I never asked to stay. "Okay," I whisper and finally find my feet.

Marcus walks in front of me, and I stare at his back, studying the ink between his shoulder blades. A skull with roses, the vines sweeping across his back and crawling up to the bottom of his neck.

"I made queso," he says, reaching for a pan on the stove like he's always lived here. "I hope you don't mind spicy."

I slip onto the stool on the other side of the island, trying to keep my distance. He's handsome, someone who would've made my heart flutter if I'd met him under different circumstances. His eyes are the darkest shade of brown, melting into the blackness of his pupils.

"I love spicy," I say, placing my hand over my stomach as it grumbles again.

He opens the drawer next to the stove, fishing out a towel, and sets it in front of me before placing the hot pan on top. "So, how was work?" he asks like we've done this a million times or are at least friends.

"The same," I tell him, fidgeting in my seat and telling myself to calm down. This is Jett's friend after all, and I'm positive he wouldn't leave me alone with someone who's questionable.

He moves toward the fridge, reaching for the handle, his back to me. "I could use a beer, you?"

"Sure."

He pulls out two beers, making quick work of twisting off the caps, and hands me one.

"What did you two do today?" I ask, trying to make small talk. At the very least, maybe I can find out about Jett and what he's been up to for the last handful of years. I can most certainly ask about the photo Marcus told me about earlier.

"Nothing unusual." He lifts the beer to his lips, taking a small sip before moving around the island to sit next to me. He pulls the bag of chips in front of us and pushes the opening toward me. "You first," he says.

I give him an impish smile, grabbing a chip and digging into the queso. I smile at Marcus, chewing slowly to avoid conversation.

I'm not a people person. I'm definitely not great with strangers, especially handsome ones I don't know.

Marcus does the same, chewing quickly before filling the silence. "Jett showed me around some of his old haunts. Places he'd told me about for years."

"There's not much to see around here."

"Everything I've seen is beautiful," he says, staring at my mouth as I lick the cheese from my lips.

I swallow, almost choking. "Florida is beautiful," I say, averting my eyes back to the steamy pan of cheese.

"You really are more beautiful than your photo."

I lean my body away from Marcus, the hairs on the back of my neck standing on their own. "Thanks," I mutter, feeling completely uncomfortable but trying not to show it.

"Jett carried that damn thing everywhere. If it wasn't above his rack, it was in his wallet. Never saw him so stupid over a chick." Marcus shakes his head, smirking. "But now, sitting here with you, I can understand the fascination."

I smile, grabbing another chip from the bag, confused about what the hell to say. I've never been the girl who men flirted with unapologetically.

"Great dip," I say, chewing on the chip, being as unladylike and not cute as possible. "Thanks for the snack, but I think I'm going to go to bed." I leave out the part about locking my door and having words with Jett tomorrow over not being comfortable with Marcus in the house. His words and the way he looks at me give me a funny feeling, and not one I welcome or enjoy.

But before I can slide off the stool, Marcus's hand is on my knee. "You know Jett and I shared a lot in California."

I turn my head and blink. "Is that so?" I ask, knowing without a doubt where this guy, who I now realize is also a sleazeball, is going.

Marcus nods, smirking at me like somehow the look alone will make me part my legs, granting him entrance. "If you're lonely tonight, I'm sure he wouldn't mind…"

I clench my teeth, avoiding stiffening or showing fear. Men like Marcus don't scare me. My dad taught me how to protect myself and take control of situations like this. I may look meek and mild, but put me in a spot I don't want to be in, and anyone, at any size, is going to be in a world of hurt.

"I'm pretty sure he would mind," I tell Marcus, my eyes narrowing on his smirk that is more creepy than sexy.

"Baby." He squeezes my knee tighter. "We've shared girls before, even girlfriends."

I slip off the stool, and so does Marcus. "Listen, while I'm flattered…" I say, but I'm not. "I know Jett isn't into sharing me, and honestly, I'm a one-man type of girl."

I try to move to the right and around him, but he moves too, blocking my way. His hands are on my shoulders, touching my bare skin. "No one likes a girl who plays hard to get."

I tilt my head, peering down at where his hands are, knowing my patience has run dry and Marcus's time to keep standing upright is over. When his hand glides across my skin and he rests his palm on my cheek, stepping closer, I know it's over.

"I'm saying no, Marcus," I tell him, giving him one more warning.

I'm cute, but looks are often deceiving. The same way a kitten can be until they swipe at you with those razor-sharp claws and draw blood.

"Come on," he says, still not getting that I don't want him to touch me, or maybe he doesn't care. I'm assuming he doesn't give two flying shits since I've given him every possible signal that this entire thing is a hard no for me.

In my short twenty-one years, I've never had to put my hands on another human being, but today, I'm breaking the seal. If anyone deserves it, it's Marcus.

"You have ten seconds to remove your hands from me and step away," I warn him, giving him one last chance to back off. "Get your things and go."

But Marcus, clearly a man who doesn't give a shit, also

doesn't do as I've asked and hoped. "Baby, you know you want me. I see the way you've been looking at me."

I snort right in his face. "Baby, this isn't the look of lust."

He crowds my space, and I know this is my time to act. The only time I'll have the proximity advantage to carry out what I need to do to make him regret ever hitting on me.

Just like I've practiced, I thrust out my arm, smashing the palm into his face, connecting with his nose. "I said no."

He staggers back, his hands moving to where I've just hit him. "Fuckin' bitch," he wails, his eyes watering.

My leg rises, my knee crashing into his balls, making him crumple forward. He's no longer worried about his nose because my bony-ass knee is wicked.

He gasps for air, one hand on his face, the other at his crotch. I'm just about to hit him with an uppercut, making him straighten, when the front door opens, and Jett appears.

His eyes snap to me then to Marcus and back to me. "What the fuck?" he hisses, running into the kitchen.

"Your friend—" I wave my hand at Marcus "—doesn't seem to understand personal boundaries."

"The fucking bitch hit me," Marcus groans.

The look of shock on Jett's face vanishes just as quickly as it came. "The fucking bitch is my girlfriend." Jett doesn't waste any time in doing what I had planned next, delivering a wicked uppercut, causing Marcus's body to fly backward.

I stand there, watching with wicked fascination as Jett kicks the shit out of his so-called best friend.

"Go get his bag for me, please," Jett says, grabbing Marcus by the collar and hauling him toward the door. "While I take out the trash."

I'm out of the kitchen a second later, running up the stairs to the spare bedroom. Marcus's bag is near the bed, only a few pieces of clothes scattered on the duvet. I jam everything inside, not giving two shits if I forget anything.

By the time I'm back downstairs, Jett has Marcus on the cement outside. "You're an asshole. You're lucky I'm letting you leave here breathing."

Although I had the situation somewhat under control, I'm happy Jett came in when he did and took over. I only had a plan to make Marcus regret touching me, but I didn't know what I'd do afterward, other than possibly grabbing Statham and making him ever regret laying his hands on me.

Jett's eyes meet mine as he grabs the pack from my hands. His gaze is filled with so much emotion—anger, sorrow, regret—and I know what he said while drugged is true.

He loves me. Maybe not the kind of love that lasts a lifetime yet, but he cares more than I realized. This isn't a fling to him. The man I never thought would settle down has fallen for me. The boy I crushed on for years is now mine.

Jett throws the pack at Marcus as he stumbles to his feet. "Get the fuck out of here. Forget I exist. If I ever see your face again..."

"Whatever, man." Marcus wipes away the blood on his lips with the back of his hand, glaring at Jett. "Can't believe you're throwing us away for some ass."

Jett's arm is around me, pulling me to his side. "You know what she means to me, but you still betrayed me and hurt the only woman I've ever really loved."

I blink, my mouth opening and closing, because hearing the words from him again still takes my breath away.

"Asshole," Marcus mumbles. "Nothing but a pussy-whipped loser."

"Marcus," I call out, finally coming to my senses.

He growls and narrows his eyes as he hoists his pack over his shoulder.

"Just remember a girl beat your ass, 'kay?" I smirk, holding back my giggles but just barely.

Those words make Jett's body relax, but his hand digs into my hip. We watch as Marcus stomps to his car, cursing and ranting with his arms waving until he gets in and peels out of the driveway like he's wanted by the cops.

"I'm so sorry," Jett says as soon as Marcus's taillights fade. He turns me, his hands on my cheeks, gazing into my eyes. "I'm so, so sorry, Lily. I never should've let him stay here."

I touch his hands, giving him a warm, kind smile. "Did you know he was like that?"

Jett shakes his head, his eyes never leaving mine. "I knew he could be a jerk, but I never saw him do anything even remotely like he did tonight. You have to believe I never would've let him stay here and be alone with you if I had."

I wrap an arm around his waist, holding on to him as my legs start to shake. The adrenaline from earlier is finally beginning to wear off. "I believe you," I whisper.

Jett smiles, leaning forward and planting a kiss on my forehead. "You kicked the shit out of him, Lily."

"I know." I giggle, remembering the way Marcus's eyes filled with water after I smashed him right in his face.

"You're pretty badass."

"I can be."

"That scares me," he admits against my skin.

I peer up, a smile on my face. "My dad taught me a few moves."

"Maybe you should be the one working at ALFA instead of me." He pulls back, bringing his lips near mine. "Lily."

"Yeah?" I whisper, staring into his eyes.

"I love you," he says. "I think I've always loved you."

My insides go squishy. "I love you too," I breathe, saying the words for the first time.

He crashes his lips down on mine, stealing the air from my lungs and my ability to stand on my own. I melt into him, giving him my weight.

His arms are under me and lifting me off the ground. "You're mine, baby," he murmurs against my lips, carrying me toward the house.

And for the first time, I feel the weight of those words. I'd always heard my father say them to my mother. Always rolled my eyes when he said them too. But hearing them slip from Jett's lips makes my stomach flutter and my heart skip.

I don't feel like this is all a dream anymore, ready to be ripped right out from underneath me.

24

JETT

"WE NEED TO TALK," Lily says while I pour myself a cup of coffee, barely awake.

"About?" My back's to her as she sits on the stool at the kitchen island.

Last night, we didn't talk much after I kicked Marcus out. We went to bed, me holding Lily, her rubbing my chest. I knew she had a million questions because Lily is rarely quiet, but last night she was unusually silent.

"Something Marcus said."

I turn, resting my mug against the granite countertop, leaning my body over the island. "What do you want to know?"

She peers up from her mug, looking every bit as cute as she always does. Her long, wavy, brown hair spills over the straps of her tank top, covering her breasts and disappearing below the counter. "You met him three years ago?"

I nod. "I was in San Diego for a year before he showed up, newly assigned to my ship."

"Had you ever seen him treating a woman poorly?"

I shake my head. "Never. I've seen him be an asshole to other men, but never to a woman." I rub the back of my neck, knowing everything that happened last night was entirely my fault. "You have to believe if I had any idea, I never would've let him stay here."

She turns the mug in her hands, her gaze dipping down. "I believe you. What he did isn't your fault."

"It is my fault," I tell her, taking full responsibility for bringing him into her life.

"He said something about you that bothered me." She peers up, her eyes filled with so many questions. "I can't stop thinking about it either."

"Ask me whatever you want, Lily. I'd never lie to you."

"Well," she says, her tongue sweeping out and over her bottom lip, "he said you two had shared women before."

I stiffen and close my eyes, knowing his words, especially those, would bother her.

"Is it true?"

I haven't lied to Lily, and I'm not about to start now. Sure, there's so much in my past I'm not proud of, but it's part of me. If we have any real chance at a future, I have to lay all my cards on the table, even the things I'm not proud of.

"Once," I admit. "Years ago."

She taps her thumb against the side of the mug, tightening her grip around the outside. "He made it seem like it was something you two did often."

"We didn't. It only happened the one time and never again."

"Will you tell me about it?"

I grimace, wishing she didn't want any details. The entire thing was a mess and not something I'm proud of. "I'll tell you anything you want, but do you really want to hear this?"

"Jett, I'm well aware I wasn't your first. I know I'm probably not even your tenth. I remember how you were in high school. I have no delusions about your sex life, but there's a giant hole between the time you graduated and showed up out of the clear blue at Inked."

I reach across the island and take her hand, wanting and needing to be connected to her. "None of them mattered," I tell her, being totally truthful. "No one mattered before you."

She gives me a small smile. "I believe you when you say those words, but I still want to know what happened."

"The details aren't important, Lily. It happened. We met a girl at a bar, she asked to sleep with us both, and we agreed. I was pretty drunk that night, and I wasn't thinking clearly or else I would've said no. But Marcus was all about banging this chick."

Lily winces at my choice of words. "Did you ever see her again?"

I shake my head, my stomach twisting over the entire conversation. "Never saw her again, babe. I also didn't fuck her. Marcus did, though."

Lily cocks her head, studying me. "You didn't have sex with her?"

"Depends on your definition. Marcus had sex with her, but I..."

"You did other things?"

I smile, loving that she's so innocent, and nod. "Something like that."

"And you only did it the one time?"

I nod again. "But Marcus did steal a girl I'd been seeing for a few weeks, fucking her when I was gone and here on leave."

"Then why were you still friends with him?" she asks incredulously.

"Well..." I wince, wondering the same thing myself, looking back on everything. "I figured he saved me a big headache. I was going to end things with her when I got back. He just made sure it happened sooner rather than later."

She blinks, studying me for a moment. "We're really nothing alike. We're doomed, aren't we?"

I jerk my head back and stare at Lily. "Why would you say such a thing? We're not doomed."

"I know you like me. God, I know you do, but Jett, come on."

I tighten my grip on her hand. "Come on, what?"

"How many women have you had a committed relationship with?" she asks.

I'd expected her to ask me this question a long time ago, and I was starting to think anyone before her didn't count anyway.

"Only a few," I tell her honestly. "The same as you."

She shakes her head. "I had one real boyfriend my entire life, and I slept with no one else. While you—"

"None of them matter."

She reaches over with her free hand, touching my face. "It's a lovely thing to say and hear." She smiles, caressing my cheek. "I know you love me too, but do you really think you have the ability to change your ways?"

"I do."

"If you have any doubt I'll be okay, I will be. I'll be sad, of course, but I don't want to trap you in something you'll regret."

"Lily?"

"Yeah?"

"Shut up," I say quickly. "There's no one else I want. I've lived enough and done enough in the last five years to know who I want, what I want, and how I want it. I want you. I want us. I want this. I'll never find someone else as good as you. Someone else as beautiful, as sweet, as caring."

"Fuckin' right, you won't." She smirks, and I finally feel like I can breathe again. "I believe you, Jett. I'm not asking you to marry me, but I want to know I'm the only one."

"You've always been the only one."

"Liar," she teases.

"Lily, I'm going to tell you a secret." I swallow hard, knowing I have to come clean so she understands the depths of my feelings for her.

"You know the photo I had of you?"

"The one the asshole told me about?" she asks, straightening on the stool and dropping her hand from my face.

I nod. "I asked Suzy to send it to me. I asked her to send a few pictures of you to me."

Her forehead wrinkles. "You what?"

"I was home just before your graduation. It was my first time back on leave from the Navy. Anyway, she started talking about the high school graduation, and I asked her to send me some photos. I wanted to see your face when you finally had your diploma in your hand."

"You did?"

"I did, baby. I wanted to see the smile on your face. I knew how important school was to you and how you'd be the valedictorian too. But nothing could've prepared me for what I saw."

"What did you see?"

"The girl of my dreams," I whisper. "The only girl I'd ever

loved, with the biggest smile, and I knew. I knew I loved you."

Tears swim in her eyes. "But why wait years to tell me?"

"I wanted you to live your life and not think about some schmuck traveling around the world. It wouldn't have been fair to tell you how I felt if I couldn't be here at your side."

"I would've waited for you."

"Exactly my point."

She wipes the corner of her eye, sniffling. "But what if I'd fallen in love with someone else?"

I move my hand to her other cheek, swiping away the moisture. "If you'd fallen for someone else, then you were never meant to be mine."

"You're crazy," she says, shaking her head. "You took a big risk."

I smirk. "Not really. I knew you'd never love anyone except me. I'd known you were mine since you were a freshman."

"You did not."

"I did," I argue.

"How?"

"One day, you left your notebook with Gigi in the lunchroom..." Her eyes widen, but I keep talking. "And I saw what you'd written on the front. Mrs. Jett Michaels was scribbled over and over again. I knew then you were mine."

"You're really insane," she says, giggling softly. "I was a dumb kid with a crush."

"And now?" I ask, brushing her hair away from her face. "Are you still a dumb kid with a crush?"

She shakes her head softly. "No. Now, I'm a stupid woman in love with a crazy man."

I release her hand, cupping her face in my palms. "No,

baby. You're not a stupid woman. You're mine. That's what you are. Mine. Only mine."

I pull her face forward, crashing my lips down on hers. She tastes of coffee, cream, and sweetness as she kisses me back, pushing her tongue between my lips, tangling it with my own.

"Always mine," I murmur against her lips between kisses. "Only mine."

Lily moans, sliding her arms around my neck. "Only yours," she repeats, solidifying what I've known and felt since the beginning.

Lily Gallo always has been and always will be mine.

"Yo," Mike, Lily's father, says as he rakes his eyes over me, looking like he wants to rip out my throat and dance on my lifeless body.

"Hey, Mr. Gallo." I'm laying it on thick, but this is Lily's father, and the last thing I want is for the man to hate me. "How are you today?"

He grunts in response.

"Daddy," Lily says, tucking herself under my arm. "Be nice."

"Michael Gallo," Mia, Mike's wife, says, walking up behind him. "Stop being rude to Jett."

"I wasn't," he grumbles and lies. "I was being as pleasant as I can be to the man who's trying to steal my girl."

Mia wraps her arms around Mike's middle, holding him as she plasters her front to his back and looks at us from the side. "You know she's not a little girl anymore."

I smile at Mia, always loving her strength in dealing with

a man like Mike, but I don't dare speak. I know better and would like to continue breathing.

"I know." He blows out a breath, relaxing his fist. "But I'm not sure I'm ready for her to grow up so fast."

"I'm twenty-one years old, Dad. It wasn't that fast."

"It felt like yesterday you were born, sweetheart. I remember rocking you to sleep every night, promising you the sun and the moon."

Lily steps away from me and grabs her dad's hand. "You gave me everything I ever wanted. I have the best dad in the world. But no matter how much you don't want me to grow up, I'm going to and already have."

Mike smiles at her like she's the most important person in the world to him. The man loves his children. Sometimes he can be a little overbearing, but his devotion to his family is evident and admirable.

"You taught me right from wrong, how to protect myself, how to love myself, and what the true meaning of family is, Dad. But you've got to let me go and let me find my happiness like you did with Mom."

Mike wraps an arm around Lily, pulling her closer. "But, sweetheart, are you sure it's him you love?"

The him is me. I can hear the unhappiness in his voice, in addition to seeing it on his face.

"Michael," Mia warns. "You know she's been in love with Jett since she was in high school, don't you?"

"But why him?"

"Why not him?" Lily asks her dad. "No one else has treated me as good as he has besides you, Dad. No one makes me feel as loved or as safe as Jett does. He makes me happy." Lily peeks over her shoulder, her cheeks pink with embarrassment.

"I love your daughter, Mr. Gallo," I say, leaving no doubt how I feel about her. "She's it for me. Always has been."

"So, all the other women you've been with…?" He raises an eyebrow.

"Would you have rather I started dating your daughter in high school?"

He shakes his head quickly. "Hell no."

I laugh. "I wanted her to finish school, live life. I knew we'd find our way to each other someday."

He scrubs a hand over his forehead, looking like he's in pain. "You made sure of it, didn't you? By coming back here, telling her you needed a roommate."

"I wasn't lying about that. I did need a roommate," I tell him, taking a step forward and wrapping my arm around Lily's middle, hauling her back against me. "But I didn't want anyone except Lily."

"I knew you had it all planned out," he says.

"Let me ask you something, Mr. G."

"Mr. Gallo," he corrects me.

"Fine. Mr. Gallo, when you met Mia, did you know she was the one?"

He places his hands over his wife's as she hugs him from behind. "I did," he whispers.

"What was that?" Mia asks. "I'm not sure I heard you." She smirks, winking at me.

"I did," he says a little louder.

"Well, so did I." Lily relaxes into me as I speak, resting her head on my shoulder as I peer down at her. "Would you have done anything to make sure she would be yours forever?" I ask, bringing my gaze back to him.

"He did," Mia answers for him. "God, he was such a

pompous asshole, but he wouldn't leave me alone, and he finally won me over."

"Lily!" my mom yells as she walks into the backyard, carrying a bowl of something she made for our first official family cookout. "You're glowing, sweetheart."

"Hey, Mrs. M." Lily smiles, leaving my arms to give my mom a kiss and take the food from her.

"Call me Sophia," Mom tells her. "Mrs. M is way too formal."

"See, baby, that's how you should be," Mia tells Mike, squeezing his waist. "Instead of being a big baby about everything. Being difficult is only going to push her away, not keep her closer."

"I'd never let that happen," I tell them. "Nothing is more important than family."

"At least he understands one thing," Mike grumbles.

"Mike," Dad says, holding out his hand to Lily's father. "You're looking better than you have in years. I may have to start working out with you."

Dad's sucking up. He's good at it, knowing exactly how much Mike Gallo loves to be complimented.

"I could get you in shape. The older we get, the more important it is we don't go soft."

"I'll never be soft," Dad argues, and I roll my eyes.

For two grown men, they act like children.

"Will you show me around the house?" Mom asks Lily, ignoring me.

"I'd love to, Sophia." Lily smiles.

Seeing Lily with my mother, and even her father and my father getting along, makes me happy. For once, I feel like my life is falling into place and everything is as it was always supposed to be.

25

LILY

"I'M SO PROUD OF YOU," Sophia says, grabbing me by the shoulders. "You two have really made this a lovely home."

I beam with pride as I look around the room, realizing this is a home. Not only because of the things in it, but because of Jett and me and the life we're building together.

"It's impressive," Aunt Suzy adds, standing next to Sophia. "I don't think I had your sense of style until I was much older."

Sophia snorts, dropping her hands from my shoulders. "You didn't have any style when we lived together, Suzy. Everything was black or white and usually whatever you could find on sale."

Aunt Suzy laughs, toying with the pendant around her neck. "I like a good deal. Hell, I still do."

"I always forget you two were roommates."

"We were fresh out of college, starting our first year of teaching, and piss-poor broke," Aunt Suzy says.

"Ah. The good times." Sophia laughs, shaking her head. "We've come a long way, babe."

"A long, long way," Suzy whispers, glancing toward Uncle Joe, Gigi, and Pike. "I wish we could turn back time to when the kids were little. I miss those days."

"Girl, don't be crazy. I remember those days, and you were a hot mess. You've conveniently blocked out all the bad shit like diapers, middle-of-the-night feedings, extreme exhaustion."

"Maybe." Suzy shrugs. "But knowing my little girl is moving on, growing up, and maybe getting married is too much for my heart."

My eyes widen. "Married?" I whisper.

Suzy shakes her head. "I know they're still a way off, but it'll happen eventually. Pike's it for her. I see the way she looks at him."

Sophia nudges Suzy. "It's the same way you looked at Joe and still do, to this day."

Suzy smiles. "He still gives me butterflies."

"Anyway," Sophia says, turning to look at me. "Are you going back to school next year, Lily?"

I shrug. "I don't think so. I'm happy at Inked."

"She's doing a wonderful job," Aunt Suzy tells Sophia. "Mike said she's really turning into a pro and the customers love her."

"I'm sure they do. Look at how cute she is." Sophia waves her hand between us. "The men have to be trampling over each other to get to her. Has to make Jett crazy."

"I don't think Jett's a big fan of all the body parts I have to touch." I wince, thinking about the first time I saw him again and had to hold his penis. "It can be awkward."

Sophia places her hand on my arm. "Then you keep doing it. Don't ever stop doing something because of a man, even if he's your man. Stick to your guns, and do what makes you happy."

"So, you would stay if you were me?" I ask her, making sure I heard her right.

"It's your family business. Your legacy. You need to live your life for you and not him."

"I love being with my family every day, but I'd also like to finish my degree."

"So, finish it, but that doesn't mean you have to use it. If having the diploma gives you a sense of accomplishment, do it, sweetheart. But don't do it because of Jett or anyone else, not even your parents."

"What about me?" Mom asks, finding her way to us at the exact moment we're talking about a topic I know is sore for her.

"We're talking about her work and school."

My mom's smile tightens. "Lily, I need to say something to you."

I turn to face her, readying myself for whatever she's going to tell me, no matter how much it may hurt. "Yeah, Mom?"

"Live your life for you. I thought you wanted to be a doctor, and I pushed you to follow in my footsteps, figuring you'd take over the clinic someday." She pauses as her smile softens. "I'm proud of you for having the courage to follow your dreams. I'd be far more upset if you didn't do something you enjoyed. I don't care where you work or what you do as long as you're happy, baby. Don't ever do something to make other people happy. It'll only make you miserable in the long run." She raises her hand, touching my face. "Your father and I are proud of the woman you've become and the courage it took for you to speak your mind and follow your heart. I don't think I could've done the same at your age."

My vision blurs as my eyes fill with tears. "You're proud of me?"

She nods, squeezing my arm. "I couldn't be prouder to have such a wonderful daughter, Lily."

I throw myself into her arms, hugging her so tight. "I love you, Mom."

"Love you too, sweetheart," she whispers into my hair.

"You two are making my mascara run," Sophia says, wiping her eyes. "Damn you."

I chuckle, pulling away from my mom's embrace. "Thanks, Mom. I needed to hear that. I've been so worried you and Dad were disappointed in me."

"I couldn't think of a better woman for my Jett. He needs someone level-headed, smart, sweet, and strong," Sophia tells me.

"Thank you, Sophia." I smile, my insides all warm, even if my eyes are filled with tears.

"What's wrong?" Jett asks, sliding his arm around my shoulders. "Why are you crying, baby?"

"They're happy tears," I say, sniffling. "Completely happy tears."

For the first time ever, I feel I can breathe and finally be me. I no longer feel as though I've let them down by my decisions.

"Who's ready to eat? Sal's manning the grill," Jett tells us.

All eyes turn toward him, wide and horrified.

"You left my grandpa at the grill?"

He nods, totally clueless.

"You know he burns everything, right?" I tell him,

shaking my head. "Like, if it isn't charcoal, it's not cooked completely."

Jett's head snaps to the side as he peers across the yard. "What? Are you serious?"

"Based on the amount of smoke pouring out of the grill, I'd say we're pretty close to being ready to eat." Suzy laughs. "I hope you have some steak sauce or something, or else we'll be chewing for hours and hours."

"I figured since your grandma is a great cook, your grandpa would be too." Jett rubs the back of his neck, looking pale. "Why didn't you warn me?"

I pat his chest, smiling up at my guy. "I thought you knew. You've been around us your entire life. You won't make the same mistake twice."

"Why didn't he say something?" Jett asks, looking between the four of us.

"Because he thinks he's a grill master," Aunt Suzy answers, covering her mouth to stifle her laughter.

"Which he's not," my mom adds. "But at least we know we won't get E. coli."

"Shit," Jett hisses, dropping his arm from my shoulder and rushing toward the grill to try to save our dinner.

"Thanks for today," I say to my mother, feeling nothing but warmth and joy.

"What are you thanking me for, baby?" she says, sweeping the hair away from my face.

"For making all of this okay."

She rubs my arm. "The only thing your father and I want for you is for you to be happy." She smiles down at me. "I've never seen you smile as big as you have today. I can see the peace you feel. I know you're home and where you're meant to be."

"I'm really happy."

"You're happy, baby girl?" Dad asks, coming into the conversation a little late. "Really, truly happy?"

I nod, my eyes filling with tears and not trusting my own voice.

He touches my chin, a sweet smile on his face. "You know we love you, right?"

I nod again, a tear sliding down my cheek.

Dad wipes it away. "We're proud of you too. I love having you at Inked with me, and I couldn't be prouder of the woman you've become."

"Thanks, Daddy," I whisper, my voice cracking.

He wraps his arms around me, giving me a bear hug. "I was blessed the day you were born, Lily. And no matter how old you get, you'll always be my baby girl."

"I wouldn't want it any other way," I whisper into his chest, hugging him tightly.

Three Weeks Later

"Hi, Lily," Sara, my mom's receptionist at the clinic, says as soon as I walk through the door.

"Hi, Sara." I smile, always loving seeing her. I've known her since I was a little girl, and I worked closely with her when I volunteered at the clinic in the summers.

Sara leans forward, placing her chin on her knuckles. "I heard you have a new special someone in your life. I saw a photo of him too, and he's a handsome devil."

I rest my hands on the counter, laughing. "He's one of the prettiest men I've ever met."

"If I were young again..." She sighs and fluffs her short

gray hair. "Just make sure he treats you right, Lily. Looks fade over time, and if he's an asshole now, you'll be left with not only an asshole, but an ugly asshole when he's older."

I giggle, covering my mouth when a woman in the waiting room gives us the side-eye. "I've missed you," I tell her.

"Miss you too, kid." She winks at me.

"Lily?" Mom says, walking up behind the desk from the exam room area. "What are you doing here, sweetie?"

I swing my gaze away from Sara and smile at my mom. "Hey, Mom. I wanted to stop by and talk to you about something."

Mom waves me back, never liking to talk about personal matters in front of patients. "What's up?" she asks as soon as I walk into the back, while her eyes sweep over me. "Are you okay?"

"I'm fine." I wave her off, not wanting her to panic. "Just wanted to talk to you about..." I lean in closer, lowering my voice. "Getting on the pill."

Mom's eyes widen just a little bit, but the rest of her face stays impartial. "Okay," she says, drawing out the word. "I'm glad you're being responsible."

I twist my hands as my belly tightens. "I always promised I'd come to you if I needed birth control."

She reaches out and grabs my hands. "I'm happy you came to me. Come on." She motions for me to follow her toward the exam rooms and stops near the bathroom. "We'll do a urine test real quick just to make sure you're healthy. Did you see Dr. Myer this year?"

I nod. "I went for my pap four months ago, and it came back normal."

"Good. Good." She nods. "You know the routine. Pee in the container, write your name on the side, and leave it on the counter."

I'm in and out of the bathroom in a hurry, somehow managing not to pee all over my hand.

"Wait in exam room one, and I'll be right back," she tells me.

"When was your last period?" Mom asks as she returns, sitting on the stool across from me with her laptop.

"About three weeks ago. You know I've always been bad at keeping track, Mom."

"You should do a better job, sweetheart."

"I never had to in the past, really. There was no reason."

"There's always a reason."

I roll my eyes. "Flo's always been consistent, and I wasn't having sex. So, I didn't…" My voice trails off because I just said I *wasn't*. The cat's out of the bag now. I am no longer a virgin.

"Well," Mom says, not making a face even though I know she didn't miss what I just said, "from now on, track it."

I nod. "Got it."

There's a knock, followed by Reva, my mom's nurse, walking into the room, carrying a sheet of paper. Reva's eyes land on me, and she gives me a tight smile. "Hey, Lil."

"Hi," I say, tucking a lock of hair behind my ear, wondering if everyone knows I'm here because I'm looking for birth control.

"Here are the urinalysis results, Mia." Reva hands the paper to my mom and gives me one more faint smile before vanishing.

"Everything okay?" Mom asks, her gaze firmly planted on the paper.

"I think so. Nothing to worry about." I place my hand on my knee, trying to stop my leg from moving.

"So, um, I can't write you a prescription for birth control," Mom says.

I jerk my head back, widening my eyes. "Why not?" I whisper.

Mom lifts her face and peers at me, blinking rapidly. "Because you're pregnant, Lily."

"I'm what?" I ask, frozen and shocked. "I can't be. We were careful."

"Well…" she mumbles, shaking her head. "Not careful enough."

"Give me that," I say, snatching the paper from her hands and scanning the results.

Fuck!

"Do it again. It has to be wrong," I tell her, shaking my head too. "We used condoms."

"They're not one hundred percent, Lily, and with his new piercing…"

"Oh shit. Oh shit. Oh shit." I start to hyperventilate.

Mom places her hand on my knee. "Breathe, sweetheart. Breathe."

I drop the paper to the floor and crumple forward, hugging my knees. "I can't be pregnant. Oh my God. I can't be. How could this happen?"

Mom moves to my side, placing her arm around my shoulders, hugging me. "There are worse things to be, Lily."

I snap my head to the side, my eyes filled with tears. "Mom, this is no time for a pep talk about being STD-free. Dad is going to kill Jett."

She smiles as she strokes the skin on my shoulder. "Your father's going to have a coronary, but he'll be fine after he gets over the shock." She giggles for a second and then sobers. "We're going to be grandparents."

I run to the garbage can on the other side of the room, my stomach twisting. Everything I'd just eaten for lunch comes hurling out, landing against the plastic. "This can't be." I gasp, wiping at my mouth. "I can't be."

She's behind me, holding on to my hair. "You are, sweetheart."

Tears stream down my cheeks, both from fear and the trauma of throwing up. "I'm not ready to be a mom," I cry.

Mom grabs my arms, pulling me upright, and turning me to face her. She has a tissue in her hand, blotting at my mouth and then my cheeks. "No one's ever ready."

"Jett's certainly not ready to be a dad. He's going to lose his shit."

"He may surprise you." She smiles, still wiping at my face like she's drying my tears after a spill on the playground.

I blink, gawking at her in complete shock. "I'm going to be a mom."

She nods, staring at me with nothing but love. There's no judgment in her gaze. No disappointment on her face. "You'll be the best mom ever."

I cry harder, gripped by fear and worry. "I don't know if I can do this."

My mother wraps her arms around me, pulling me in for a hug and wrapping me up in the safety of her embrace. "You can do anything you put your mind to, baby," she whispers in my ear, rubbing my back. "And I'll be here every step of the way."

I sob against her shoulder. Twenty-one years of virginity and virtue instantly wiped away by becoming the first of my generation to get pregnant—and out of wedlock, no less. I always thought Tamara would be the first one to get knocked up, but no, fate had other plans.

"Want me to help you tell Jett tonight?" she asks.

"I can tell him, but I can't tell Dad." I shake my head. "I can't." I sniffle, rubbing the back of my hand across my wet cheeks. "You can't tell him, Mom. He can't know before Jett."

Mom nods as her lips twist. "I won't, but this is one hell of a secret to keep."

"Please, Mom," I beg, grabbing her arm. "Promise me you won't tell him before I tell Jett?"

"Your secret's safe with me, sweetheart." Mom smiles softly. "I'm going to be a grandma," she whispers. "A grandma."

"Stop saying that," I tell her, shaking my head. "You're freaking me out."

She laughs. Freaking laughs.

"We should do a blood test."

Mom nods. "Whatever will make you happy."

I wave my hand in front of my body, stopping in front of my abdomen. "This doesn't make me happy."

"Someday, you'll look back on this day and laugh."

I blink, wondering who this person is in front of me. She's being way too cool about me getting knocked up. "I don't think I'll ever laugh about today."

"You will."

"I'm going to be an unwed mom," I mumble, the words sounding foreign and crude. "And a college dropout." My stomach flips, and the reality slaps me right in the face.

"Come over tonight, and we can tell your Dad together, sweetheart. It's better to tell him now than have him find out later."

"I'll see," I whisper, wiping away the tears streaming down my face.

I'm going to be a mom.

Fuuuuuuuck.

26

JETT

LILY WALKS through the front door and is as white as a sheet. I rush to her side before she has a chance to drop her purse on to the table. "What's wrong, baby?" I ask, studying her face as she stands there, frozen like a statue.

Her eyes are glazed over, and she's barely blinking. "I'm… I'm…" She pauses as her gaze moves to my face, but it's like she's looking through me instead of at me, completely lost. "I'm…"

"You're what?" Panic crawls up my spine as I clasp her cheeks in my hands. "What's wrong? Are you sick?"

"My mom." She pauses. "I'm… Oh God," she whispers, tears forming in her eyes.

I drop my hands from her face, pulling her into my arms, trying to comfort her. "What happened to Mia?"

"It's not… She's…"

My stomach knots, but I do everything in my power to stay calm and be her rock. "Lily, baby," I whisper in her ear, holding her tight. "You're not making any sense. You're scaring me."

Lily rears back, tears staining her cheeks. "I'm pregnant," she blurts out and her eyes widen.

I jerk my head back, and my eyes widen too. "What?"

"I'm pregnant," she repeats, crying harder. "We're pregnant."

I almost stagger back, but I catch her by the arms, digging my fingers into her biceps. "We're pregnant?" I whisper, never dreaming I'd be saying the words anytime soon. My heart skips, feeling weird in my chest as the realization of her words finally hits me.

Lily isn't one to play jokes and never about something so serious or life-changing. I knew the minute she walked in the door something was off, but never in a million years did I think she was going to say she was having my baby.

My baby.

She's officially my baby mama.

Does it make me a bad person because there's a part of me that's over-the-moon excited about the fact that Lily and I will be tied together forever?

I can already see a dark-haired little girl with her blue eyes, giggling as I throw her in the air. A mini Lily, all full of joy and innocent as can be.

Lily nods, her body shaking in my grip. "I'm so sorry. So, so, so, so, so sorry. I don't know how this happened."

"You're sorry?" I ask as a smile slides across my lips.

"Please don't hate me," she begs, curling her fingers into the material of my T-shirt.

I slide my hands back to her face, wiping away her tears. "I can never hate you, baby."

"What do you want to do?" she asks and is dead serious with the question.

"What do I want to do?" I'm confused. *What is there to do? We're having a baby.*

A little human with ten toes on little feet to snuggle and love. What could there be to do about something so wonderful?

"I know you don't want to have kids right now, so we can…"

I place my finger over her lips. "Stop it right now, Lily Gallo."

Her eyes widen, and her lips part behind my finger. "I don't want to ruin your…"

I shake my head. "You're not ruining anything. I love you. Do you love me?"

She nods, not speaking, which, for Lily, isn't easy.

"We're having a baby," I tell her, smiling so damn big because we're having a freaking baby.

"You're not mad?" she mumbles behind my finger.

It's my turn to shake my head. "I'm not mad. You're okay. Your mom's okay. Sure, life is going to change, but it's a baby. A little human. A tiny piece of both of us." I study her, because the color still hasn't returned to her face besides the splotches near her eyes from the tears. "Are you okay?"

She throws her arms around me, hugging me tight and crying harder. "I'm okay," she sniffles. "I'm scared. I was scared, but now…" She burrows her face in my chest. "I think I'm okay." There is a long pause as we hold each other. "We're going to be parents, Jett."

I rub her back, still in shock. "We are." I know what she's saying is true, but it still feels surreal. What does it even mean to be a parent?

Sure, I know late-night feedings, being responsible for

another human, but the reality has to be so much more, so much bigger.

"My father's going to kill you," she whispers into the material of my shirt. "We can't tell him. Not ever."

I laugh for a moment and then sober, knowing Michael Gallo is going to beat me to a bloody pulp. "He'll be okay. Your dad will be happy," I lie.

"We can hide it, right? I mean, at least for, like, six months or so."

I shake my head. "Baby, your dad is going to know. We might as well rip off the Band-Aid and tell him now. What's the worst thing that could happen?"

THE DOOR OPENS, and Mike's eyes swing from Lily to me and back to Lily. "What's wrong?" he asks immediately, knowing his daughter better than anyone else in the world.

"Nothing, Daddy," Lily says, somehow plastering a smile on her face. "We just thought we'd stop by and say hi."

Michael's eyes narrow on me. "And you brought him because…?"

I swallow, knowing this may well be my last minute left with the ability to walk or, at the very least, the ability to eat without the help of a straw because my jaw has been wired shut. "Hi, Mr. Gallo," I say, smiling, trying to hide the fear from my voice.

"Michael, let the kids in," Mia says in the background. "Lily told me they were coming by."

Mr. Gallo turns his head, but his wide neck barely moves. "Why didn't you tell me?"

"I know you love surprises, especially when it involves Lily."

Mike grumbles under his breath as he turns back to face me. "When Lily is involved, yeah. But him…"

"Daddy." Lily places her hand on his chest, smiling up at him with so much love. "Be nice. For me… please."

"For you, baby, always," he says, scooping her up into a hug. "I'll try, at least."

Mike stalks backward, still holding Lily in his arms, leaving me on the front step. I follow, not saying a word as we walk into the living room where Mia's curled up on the couch with a book resting on her leg. "Come sit," she says to me, patting the open spot next to her.

I sit, and Mia grabs my hand, giving it a tight squeeze. "It'll be okay," she whispers while Lily and Mike are busy chatting about nonsense. "Just breathe, kid."

I give her a tight smile as my stomach turns and fear sets in. I run my free hand along my jeans, trying to dry the sweat that hasn't seemed to calm the hell down since Lily told me the news.

"So," Mia says, looking at Lily and Mike as they sit on the couch across from us. She's so tiny compared to her father, but I see bits of him in her features even though she's a dead ringer for her mother. "What brings you kids by?"

"Um, just wanted to say hey. I haven't seen you two in a while," Lily lies, and Mike eyes her, knowing she's totally full of shit.

"Lil, I just saw you at work. So, what gives?" There's confusion all over his mean-looking mug.

Mia chuckles, uncurling her legs and sitting up. "You know young people, sweetheart."

Mike's eyes move to his wife, forehead wrinkled in more confusion. "What's wrong? What aren't you telling me?"

"Nothing, Daddy," Lily whispers, tucking a lock of hair behind her ear as she peers at the hardwood floor beneath her sandals.

"Oh. My. God. Are you sick?" he asks, his tone panicked. He reaches out, grabbing her hands and covering them with his own. "Tell me. Are you sick, baby?"

Lily shakes her head, unable to look up at her father. I know how she feels about him, never wanting to disappoint the man she's always loved the most. "I'm not sick, Dad."

"Someone better start talking and quick." He slices his eyes to me, and I gulp. "Because I'm getting the feeling everyone knows something I don't. You know how I feel about that too."

"Well, I…" I run my hand back across my hair, knowing I've got to man up. I should be the one to break the news that I knocked up his daughter. I won't say it in those words, but that's what happened. I slept with his virgin baby girl, and in the end, she's now carrying my baby.

Lily shakes her head and glares at me.

"Lily?" Mike asks, seeing her movement out of the corner of his eye. "Tell me, baby. You know nothing you can say will ever make me mad."

Lily moves her body toward him, gripping his hands tighter. "Okay, Daddy. Promise you won't freak?"

Oh God. That's code for freak the fuck out.

Mike raises an eyebrow. "I'll reserve my right to freak until after you tell me."

"Promise you won't kill Jett?"

That gets me a look of death from the man who used to beat people half to death for the fun of it.

"I won't kill Jett, but I'm not promising anything more."

"I'm pregnant," she blurts out again. Same tone. Same words. Same sweetness as when she told me.

But Mike's head doesn't jerk back. His body doesn't move. He doesn't even blink. He sits there, motionless. I'm not even sure he's breathing at this point. "You're what?"

"Pregnant." She smiles nervously.

"Like a baby?" he asks and finally blinks.

"What other pregnant is there, Michael?" Mia says, rolling her eyes. "Of course, she's having a baby. You're going to be a grandpa."

With the one word, Michael gasps as he looks around the room as if he's lost. "Grandpa?" he whispers so softly I barely hear him. "I'm going to be a grandpa."

I lock all my joints, readying myself for him to throw his body across the coffee table and choke me out. I know it's coming. It has to be. This is Lily, and I not only deflowered her but put my baby inside her too.

"Don't be mad. I'm so sorry, Dad. I never meant..."

Mike shakes his head, releasing her hands and covering his face. "Don't talk for a minute," he tells her.

She snaps her mouth shut, gawking at me in total fear.

"Do I run?" I mouth to her.

She shrugs with a grimace.

But my question is answered when Mia places her hand on my leg and says, "Stay calm and don't move." God, she makes it sound like there's a wild animal across the room and I should try my best not to spook it into attacking me.

"Grandpa," Mike mutters into his palm. "Grandpa. Grandpa. Grandpa." He repeats the word almost a dozen times without moving.

"Dad." Lily touches his shoulder. "Are you okay?"

He drops his hands away from his face, but there's no anger. "Am I okay?" He smiles. "I'm going to be a grandpa."

I breathe a momentary sigh of relief because I can see he's happy, but I know the joy is geared toward Lily and not me.

"So, you're okay with…" Lily glances down, moving a hand over her stomach. "With this."

Mike's arms are around her, pulling her to his body. "I'm excited, baby. So excited. We're having the first Gallo great-grandchild. I'm going to be a grandpa."

Lily smiles at me over her father's shoulder, and I can see the relief all over her features. She was so worried about telling him, I thought she was going to pass out from hyperventilating on the way to their house.

"And you," Mike says after releasing Lily and turning to face me.

I freeze, gripping the couch and closing one eye, waiting for his fist to strike. I've seen videos of his nasty uppercut, and I'm pretty sure my head would come clean off if he hit me the right way.

"I'm sorry," I say quickly, my voice squeaking as I ready myself for the worst ass-beating I'll ever receive.

Mike stands and stalks around the coffee table as I crane my neck back, waiting for the moment. I squeeze my eyes shut as he gets closer and I see his upper body move my way.

This is it. The end.

I had a good run.

Life has been fantastic until this moment.

I served in the military. Traveled the world. Made the girl I've loved forever mine.

But tragically and suddenly, everything must come to an end.

Mike looms over me, hands fisted at his sides like he's about to swing on me.

"I've hated you from the moment you stole my daughter, Jett."

"Daddy," Lily chides him. "Don't say that."

"And today...I still hate you."

"I'm sorry."

He narrows his eyes for a moment before his face softens. "I'm not happy about how this happened. Not happy you knocked up my daughter. Not happy that you're not married. But this is a baby, and I will love this child because it's my blood."

"You're happy?" I almost choke on the words. "You aren't going to kill me?"

"No. Not yet, at least, but if you break her heart or skip out on your responsibilities as a father, I will rip your limbs from your body."

Mia's off the couch, tucking herself under his arm and placing her hand on his chest. "I can't wait for that new baby smell again," she says to him.

"Babysitting's where it's at, sweetheart," Mike tells her. "We get all the perks and then get to send the kid home."

I blink, my heart thumping in my chest as I try to catch my breath. Lily's at my side a moment later, tucking herself under my arm exactly like her mother did with her father.

I peer down, smiling at my girl, who looks like she can breathe for the first time in hours. "I love you, Lily," I whisper.

"Love you too, Daddy." She winks, and my belly flops, knowing soon...someone is going to call me that same name.

My phone vibrates in my back pocket, and I nearly jump, still on edge.

"Answer it," Lily tells me when I don't reach for it right away.

"Fine." I groan, hating to ruin the moment. But when I pull out my phone and look at the screen, I see Mammoth's name on the screen. "Yo."

"Yo, man. I need you," he says in a rushed voice.

"What's wrong?"

Lily's eyebrows furrow, and her happiness evaporates.

"I'm on your side of the state and need some backup. Pike's headed my way, but I need you too."

"Whatever you need, I'm there."

Lily curls into me, staring up at me with wide eyes. "What's wrong?"

I shake my head, listening to Mammoth's instructions.

"Be there in an hour," I tell him before disconnecting the call.

"Jett, tell me what's wrong," Lily begs as her parents fall silent, and then three sets of eyes are on me.

I lean down, kissing Lily's forehead as I jam my phone back into my pocket. "Mammoth's in trouble. I have to go, baby. He needs my help. Pike's on the way too."

"I should come," Mike offers, stepping forward.

I shake my head, and Mike stops moving. "Stay with the girls. I got this. There's no need to worry. I'm sure it's nothing."

Lily slides her hand into her purse. "Take Statham. He's always been lucky for me."

I put my hand over hers as she pulls out her cute-ass pink Glock. "Keep it, baby. I got my own. I want to know you're protected."

She places the gun back in her purse before she grips my

shirt and rests her cheek against my chest. "Be careful," she tells me and peers up. "We need you."

"I promise to come back, Lily. I love you," I whisper, hoping I'm not lying to the girl I love and the mother of my future baby.

The family saga continues in Ignite, Men of Inked Heatwave #5. Visit menofinked.com/ignite for more information.

ABOUT THE AUTHOR

Chelle hails from the Ohio, but currently lives near the beach in Florida even though she hates sand.

She's a full-time writer, time-waster extraordinaire, social media addict, coffee fiend, and ex-history teacher.

She loves spending time with her two cats, sometimes pain in the ass alpha boyfriend, and chatting with readers.

To learn more about Chelle's books, please visit menofinked.com.

Join my newsletter at menofinked.com/alert

Text Notifications (US only)
➔ Text **BLISS** to **24587**

Where to Follow Me:

facebook.com/authorchellebliss1
bookbub.com/authors/chelle-bliss
instagram.com/authorchellebliss
twitter.com/ChelleBliss1
goodreads.com/chellebliss
amazon.com/author/chellebliss
pinterest.com/chellebliss10

Are you ready for more Inked?

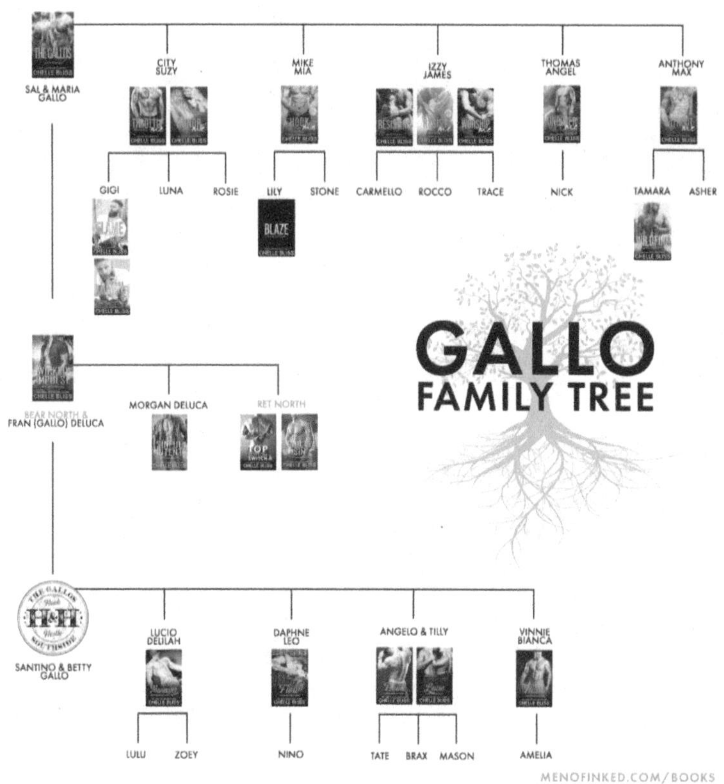

Learn more at menofinked.com/books

View Chelle's entire collection of books at **menofinked.com/books**

Original Men of Inked Series

Join the Gallo siblings as their lives are turned upside down by irresistible chemistry and unexpected love. A sizzling USA Today bestselling series!

Throttle Me - Book 1 (Free Download)

Ambitious Suzy has her life planned out, but everything changes when she meets tattooed bad boy **Joseph Gallo**. Could their one-night stand ever turn into the real thing?

Hook Me - Book 2

Michael Gallo has been working toward his dream of winning a MMA championship, but when he meets a sexy doctor who loathes violence, his plans may get derailed.

Resist Me - Book 3

After growing up with four older brothers, **Izzy Gallo** refuses to be ordered around by anyone. So when hot, bossy James Caldo saves her from trouble, will she be able to give up control?

Uncover Me - Book 4

Roxanne has been part of the dangerous Sun Devils motorcycle club all of her life, while **Thomas Gallo** has been deep undercover for so long, he's forgotten who he truly is. Can they find redemption and save each other?

Without Me - Book 5

Anthony Gallo never thought he'd fall in love, but when he meets the only woman who doesn't fall to her knees in front of him, he's instantly smitten.

Honor Me - Book 6

Joe and Suzy Gallo have everything they ever wanted and are living the American dream. Just when life has evened out, a familiar enemy comes back to haunt them.

Worship Me - Book 7

James Caldo needs to control everything in his life, even his wife. But **Izzy Gallo**'s stubborn and is constantly testing her husband's limits as much as he pushes hers.

Men of Inked: Heatwave Series

The Gallo's Next Generation

Flame - Book 1

Gigi Gallo's childhood was filled with the roar of a motorcycle and the hum of a tattoo gun. Fresh out of college, she never expected to run into someone tall, dark, and totally sexy from her not-so-innocent past.

Burn - Book 2

Gigi Gallo thought she'd never fall in love, but then he rode into her world covered in ink and wrapped in chaos. Pike Moore never expected his past to follow him into his future, but nothing stays hidden for long.

Wildfire - Book 3

Tamara Gallo knew she was missing something in life. Looking for adventure, she takes off, searching for a hot biker who can deliver more than a good time. But once inside the Disciples, she may get more than she bargained for.

Blaze - Book 4

Lily Gallo has never been a wild child, but when she reconnects with an old friend, someone she's always had a crush on, she's about to change.

Men of Inked: Southside Series

The Chicago side of the Gallo Family

Maneuver - Book 1

Poor single mother Delilah is suspicious when sexy **Lucio Gallo** offers her and her baby a place to live. But soon the muscular bar owner is working his way into her heart — and into her bed…

Flow - Book 2

The moment **Daphne Gallo** looked into his eyes, she knew she was in trouble. Their fathers were enemies--Chicago crime bosses from rival families. But that didn't stop Leo Conti from pursuing her.

Hook - Book 3

Nothing prepared **Angelo Gallo** for losing his wife. He promised her that he'd love again. Find someone to mend his broken heart. And that seemed impossible, until the day that he walked into Tilly Carter's cupcake shop.

Hustle - Book 4

Vinnie Gallo's the hottest rookie in professional football. He's a smooth-talker, good with his hands, and knows how to score. Nothing will stop Vinnie from getting the girl—not a crazy stalker or the fear he's falling in love.

Love - Book 5

Finding love once is hard, but twice is almost impossible. **Angelo Gallo** had almost given up, but then Tilly Carter walked into his life and the sweet talkin' Southern girl stole his heart forever.

ALFA Investigations Series

A sexy, suspenseful Men of Inked Spin-off series...

Sinful Intent - Book 1

Out of the army and back to civilian life, **Morgan DeLuca** takes a job with a private investigation firm. When he meets his first client, one night of passion blurs the line between business and pleasure...

Unlawful Desire - Book 2

Frisco Jones was never lucky in love and had finally given up, diving into his new job at ALFA Investigations. But when a dirty-mouthed temptress crossed his path, he questioned everything.

Wicked Impulse - Book 3

Bear North, ALFA's resident bad boy, had always lived by the friend's code of honor—Never sleep with a buddy's sister, and family was totally off-limits. But that was before **Fran DeLuca**, his best friend's mom, seduced him.

Guilty Sin - Book 4

When a mission puts a woman under **Ret North**'s protection, he and his longtime girlfriend Alese welcome her into their home. What starts out as a friendship rooted in trust ignites into a romance far bigger than any of them expect.

Single Novels

Enshrine

When Callie's life crumbles around her, can she trust her attraction to ruthless Bruno?

Mend

Before senior year, I was forced to move away, leaving behind the only man I ever loved. He promised he'd love me forever. He vowed nothing would tear us apart. He swore he'd wait for me, but Jack lied.

Rebound

After having his heart broken, **Flash** heads to New Orleans to lose himself, but ends up finding so much more!

Acquisition - Takeover 1

Rival CEO Antonio Forte is arrogant, controlling, and sexy as hell. He'll stop at nothing to get control of Lauren's company.The only problem? He's also the one-night stand she can't forget. And Antonio not only wants her company, he wants her as part of the acquisition.

Merger - Takeover 2

Antonio Forte has always put business before pleasure, but ever since he met the gorgeous CEO of Interstellar Corp, he finds himself wanting both. And he's hoping she won't be able to refuse his latest offer.

Top Bottom Switch

Ret North knows exactly who he is—a Dominant male with an insatiable sexual appetite. He's always been a top, searching for his bottom...until a notorious switch catches his eye.

Love at Last Series

Untangle Me - Book 1

Kayden Michaels is a bad boy that never played by the rules. **Sophia** has always been the quintessential good girl, living a life filled with disappointment. Everything changes when their lives become intertwined through a chance encounter online.

Kayden the Past - Book 2

Kayden has a past filled with sex, addiction, and heartache. Needing to get his addictions in check and gain control of his life for the sake of his family, Kayden is forced to confront his past and make amends for the path he's walked.

www.ingramcontent.com/pod-product-compliance
Lightning Source LLC
Chambersburg PA
CBHW010447310726
48979CB00018B/2843/J

* 9 7 8 1 9 5 0 0 2 3 8 9 9 *